"Miss Canville," firmly, "do you really have any idea exactly what the duties of such a position entail?"

"Exactly?" She blushed. "No. Not exactly. Is that a problem?"

"That a young lady such as yourself does not know…? No. Definitely not a problem. I should be quite shocked if you did."

She held out her hands in front of her. "I had rather hoped that this was the sort of thing one could learn by doing. Is there anything about me that would lead you to suspect I wouldn't be able to do the job as required?"

It was as if he was looking at her for the first time. She had a sweet face, with soft, full lips, and pale skin that hinted at roses underneath. She'd thrown off her cloak and sat before him in a modest and rather ugly gown, but the plain fabric and high neck hid what appeared to be a fine bosom. He imagined the full breasts, the curve of her hip, the way her legs would wrap around him, and the feel of her flowing blond hair as he ran his fingers through it to pull that mouth up to his.…

* * *

An Unladylike Offer
Harlequin® Historical #862—August 2007

Author Note

I'm overjoyed to revisit the characters from my last book and to tell St. John's side of the story.

I spent far too much time arguing with people while writing *The Inconvenient Duchess,* insisting that St. John could not possibly be the book's antagonist, because none of what happened was his fault. He was just an innocent victim of circumstance.

Of course, you have to have a very flexible definition of innocence.

I was convinced that he was a hopeless romantic, and that the right girl would make him settle down. He needed someone with a sense of adventure, someone who was not too concerned with propriety and who wouldn't stand for any of his nonsense.

And then I met Esme Canville. St. John didn't have a chance.

Enjoy!

CHRISTINE MERRILL

An Unladylike Offer

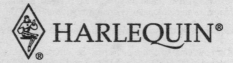

TORONTO • NEW YORK • LONDON
AMSTERDAM • PARIS • SYDNEY • HAMBURG
STOCKHOLM • ATHENS • TOKYO • MILAN • MADRID
PRAGUE • WARSAW • BUDAPEST • AUCKLAND

ISBN-13: 978-0-373-29462-6
ISBN-10:   0-373-29462-X

AN UNLADYLIKE OFFER

Copyright © 2007 by Christine Merrill

First North American Publication 2007

This edition published by arrangement with Harlequin Books S.A.

® and TM are trademarks of the publisher. Trademarks indicated with
® are registered in the United States Patent and Trademark Office, the
Canadian Trade Marks Office and in other countries.

www.eHarlequin.com

Printed in U.S.A.

**DON'T MISS THESE OTHER
NOVELS AVAILABLE NOW:**

To Barb, Betsy, Cory, Deb, Heidi, Katy, Kim, Michele, Pat, Pokey and Robin.

If they ever get tired of listening to me whine, they are all too sweet to admit it.

Chapter One

'If you're cold, Miss Esme, I could ask a footman to lay the fire.'

Esme Canville resisted the impulse to gather her shawl more tightly around her. 'No, Meg. I am quite comfortable. No need for a fire. No need for anything, actually. I am content.'

The maid continued to bustle around the room, straightening things that had been straight enough for hours. 'You're sure, miss? Because it seems a bit chill.'

'No, really. I am fine. You may go.' She tried to sound firm without drawing attention. 'I wish to spend the morning reading.'

Was the maid watching her with too much interest? It was so hard to be sure. Meg was new, and quite devoted to the master of the house. Certainly not someone Esme could consider an ally. But not an enemy, either, she hoped. Still, if her father had requested a report on any unusual behaviour, it was best not to provide fodder. She moved to the settee, and picked up her book.

Meg hesitated, and then said, 'If you're sure, then. But it is still quite cold.'

Esme gathered as much hauteur as she could muster. It would not do to allow her lady's maid to decide for her. 'I find it invigorating. And most economic. I am sure my father would not approve of me wasting coal in the morning, when the afternoon will be temperate.'

Meg nodded, approving of anything that Mr Canville approved of. 'If that is what your father wants, then of course, miss. But you'll ring…'

'If I need anything. Certainly. You may go, Meg.'

The maid let herself out of the room and Esme breathed a sigh of relief as she hurried to the fireplace. Meg took her new duties far too seriously. It had been better when Bess had held the job. But then, Bess had been too good a friend to Esme for her father's taste. And when service to her lady had smacked of disobedience to her master, that had been the end of her. And now, the much more cooperative Meg was trying to lay fires where none were needed.

Esme dropped her shawl carefully on the hearth in front of her and knelt on it, silently thanking the staff for the cleanliness of the slate. What ashes there were would hardly show on the shawl's grey wool. She opened the damper and leaned her cheek against the bricks at the back of the fireplace.

Voices travelled faintly up from the room below. Her father's study was just as cold and fireless as her bedroom, and it shared a chimney. Esme closed her eyes, trying to imagine the men below.

'...for coming here today. I am sure we can find an arrangement that is agreeable to all parties concerned.' Her father was speaking.

'But without even a meeting? Are you sure...?' The visitor's voice trailed off as he walked away from the fireplace.

Esme hissed in frustration. If they didn't stand still, how was she to hear?

'A meeting is not necessary.' She could almost see her father waving a hand in dismissal. 'She will do as she's told in the matter. And you have seen the miniature, have you not? I assure you it is a good likeness.'

Esme touched her own hair. The portrait was a fair likeness of her at best. And done several years ago. At twenty, she was hardly on the shelf, but she was not the wide-eyed innocent in the little painting.

'...lovely.' The man was walking back towards the fireplace again and his voice grew louder. 'Very much to my taste. And she will agree? You're certain of it?'

'I fail to see how it signifies. She will do as she's told, or face the consequences. And since it is you or no one, she'll soon see the wisdom of cooperation. It is more than a favourable match, milord. She would be a fool to hope for better.'

The voices faded away again as the men in the room below walked towards the desk. Esme's mouth compressed to a thin white line. How could she hope for better? She was not to be allowed a Season. Ever. Or to travel unescorted by her father into any of the social circles that other young ladies were permitted to as a matter of course. Evenings were spent at home or in the company of her father and his friends, who were almost all as old as he. Certainly not marriage material.

She hoped.

'And I would be well pleased with one so young and lovely as your daughter.'

Young. He found her young enough to comment on it. This could not be good. She strained her ears, trying to guess the nature of the man from the voice that echoed up through the brickwork. His tone told nothing, although she could not say the sound of it pleased her. There had been no passion in it as he'd examined her likeness, only cool appraisal. He could as easily have been choosing furniture as a wife.

'She will be honoured by your suit, Lord Halverston.'

A lord. But of course. Her father would wish a match that would advance the family. But her future husband's rank did not signify if she could not find room for him in her heart.

The voices increased in volume again. '…and obedient, you say? Girls these days are too wilful by half, and I'll have none of that in a prospective wife.' They were walking away from the fireplace again as he continued his diatribe against youth, female youth in particular.

And there was the first emotion she'd heard from

him, for his increased volume carried the words to her as he enumerated the faults of other prospective brides, compared with the agreeability of making a match without having to contend with the fractious personality of a girl.

Her heart sank.

Her father responded. 'I'm sure you will have no problem there. She knows her duty.'

'Or she soon will,' Halverston responded.

Both men laughed.

She stood up, heart pounding. It was inevitable, was it not? Of course, her father would find her a husband and make the decision himself. And he would choose someone of a like mind to his own. Someone who believed in the need to use a closed fist to explain one's duty. Someone who was sure that nothing refreshed the memory of a disobedient daughter or a wayward wife like the sting of the razor strop on her back.

She gripped the mantelpiece and tried to steady her breathing. It was possible that the situation was not as bad as it sounded. Without meeting Lord Halverston, it was unfair to judge him. And she was making many assumptions, based on what little she'd managed to overhear of a single conversation.

Her father and Halverston had come to an agreement and were moving out of the study and into the front hall. She brushed the soot from her skirt and hurried out on to the balcony, staying close to the wall so as not to be spied from the street. After a brief farewell, the man would call for his hat and stick and he would come through the door beneath her.

And then she would catch her first glimpse of the man her father intended her to marry. His carriage was already waiting on the street below and she admired the fine matched bays with silver on their harnesses. The body of the carriage was rich, and she could see the well-upholstered squabs, and almost smell the leather. Her future husband would be wealthy. And she would share in his wealth. It would not be all bad. She would have gowns, jewels, and a fine house to live in. Houses, perhaps.

She heard the door closing and watched as the driver and grooms straightened as their master approached. With respect, she hoped, and not fear of punishment for idleness. She would have servants, she reminded herself. Perhaps a maid that answered to her before her father.

Esme bit her lip. All that was well and good. But was it too much to hope that her husband would be gentle, as well as a gentleman? She forced the thought from her mind, trying not to let the snippets of conversation she'd heard affect her opinions.

And then she saw the man step up and into the carriage and she moved forward for a better look.

He was old. She could tell it from the stoop of his shoulders. His gait was steady, but stiff and measured, and his body tall and unnaturally thin, as though wasted by illness. The fingers that he spread on the dark leather of the seat looked bony and twisted, more claw than hand.

She stifled her disappointment. It would have been foolish to hope for a young man, after seeing the carriage. It must have taken time to get the wealth necessary to own such a fine thing. Of course, he would be older than herself.

But if he were as old as he appeared… She shuddered at the thought of him coming to her in the night, and could almost feel the bony hands as they plucked at her hair and touched her bare skin. He was older than her father. And she might soon be a widow.

It was horrible to think such a thing. Perhaps her father was right to punish her, for she truly was wicked.

But the voice inside her refused to be silent. *You are not wicked. You know you are not. He is old, but you are young. And your father is doing this to be sure that you never enjoy that youth.*

As though he sensed her eyes upon him, Lord Halverston lifted his head and spied her on the balcony.

She held still as he looked at her, and tried not to let the fear of him show on her face.

He held up a staying hand to the driver, and stared at her for what seemed like a long time. And she could feel his eyes, lingering on her body, travelling slowly over her belly, her breasts and her throat, before coming to rest on her face. Then he smiled at her, seeing her without acknowledging her, and there was not a trace of warmth in his face.

She watched as his hand began to twitch and then to stroke the leather of the seat, palm cupping the curves of the upholstery and fingers stroking and thrusting again and again into the crevices between the cushions.

Then he signalled to the driver in a voice that was harsh and excited, and the coach pulled away.

She sagged against the stone of the house and felt her knees trembling beneath her. Perhaps she was imagining his expression. It was the distance, the smells of the street, and the sun in her eyes, combining to overheat her imagination. He could have been thinking about other things entirely than marriage to her. He could have been searching for a key, or a coin, or some other small thing on the seat beside him.

And it was merely the devil in her, as her father had so often claimed, that made her feel that hand travelling over her body. Stroking. Grasping. Thrusting.

She gripped the balustrade and fought down a wave of sickness, taking in great gasps of air. She could not do it. She simply could not. Her father must listen to reason, just this once. Perhaps if she promised to be good, from now on. Not to anger him as she always seemed to. If she agreed to marry any man he chose. Any man other than the Earl of Halverston...

A sudden crash roused her from the waking nightmare of her future. A pane of glass had shattered in the French doors on the balcony across the street. As she watched, a man threw the doors open and stood in the opening with his back to her. He had a military bearing, and, when he spoke, his pleasant baritone was loud without shouting and carried clearly to her, despite the distance.

'I believe this proves my point. Let us keep these open and spare the rest of the window glass from your little moods.'

A projectile sailed past him and into the street. Then another, which he turned and caught as it narrowly missed his head. He waved it in the air next to him, and she could see that it was a lady's silk slipper.

He spoke again. 'And what, pray tell, was the point of that? Even if you'd hit me, it would have done no real damage. Since you missed, you've lost one shoe and must hop home, for I'll be damned before I go into the street to retrieve the one you threw at me.'

The owner of the slippers responded with an angry tirade of what sounded to her uneducated ears like Spanish.

The man folded his arms in front of him and leaned against the door-frame, giving Esme a view of a fine profile and a sardonic smile. 'No. That would not be technically accurate. My mother assured me that I was legitimate. Not that my parentage has done me a lick of good.'

There was more Spanish and another crash of breaking glass, but this time from inside the apartment.

'And now you have broken the mirror, and are left to dance in the shards in your bare feet.' He tossed the shoe back into the room with no great force in the general direction of his opponent. 'Why I ever chose to keep such a goose-brained creature…' He looked into the room for a moment. 'Well, of course, it's plain why I chose you…but insufficient reason to keep you now.

Cara, as I told you before, the apartment is yours until the end of the month. It should not be hard to find another protector, for you are a great beauty and quite charming when you are not breaking glass and throwing the expensive baubles I've bought you back in my face.'

The woman in the house released another torrent of offended and unintelligible speech.

Esme sank beneath the balcony rail, embarrassed by her own eavesdropping. But it was hard to look away from so interesting a performance. And so public a one as well. It was quite the most exciting thing she'd seen in years, and she did not even have to leave her room to enjoy it.

Her father had warned her about the new neighbour. The scandalous Captain St John Radwell, just back from the Peninsula. It had been rumoured that he'd bought his commission with stolen family jewels, on the run from one of his many disastrous affairs. If there was any truth to the story, it wouldn't have come from his brother, the Duke of Haughleigh, who, when questioned, refused to acknowledge he had a brother at all.

Captain Radwell was another of the many things her father railed about, and warned her against. And here was the devil in the flesh, casting off his mistress in broad daylight in a decent neighbourhood, and loud enough for the whole street to hear.

She peeped over the railing at him, unable to look away.

When the irate woman in the room opposite paused for breath, Radwell retorted, 'Then sell the bracelet. Or perhaps the earrings. They cost a pretty penny, as I well know, and should keep you comfortably until another fool comes along to take my place. But this interview is at an end.'

She could hear the sound of angry sobbing in the distance, followed by slamming doors.

Her own troubles were forgotten as she smiled wickedly to herself. It was nice to see that one of her father's irrational ravings had a basis in fact.

Without warning, St John Radwell turned to face her, and caught her staring.

He wasn't merely a devil. He was Lucifer himself, with his hair, golden in the sunlight, waved to cover his temple, a straight nose and a slightly crooked grin. His eyes must be blue, although she could not see the colour from this distance, for clear blue eyes would suit the face. The cut of his coat and smooth fit of his breeches accented a well-muscled body and straight back. He gave every indication of perfection as he stood framed in the windows of his apartments. The sight left her breathless.

And then he stared back, holding her gaze before turning his attention to the rest of her. He examined her at length and at last he smiled, and she felt the rioting in her stomach turn to the gentle flutter of butterflies.

He tapped the side of his nose and nodded significantly.

But significant of what? His gesture was strange.

Not a scold at her rudeness, but an indication of something. She shook her head in confusion.

With a flourish, he pulled a handkerchief from his pocket, unfolded it with a snap and wiped his own face, then gestured to her.

Her hands flew to her cheeks, and she rubbed once. When she held them in front of her, they showed traces of soot. Not only was she eavesdropping on the neighbours, she was as dirty as a chimney sweep.

He waved the handkerchief in triumph, seeing that his message had been understood, bowed to her with a grin, then turned and re-entered his apartment, shutting the windows behind him.

Her heart was pounding as she stepped back into her own room and shut the balcony doors. Oh, the horrible man, to make such a scene and then tease her for her impertinence. He seemed not the least bit perturbed to be caught in an indiscretion, or to catch her as well.

It must be delightful to know such freedom, to not give a damn for society and do just as you liked.

The plan was forming in her mind before she even realised it. It was daring, and the most improper thing she had ever imagined. She was shameless, and now the world would know it. It would serve her father right, if his only daughter came to such. And it would certainly make marriage to the earl out of the question. It would be easier to accomplish if she waited for darkness, but in a few short hours, with the help of the scandalous Captain St John Radwell, she could be free of her father, this house *and* the earl. She would do it.

Chapter Two

'No, thank you, Toby. I'll not need you tonight. It's another quiet evening at home for me. Relaxing in front of the fire. And perhaps a brandy before bed. Don't bother. I'll get it. You should know, after Portugal, that I'm able to manage for myself.'

The valet left the room and St John threw himself into a chair, staring into the fire. Relaxing, indeed. It was damned boring. But considering the contents of his purse, or lack thereof, it was all he could afford. The risk of creating new debt at White's was greater than the chance that he'd win and refill the coffers. And his credit was stretched uncomfortably thin already.

He was due a reversal in fortune. It had been all but guaranteed to him—if he kept his nose clean, of course. When he'd been presented at court to be decorated, the regent had hinted that rich rewards would be given to those who'd served their country so well. If, that was, they could also manage to navigate society without embarrassing themselves and their patrons. How had Prinny put it?

'A man who can survive the French must also be able to survive a Season in London without getting himself shot by jealous husbands or his own brother for conduct unbecoming. Steer clear of trouble and Haughleigh. The Earl of Stanton is turning eighty, and not likely to get an heir at this late date. There is a nice little piece of land attached to that title and I'd like to award it to someone who can prove himself worthy of the honour.'

St John Radwell, Earl of Stanton. He said the words to himself on nights like this, when the old desires arose to tempt him. But he was not an earl yet. And he would never be one if he landed himself in scandal, or gambled away the entail before receiving it. Better to be circumspect in all things, at least for a while. He must remember that he was a respectable man about town, and a distinguished Peninsular veteran, ready to live a quiet life in the country. There would be no awards to the scapegrace brother of the Duke of Haughleigh, with pockets to let and a list of sins long enough to get him permanently banned from the family estates.

He sighed. After five years in Portugal and Spain, he missed home. He'd found that he even missed his brother, which was a thing he'd never have believed possible. He'd often thought, in the hours before a battle, of the things he might never be able to say to·Marcus or his wife Miranda, should things go badly. And despite the end he'd expected and sometimes felt he deserved, he'd escaped with a whole skin. It seemed he might still have his chance to heal the breach between them.

And his apologies might ring with more truth, should he arrive at Haughleigh with his own title and perhaps a wife at his side. Lord knew, he did not want to marry. But it would be necessary. He would want heirs. A family of his own would be proof positive that he was no threat to his brother's marriage and that old rivalries over the Haughleigh succession might be permanently buried.

But he needn't worry about any of it now. The current plans might take years to bear fruit, and it did no good to wish on it. Until then there would be many more quiet nights at home, biding his time and letting the scandals die and his old reputation be forgotten. And with not even the solace of female distraction, now that he'd cast off Cara as too volatile and far too expensive.

Of course, the old St John would have appealed to his brother for funds to tide him over, offering his newly reformed character as collateral, oblivious of the reaction it would provoke from the duke. The thought was so amusing, he laughed out loud.

There was a discreet cough behind him.

'Yes, Toby.'

'You have a guest, sir. A lady.'

'A lady?' No lady, certainly, if she was visiting at this hour. But there was no trace of irony in the word as Toby spoke it. 'Show her up, then. And bring that brandy after all.'

St John detected a hint of disapproval in the set of his valet's shoulders, at the idea of bringing the female upstairs. But, whoever she was, she must know full well what she was getting into, and if Toby cared more for her reputation than she did, he could keep his tongue in his head.

The door opened shortly and Toby announced, 'Miss Esme Canville.'

'Who?' It was rude, but he couldn't help himself. The name did not register in any corner of his brain, and certainly didn't match any of the discreet widows or straying wives he'd expected to darken his doorway at so late an hour.

She stepped into the room and curtsied politely and he was on his feet, offering her a chair and trying to conceal his confusion. It was the damned nosy chit from across the street. Whatever would bring her here? 'I beg your pardon, Miss Canville. But you quite have the better of me. Toby?' He'd hoped to keep the servant in the room, although it would hardly cover the impropriety of the situation, should the girl's father get wind of this. But Toby had left the brandy and retreated to the kitchen.

'No. Please, Captain Radwell. I would prefer that our conversation be private, if that is possible.'

Dear God, he couldn't be alone with her. But perhaps if she said her piece, whatever it was, he could get her back out of the house before anyone guessed her whereabouts. 'All right. And I do admit to a certain curiosity on that count. Just what is it that brings a gently bred female to my chambers at this late hour? I don't believe we have even been formally introduced.'

'No.' She had the sense to look embarrassed. 'We have not actually met. Although earlier today...I couldn't help but overhear... And I certainly know of you, Captain Radwell. By reputation.'

'I suppose I should assure you, at this point, that the reputation is undeserved, but, alas, I cannot. I'm sure I've done most of the things attributed to me over the years. And if not? Well, I've probably done worse, but not been caught.' He almost smiled before remembering that there was no reason to boast. 'You understand, Miss Canville, that you put yourself in a very dangerous position by coming here alone?'

Her chin rose a fraction of a degree and she looked into his eyes without flinching. 'If I cared at all for my reputation, that would be the case. But circumstances force me to take drastic action on that front, Captain Radwell. I find myself in a difficult situation and had hoped that perhaps you might be able to help me.'

'Help you?' He straightened. 'Why you should choose me to aid you, I have no idea. But as an officer and—' he cleared his throat at the unfamiliar idea '—a...ah...gentleman, I will certainly do everything in my power to aid you.'

Her confidence was short lived, and he sensed that she must be near to telling him the reason for her visit. She removed a handkerchief from her reticule and twisted it in nervous hands. 'Well, yes. I was seeking your aid, after a fashion, but not precisely as an officer and a gentleman. I think the term I am searching for is protection.' Her eyes were full of hope as she looked up into his. 'If you could see fit to offer me your protection…'

At first he had the outlandish idea that she meant him to draw sword and stand between her and a foe. Protection? What did she need protection from? Certainly not her father, for he hardly looked the sort to do violence…

Protection. An ungentlemanly offer of protection?

He sprang from his seat to put as much distance between himself and the young lady as possible. 'I say. You can't mean… You don't think that I would…'

'I couldn't help but hear you arguing with your…' she searched for a word '—paramour earlier in the day. It was most plain that you were casting her off. And I assumed that that might mean that there was a position open…'

'Position? Dear God, woman. You are not hiring yourself out as a governess.'

'Well, I know that, of course. I could never have a job as a governess without my father becoming aware of it. Even securing the necessary references would be impossible.' She explained it as though it should be the most obvious thing in the world.

'I seriously doubt that you have references for the position you're inquiring after now.'

'Are references required?' She looked more alarmed

by that prospect than she did by the situation, which he found more than alarming enough for both of them.

'Not references, per se. But I would hope that you are lacking in previous experience.' He sat down next to her, and looked gravely into her face. 'I mean, Miss Canville—'

'Please call me Esme.'

'Miss Canville,' he responded firmly. 'Do you really have any idea exactly what the duties of such a position entail?'

'Exactly?' She blushed. 'No. Not exactly. Is that a problem?'

'That a young lady such as yourself does not know… No. Definitely not a problem. I should be quite shocked if you did.'

She held out her hands in front of her. 'I had rather hoped that this was the sort of thing that one could learn by doing. Is there anything about me that would lead you to suspect I wouldn't be able to do the job, as required?'

It was as if he was looking at her for the first time. She had a sweet face, with soft, full lips, and pale skin that hinted at roses underneath. She'd thrown off her cloak and sat before him in a modest and rather ugly gown, but the plain fabric and high neck hid what appeared to be a fine bosom. He imagined the full breasts, the curve of her hip, the way her legs would rap around him, and feel of her flowing blonde hair as he ran his fingers through it to pull that mouth up to his…

He stood again and paced across the room. 'No.

No. No, there is absolutely nothing about you that would make me think you unfit or unable. But that is not the point. What I think you might be capable of should be no concern of yours, for I am a rather base and untrustworthy fellow, and could eat a little lamb like you for breakfast and have no compunction about leaving you after.'

The girl said, 'But I seriously doubt that is the case. I watched you today, as you argued with the lady in your chambers. She did several things that might have provoked a lesser man to violence, but you were the picture of reason. You also made it clear that you'd left her with sufficient funds to care for herself, until she could find another position.' She smiled. 'And she was most unreasonable about the whole thing, I might add. You need have no fear, when the time comes to cast me off, that I will throw such unladylike fits about it.'

'Cast you off? Dear God, woman. I have no intention of taking you on, so I need never worry about casting you off.' He made a shooing gesture. 'Run home to your father, now, before someone realises you are gone, and we're both in the soup.'

She shook her head. 'That is quite impossible. I am not going back, no matter what you might say in the matter.'

'Then I shall carry you there myself.'

She planted her hands on her hips. 'You shall not. For if you do, I will tell my father where I have been, with the addition of certain colourful and inaccurate details, and you shall be the only one in the soup, Captain Radwell. I doubt it would be possible for *my* life to be any worse than it already is, but *you* would run the risk of being saddled with me, and society would require a more permanent union than the one I am suggesting.'

She was right, damn her. But the situation was even worse than she threatened. Should word of this get out, it would not matter if he married her or not. There would be no title in his future. And Prinny's displeasure would be the least of his worries. He could well imagine the look on his brother's face, if he tried to gain entrance to the family home with an empty purse and a broken reputation, out of favour with the regent and two steps ahead of Esme Canville's angry papa, but claiming that it was all a horrible mistake. 'You think, if I take you back, that I can be forced to marry you. But if I don't, you would permit me to do as I will with you, without the benefit of marriage?' And for a moment he was tempted. He shook his head. It mattered not that her charms were considerable—they would not outweigh their cost.

'Of course, I would expect similar compensation to the woman who left your employ earlier in the day. Not so much, perhaps, since I am inexperienced,' she reassured.

'No.'

'I do not eat much, and I am not vain about clothing or jewelry. Nor do I require much space to be happy. I dare say I shall be much less expensive to keep than your last mistress.'

'No!'

'Then perhaps you could arrange an introduction to one of your friends? Someone of a similar temperament, but also in need of female companionship?'

'And now you expect me to turn panderer? Oh, this is too rich, madam. I know that my reputation is black, but I never had anyone suggest that I should become a procurer for my friends.'

'I am so sorry,' she responded. 'I never meant to offend you.'

He shook his head. 'And a virgin, no less.' He reached for the brandy with a shaking hand and watched her eyes follow his movement. 'Would you care for a glass?'

'No, thank you. I do not drink spirits.'

'That you are able to come up with a hare-brained notion such as this stone-cold sober astounds me. Besides, I could never consider someone teetotal for the job you are seeking.'

She set her chin. 'Then pour me a glass, sir, for I assure you, I am serious in my request. Although I would much prefer it to be you, since I must admit I admire you greatly, I *will* find another willing man if I must.' Her voice fell to a whisper. 'Surely someone would want me. I cannot be so bad as all that. But, whatever the outcome, I will not return home.'

He poured a jot of brandy into a snifter and carefully added a few drops from the flask in his pocket, swirling the liquid to mix the contents.

She watched him with curiosity. 'What is that you have added to your drink?'

'Nothing you need be concerned about. I find it sometimes necessary to take laudanum to quiet my nerves, and I must say that your behaviour is quite shocking enough to unbalance a man stronger than myself.'

She laughed. 'What have you to be afraid of? You seem most steady to me. If you are as bad as you claim, than there should be nothing particularly fearsome in finding a woman in your rooms.'

She stepped closer to him, and his breath felt thick in his lungs. She was right, of course. There was nothing to be afraid of in the thought of a woman, soft and willing in his arms. And the night always passed more easily when he was not alone.

Her voice was husky and low as she said, 'As you have pointed out, it is I who should be afraid of you. For you know exactly what is to happen to me tonight, while I know only whispers and rumours of what goes on between a man and a woman at a time like this.'

She came the rest of the way to him, standing within easy reach, and he stood rooted to the spot, watching her in fascination.

She tilted her head to look into his eyes. 'Is it true that it can be both pleasant and painful? I've always wondered how that could be possible. I know much of pain, but very little of pleasure.'

He could certainly show her pleasure, if that was what she was seeking. It was late, they were alone, and no one would expect to find her here. He could give her what she wanted, and send her home and none need be the wiser. He could feel the offer forming in his mind and bit his tongue to keep from saying the words, but he could not bring himself to step away as she came closer still and the fabric of her gown brushed against his shirtfront.

'Since you are, as you say, an officer and a gentleman, I would hope that you take into account my inexperience as we proceed, and to be as gentle as possible, for I will admit to being somewhat frightened, now that the time has come. I suspect that my nerves are even more unsteady than yours.'

Without warning, she reached out and snatched the brandy from his hand and drained the glass, laudanum and all. She coughed once, and her eyes watered at the strength of the drink. Then she set it carefully on the table beside them, and stepped away from him to sit on the sofa, leaning back into the cushions.

'Dear God, Miss Canville.' He dropped his hands to his sides helplessly. Even as he cursed himself for a fool, he could feel his body missing the warmth of hers as she stood close. He'd seen only the woman, pretty and willing, and ignored the mind, sharper and more devious than he'd expected in one so young. And now the slip of a girl had outfoxed him, and there was little he could do to undo what had been done.

He smiled his best and most seductive smile and stepped closer to look down upon her. 'Very well, if you are intent on doing what you seem to wish, you are right that it could be a difficult and rather painful experience. It will go easier on both of us if we wait until you are fully relaxed.'

She looked at him with large, frightened eyes and said, 'Do as you will. I am prepared.'

And he hated himself for seeing her as such a bold temptress, only a few moments before. The girl was terrified of what was about to happen, and that he had allowed himself to consider her request even for a moment proved that he had as black a soul as others claimed. He sat down on the sofa near her and took her hand. 'Not yet, I think. A little while longer.'

St John watched as her limbs began to relax and the brandy brought a flush to her cheeks. 'How long? Before I begin to feel the effects?' Her breathing steadied and she moistened her parted lips with the tip of her tongue.

And to his shame, he felt his body stirring in response. He could feel the grasp of her hand relaxing in his as the drug took effect and gave it what he hoped was an encouraging pat. 'Not very.'

'That is good. And I'm sure you are right. It will be easier this way.' Esme shook her head a little and smiled. 'Oh, how odd. It is as if I cannot feel my body. It is so wonderful not to feel any more.'

He smiled in sympathy. 'You understand too well, little one.'

She closed her eyes and murmured, 'If I had the contents of your little bottle in my possession before coming here, this might not have been necessary. Of course, I doubt I'd have stopped at a few drops.' And her head drooped to the side and she was lost to the world.

St John forced himself not to pace the marble floor of the entryway. In another house, he would not have been left standing in the hall. The servants would have had the decency to show him to a parlour somewhere, to wait before the fire. Of course, in most other houses, he was not total anathema. And he'd never arrived so late in the evening and with such an unusual problem.

The butler was returning with the lady of the house a discreet step behind him. When she saw him, her voice was low and full of warning. 'St John.'

'Miranda.' He bowed low, hoping that the she did not notice the look in his eyes. She had grown even lovelier in the five years since he'd last seen her. Marriage to his brother had been kind to her.

Jealousy flashed within him, and he crushed it. She was happy here. It was what he'd wished for her, certainly what she deserved, and he would not spoil it now.

'How much?' Her tone was all business.

'I beg your pardon?'

'How much do you need? To make you go away again. For I swear, St John, if Marcus realises you are here, this time I will not be able to protect you.'

'And how is my brother?'

'Well,' she answered without thinking. 'As are the children.'

'My nephew and my niece.' He smiled as he tasted the unfamiliar words on his tongue. 'I meant to congratulate you on their births, but was not sure it would be welcome.'

She shook her head in disapproval. 'You know well it would not have been. But you are not here, at this advanced hour, to enquire after the health of the family. How much do you need, St John?'

He snorted. 'I'm sorry to admit that I have a problem that cannot be solved by an open purse.'

He stepped to the side and revealed the bundle on the bench beside the door.

Miranda rushed to the girl, throwing back her cloak and touching her cheek, feeling at her throat for a pulse. She glared up at him. 'Oh, dear God, St John. What have you done to her?'

'Nothing. I swear. She is only drugged. And untouched. On my—' He stopped. Swearing on non-existent honour would be worse than useless in this house. 'On Marcus's honour, shall we say? Let me swear in a coin that has some worth to you. I brought her here because it was the most respectable place I could think of. I had barely a passing acquaintance with the girl before this evening. She arrived on my doorstep suggesting… I hesitate to say it to a lady.'

Miranda arched a sceptical eyebrow.

'In truth, she was suggesting I take her as mistress. And she was damned insistent about it, too. Said if it wasn't me, then it would be someone else, but that she couldn't go home. She chose to take the laudanum. I swear it was accidental. But there at the end, when her mind was relaxed and her speech unguarded, she was hinting that she'd do away with herself, given the opportunity. I couldn't take her home. Even being seen in my presence might be enough to ruin her. I couldn't talk sense into her. I couldn't even manage to frighten her. She took my glass and drank the drug without a qualm. Then she laid back on the sofa, ready to let me—' He broke off in embarrassment. 'It was dashed strange. When I was sure she was fully unconscious, I took her down the back stairs and brought her here in a closed carriage. I needed to find a place of safety for her. For her reputation's sake, no one must know I had anything to do with her condition. And I thought—'

'That your brother could dispose of the woman you kidnapped?' Miranda's voice was rising now.

St John shook his head. 'It was not a kidnapping. Not intentionally, at least. She needed to be rescued from herself.'

'Miranda, why on earth are you shouting in the hall?'

St John stiffened himself against what was to come. Now, of all times, was not the moment for the tender reunion he had wanted with his brother. 'Marcus.'

'Pistols or swords, St John?'

'I really don't think that will be—'

'It was a statement, not a request. Choose a weapon. And choose your second.'

'No.'

'How dare you?' Marcus reached for him, ready to strike.

St John fought every instinct that had been honed for five years on the battlefield and stepped into range of his enemy's attack, holding his hands empty at his side. The blow caught him across the cheek, a backhanded slap that sent him staggering. And he let it connect, making no effort to block, fighting the urge to strike back, not allowing himself even the desire to grip his brother's shoulder to stay on his feet. St John let the force of the blow drive him back into the wall and dropped to his knees, waiting for the ringing in his head to clear.

He looked up into his brother's rage-contorted face. 'And I said, no. I will not fight you. If you strike me, I will not strike back. If you kill me, it will be in cold blood. Throw me into the street if you must. But if you do, let me go alone.' He looked pointedly at Miranda.

'Marcus, wait.' Miranda grabbed her husband's arm before he could strike again. 'He has a legitimate reason for coming to us.'

'You were always quick to defend him, Miranda.'

'Marcus, you ninny,' St John said in exasperation. 'if it makes you feel any better, then hit me again. But do not take that tone with your wife in front of me. She has never been anything but loyal to you, much to my disappointment. If it were just for me, I would never have come near you or your family. But I have here someone who needs the protection of an honourable man. And all the little fool could find was me. Take care of her, will you? But do not send her home until you have obtained the truth from her, for there is something there so horrible that she would die rather than face it.'

His eyes locked with Marcus's, and he waited for a moment to see what reaction his words would receive. His brother looked more tired than angry, as if the single blow had taken all his strength. And his expression held the same disappointment that St John had seen so many times before—the look that said St John had failed the family and shamed himself and now the duke must avert another scandal. And here was another proof that he could not manage his own affairs.

But then Marcus looked to the girl, and gave an almost imperceptible nod.

St John tasted gall along with the relief, and nodded in return. 'Now, if you will excuse me? I'll take myself out of your life and hers and trouble you no further.' And he turned stiffly, without glancing at Esme Canville, and walked out the door and into the street.

Chapter Three

Esme opened her eyes cautiously and looked at the canopy above her. It most certainly was not her own room, but neither was it what she expected to find in the bachelor's quarters of Captain St John Radwell. And she did not remember travelling anywhere else. She moved her head and winced. Ah, yes. The brandy had been drugged. He'd said she needed to relax, but she had not expected to be totally unconscious, when the moment came. Had it been pleasant for him, she wondered? She must have been almost corpse-like; if the Spanish lady from yesterday was any indication, he was accustomed to someone a trifle more animated.

Unless…

She frowned. She did not feel any different, other than the headache. She knew only the vaguest details of the process, but there was supposed to be blood, and pain. And she remembered neither. There was not even an indication that he'd disarranged her clothes, for she was sleeping *sans* shoes, but still in her gown.

'You are awake, I see. Let me offer you tea. Or would you prefer chocolate?'

The voice was pleasant and female and Esme craned her neck to get a look at the speaker. The woman had chestnut hair arranged in attractive curls, and the graceful posture of a swan. Her clothing was simple, but well cut and expensive. Esme scanned the room. Also expensive. Whatever she'd been expecting to see when she awoke, this was certainly not it.

The woman spoke again. 'You are, no doubt, wondering where you are. I am the wife of St John's brother, and you are in my home.'

Esme sat up quickly. 'But his brother is the Duke of Haughleigh. And you must be…'

'Miranda. That is sufficient, I think. You may call me Miranda. But what am I to call you? St John was most remiss on that point.'

'Esme Canville, your Grace.'

The woman laughed. 'Please, as I told you before, let us not bring my grace into discussion. I am Miranda. May I call you Esme?'

'Of, course, Miranda.' How strange. She thought carefully before she spoke. 'How came I to be here? You say Captain Radwell brought me, but I understood that there was an estrangement between the brothers. I certainly did not expect—'

'The estrangement was temporarily mended, because St John was concerned for your welfare. And rightly so. Perhaps you do not realise what risk you put your reputation in when you sought out help from him.'

Esme sat up and took the cup that was offered by Miranda. 'Oh, no. I was quite aware of it. As a matter of fact, it was precisely what I was looking for. When one wishes to be dishonoured, it makes no sense to go to a gentleman.'

'You wish for dishonour?' Miranda's own cup had stopped halfway to her mouth.

'I wish, just once, to be guilty of the crimes for which I'm punished. Does that sound strange to you?' She paused. 'I suppose it does. Let me try to explain. My father is a proud and upright man. He believes in living simply, not courting vanity or ornament, and shuns society as foolish and dangerous to the soul. And he believes that it is a suitable life for me as well. Silks and fripperies are a waste of money. Lavish dinners and dancing are merely an excuse to indulge the sins of the flesh and must be avoided at all costs.'

'Well…' Miranda was obviously searching for a way to proceed with the conversation without censuring Esme's family '…it is a noble aspiration to keep one's soul pure and avoid excesses.'

'Perhaps if we all avoided such excesses, the world would be a paradise. But I speak from experience when I tell you that it would be incredibly dull.'

Miranda's mouth thinned in disapproval. 'Boredom is not the worst fate that could befall a young lady.'

'No, it is not. I suspect that it will be far worse to be bound in marriage to a man I have never met, who is old enough to be my father. While I cannot be sure of the fact, judging by the look he gave me yesterday when I spied him in the street, he does not wish to spend our evenings together in prayer and reflection.'

'Oh.' Miranda chose her next words carefully. 'But there would be the benefit of marriage. And certainly the kind of life that St John would offer…'

'I have seen the life that St John might offer, for I have seen him with his mistress.'

'Surely not…?'

'In flagrante delicto?' Esme smiled. 'No. Merely in argument. She was throwing shoes and breaking glass, and he appeared to be bearing it with a great deal of patience and good humour. I did not see him strike her for uttering an impertinence, or beat her for imagined transgressions, or lock her in her room to ensure obedience. This is the life I am accustomed to, and I suspect that my father has chosen a husband for me who is much in the same mould.' She felt a tear on her own check and ignored it. 'Because he has my welfare for ever in mind.'

'And what of your mother? Can she do nothing to help you? Or is she no longer with us?'

'She is no longer with me, certainly, for she ran away with a dancing master when I was fourteen. I do not know whether she is alive or dead, but, wherever she is, I suspect she is happier than she was with my father. He is much older than she, and he treated her much the same way he treats me now.' There was another tear on her cheek, and she wiped it away, hoping that the gesture did not draw too much attention. 'I do not know whether my life might have been different, if she had stayed. But there might have been a chance for a Season, marriage, and escape if he had no reason to be ever vigilant of my character. Which, despite my efforts to the contrary, seems to need continual correction. He says I am much like my mother, and he will not make the same mistakes with me that he did with her and that what he does to me is for the honour of the house and my own good.' More tears were coming and she swallowed hard to drive them back. 'I swear, I never give him cause. I am not vain because I know I have no reason. I do not flirt. I do not seek the attentions of suitors. How can I when I am never in the company of anyone who might want me? And yet he punishes me and says it is for things I might do, if given the opportunity. I know you must think me horrible, but I would much prefer to live in comfort as the paid companion of a rake than to live another moment in the life set out for me. When I die, I will burn for my sins, but at least there will be a chance for a moment's pleasure in life.' She took a sip of tea and felt the cup rattle on the saucer as her hands shook, so she set it down. 'I am sorry to bother you with my problems. Indeed, I never intended it. But I cannot bear it any longer. I simply cannot.' She looked down at her hands, which were still shaking, and clasped them together in front of her.

Miranda's voice was strangely distant. 'And what was your plan, if and when St John turned you away? For that is what happens in the end, when you accept a *carte blanche.*'

'Then I would find another such offer, or throw myself into the Thames. It was my plan last night as well. It matters very little to me any more. If I go home, I will get such a beating that a quick end might be preferable.' Another tear fell. Once they started in earnest she would not be able to stop them. She raised her hands to cover her face, wishing she could force the emotions back into hiding.

She felt the cool air on her wrists as her sleeves crept up to reveal the flesh of her forearms.

There was a sharp gasp from the duchess.

Esme lowered her arms and tugged her dress back into place, but it was too late to hide the vivid bruises that were the marks of her father's hands upon her.

She hung her head. 'I was choosing a book from the study, and he wanted me to go back to my room. A guest was coming, and he did not wish me to be present. I did not move quickly enough. So he took me by the wrists to encourage me.' She lifted her head again, to stare into the duchess's concerned eyes.

'Please, do not tell anyone of this. The simplicity of my dress is not for modesty alone. Much can be hidden with high necklines and long sleeves. And I am so ashamed.' She closed her eyes so she would not have to see Miranda's expression turn from pity to disgust. She had hoped to hide the truth a little longer, at least from the fine lady sitting in front of her. She was marked by punishment, in body and spirit. Next to the Duchess of Haughleigh, with her graceful white throat, smooth unmarked arms, and serene disposition, Esme felt coarse and unclean. And now the tears were squeezing out from between her lashes, embarrassing her further.

Then, the strangest thing happened. She felt a weight on the bed, and the duchess's arms about her, hands stroking her hair and her melodic voice promising that everything would be all right and that she needn't worry any more. And Esme sagged in relief, laid her head upon Miranda's shoulder and wept.

Miranda looked at her brother-in-law lounging insolently in a chair, and her husband sitting in stony silence behind his desk. This might go more easily, if it were just she and Marcus. But for all his apparent innocence in the matter, it was St John's business, as much as theirs.

Even if St John did not see it that way. 'I do not understand why I have been called to account for this. The girl is better off, is she not, if I stay far, far away from her?'

'Much as you are better off if you stay far from me,' responded Marcus.

'I was endeavouring to do just that, brother, until your wife summoned me back this morning. Would you have me flout her wishes? Perhaps you would. And I should defer to the peer, should I not? I beg your pardon, your Grace.'

'And now you throw my title back in my face?'

'If you wish to play the role, then how am I to ignore it?'

'Enough!' Miranda stepped between them. 'St John, I did not send for you because I wished to listen to the two of you argue. Marcus, you as well should mind your tongue and listen to what I have to say. For we are all in a pretty pickle because of the young lady upstairs and it will take more heads than mine to get us out of it.' She looked to her husband. 'If the girl is to be believed, and I think she is, she had little to no prior acquaintance with St John before last night. What she knew of him was from reputation and from spying on his apartments across the street from her home. She sought him out because she believed that he was the sort who would stoop to ruining a young lady under the very nose of her father and might think it good sport to set her up somewhere…'

'And I disappointed her,' remarked St John. 'See, Marcus? I am not so bad as you paint me. Or as stupid. I have more honour and sense than that.'

'It is too late to brag to me about your new-found good sense. Bitter experience has taught me the depths to which you will stoop—'

Miranda glared at the interruption and spoke over it. '…until such time as he tired of her, whereupon she meant to find another or end her life.'

The two men fell silent.

'She does not want to return home, fearing punishment, and I must agree that it would be unwise. From what she describes, her father's response will be swift and severe. If we send her back, we can rest sure in the knowledge that she will be soundly beaten and locked in her room until such time as she can be married against her wishes to an elderly gentleman of her father's choosing.'

She noted, with some satisfaction, that the glances passing between the two brothers showed alarm at the girl's condition and had nothing to do with their previous quarrel. 'I am sorry,' began St John, 'to involve you in this. But last night I had no idea what to do with the chit, other than to return her to her home. She was spouting such a variety of nonsense that it did seem, at first, to be the best plan. But her talk was wild. It worried me. And then she took my drugged brandy and drank it before I could stop her. What if she ran away again when the laudanum wore off? Or did herself an injury? Or was found in her drugged condition by someone with even fewer scruples than myself?' He held out open hands to his brother. 'I did not want to be responsible for the ruin of an innocent. So I brought her to you. I thought that she would see reason in the morning, and her virtue would be intact. No father could argue that a night spent in so august a household could be anything but an honour. And her name would not be linked in shame with mine because all the world knows we are estranged. This must be the last place that I would bring her.'

Marcus nodded. 'It makes sense, when you explain it thus. This would be the last place she'd end up, if you were involved. But what are we to do with her, now we've got her?'

Miranda cleared her throat. 'I have a suggestion. It

is rather unorthodox, and only a temporary solution to the girl's troubles. And it will require her co-operation and some time getting the story straight between us.' She looked at St John. 'If anyone asks you, last night, you retired early and alone. You saw nothing of Esme Canville. Do your servants gossip?'

St John shrugged. 'All servants gossip.'

She looked to Marcus. 'Then we must see that St John's are generously rewarded to hold their tongues. The Canville household must get no wind of her true behaviour last night. I suspect that St John is in no financial position to do this, and we will help him.'

Marcus hesitated for a moment, then nodded.

'Marcus, last night we were travelling by carriage in the neighborhood of the Canville home. It matters not why. And we found a strange girl, dazed and wandering in the street.' She snapped her fingers. 'And feverish. Which is why she cannot return immediately home. She was taken ill in the night and somehow wandered away from home in her delirium.'

St John grinned. 'I say, Miranda, that's a cracking good yarn. Have you considered writing for the stage?'

Marcus's eyes flashed at the impertinence and Miranda leapt into the conversational gap before he could respond. 'And you, Marcus, have managed to discover her direction, and will go to the Canville household with the sad news of the illness. You will assure her father that we will care for her until she is better. I think it shall be several weeks before she is fully recovered. It might be best done in Devon, where the air is clean and the noise of the city does not prey upon her nerves. Go in your most severe black suit, for Mr Canville disapproves of artifice and ornament. But go with full livery and the best carriage—I doubt his disdain will extend to your title.'

Marcus grinned, and she noted that the two brothers looked very alike when they smiled, although they would never believe it.

'All right. I frighten Lord Canville into giving us his only child, or bludgeon him into co-operation with my title. What are we to do with Esme Canville and her imaginary fever?'

'We will take her out of the city, far away from the loving attentions of her father and the suitor he has chosen for her. We entertain lavishly and introduce her to all the families in the area. Even in brief conversation with her, I find her to be a girl of surpassing wit and no little beauty. But her father has taken pains to ensure that she never meets with the opposite gender and so she has never been courted by them. We find a match to her satisfaction and she need never return home. She is nearing the age of consent. It is only her father's control that has prevented her from finding someone appropriate. If we find such a man, we lean on her father until he sees reason, or stall her return until she is of age. And thus we solve all her problems.'

Marcus's smile faded. 'While I agree that we must work to preserve the girl's reputation, we do not have the right to separate her from her family and reshape her future. If her father wishes to keep her apart from society, then who are we to say he is wrong?'

Miranda bit her lip. This had been a mistake. She should have spoken to her husband in private, revealed all and obtained his approval. She could not very well betray the girl's confidence and parade her bruises in front of the family to win the argument. 'Marcus, I understand we have no legal right. But we do have a moral obligation to do all we can for her. You must trust me when I say we cannot just make up some fustian to cover last night, and then send her home. While her father may have the right, he is not in the right. Not in the eyes of God or man. Even a few weeks apart from her may be enough to calm his temper and persuade him to see reason.' *At least it will heal the marks on her arms.*

Marcus looked into her eyes, searching for an explanation, and then said at last, 'Very well. I trust you in all things. If you feel this strongly about it, then be damned to society. We will do what you feel is necessary. But I will also consult our solicitor, so that we might raise a defence should this go awry.'

She nodded, relieved.

'Then it's off to Devon for you and the girl, and I am well clear of things, as soon as I gain control of the servants.' St John rose to go.

Miranda turned to him. 'There is some little dispute on that matter.'

He dropped back into his chair.

She smiled. 'While I do not begrudge helping her,

you have caused much difficulty by bringing the girl to our house. I don't think you should get off scot free in this.'

'But what can I do to assist?' St John looked suspicious.

She looked from St John to Marcus and proceeded with caution. 'After a week or two, you might retire quietly to the country as well, St John. For your health. Or your pocket. The girl seems to have developed a small *tendre* for you, and the quickest way to cure her of it might be for her to get to know you better. Then she will see how hopeless a thing that is, and be more amenable to the suitors we will choose for her.'

He drew himself up in his chair, no longer the indolent young noble. 'Prolonged contact with me is so odious?'

Miranda smiled. 'Well, you must admit that it is quite easy to see through your advances, once one knows which way the wind blows. And Esme Canville might be sheltered, but she's no fool. When she sees that you are not interested in her—'

Miranda was pleased to see the shadow of doubt that passed over St John's face.

'—and that all you can offer is dishonour, but that there is a chance for a decent union with some respectable young man in the neighbourhood, she'll soon be set right.'

'I am not so easy to see through as all that.' St John seemed genuinely put out. 'I've a good mind to come down to Devon and show you just how charming I can be, when on my best behaviour.'

'But we do not need your best behaviour, St John. We need for you to be a fate worse than death. She must be disabused of any romantic notions she might have of a glamorous life in the *demimonde*. While I am fully capable of telling her, this is a lesson that will be better learned from you. I recommend that you do not break her heart, only damage it a little. Send her into the arms of a young man of our mutual agreement, and we all end happily.'

St John shook his head. 'This is a plot of surpassing deviousness, Miranda. I am surprised at you. Prolonged association with my brother has warped your character.'

Marcus darkened, but then smiled as he said, 'For once, I must agree with St John. It is a most convoluted plan, but I see no reason why it might not work.'

There was at least one glaring reason, and Miranda was pleased to note that the men had not noticed it.

'Very well, then. I retire to the country. In advance of you, I think—that will seem less suspicious. I will set myself up at the inn near Haughleigh. If you have no objections,' St John added, looking to the duke.

Miranda felt a brief flare of hope. The St John she knew of old had been quick enough to ignore his banishment from the family lands and would never have asked for the duke's permission before returning. His last comment had almost sounded like sincere respect for Marcus's wishes. Was it too much to hope that his service in Portugal had changed him for the better?

Marcus looked at the desk blotter, not his brother,

as he said, 'If you retire to Devon, you might as well go straight to the house. No reason for you to pay an innkeeper when the family manor stands empty. I will write to the servants, informing them of the change.'

Miranda started, and concealed her smile. Her husband was being unusually generous of spirit, possibly because of St John's circumspect and polite behaviour. So they would all be staying at the house together? All the better, for she might kill both birds with one stone. If things went according to her plans, there would be a reconciliation between the brothers before the summer was through.

And Esme Canville would find a way out of her difficulties as well. For unless she missed her guess, Miranda had already found a suitor who would meet with Esme's approval, and he was sitting in the room with them.

Chapter Four

St John turned his face into the pillow, away from the spring sunlight streaming through the window. Things had changed at Haughleigh under the care of his sister-in-law. For one thing, he didn't remember it as being so damned bright when his mother had been in charge. He had come to his old home, hoping to nurse his dark moods in the gloom. But everywhere he turned there was sunshine and fresh air. It was most disconcerting.

He sat up and took his tea from the waiting valet. The food was good, as well. It was all too comfortable and it put him on his guard.

Not that he expected his brother to be laying traps for him. This was not the Peninsula, after all, with danger at every turn and spies in the bushes. Marcus was much more straightforward then that. If there was to be an attack from Marcus, it would be full on and from the front, not preceded by peaceful overtures and tea in his old bedroom. He was here at the invitation of the duke, and could take it at face value. Perhaps the blow in the hallway had been enough to settle the score between them.

But he doubted it. Letting his brother strike him had been enough to allow him entrance to the house. To allow him back into the family would take something more. Time, money and apologies. And while he had all the time in the world, he was at a loss as to how to carry on with the rest.

If he had to dance to Miranda's tune for a while, and get the Canville chit properly married, so be it. It was an odd scheme, but it fit well with his own plans for reconciliation with his family. It would be much easier to demonstrate his repentance while living under the nose of his brother. The family was scheduled to arrive today and he had done nothing so far to arouse comment from servants or neighbours. He expected that Marcus would quiz the staff on his behaviour when unobserved by family. The report should be most favourable, since he had taken great pains to appear to be nothing more than the circumspect gentleman he was.

He could hear the carriages in the distance, and hurried with his dressing, not wanting to be caught unprepared when his host arrived.

St John wandered down the corridor to the sound of Marcus's voice booming orders in the hallway. It still had the tone of command, but with less bluster than when St John had last heard it. There was laughter in his brother's nature that had not been there before. And Miranda's as well, sweet and clear, happy to be home.

He froze at the next sounds. The laughter of children—a boy and a girl. Of course he knew of them, he'd read the announcement of the births in *The Times*. He'd just doubted he would ever be allowed to meet them. It was a shock to hear them so close.

St John walked slowly down the stairs, into the bustle of the homecoming, and felt it stop around him. Miranda, at least, appeared happy to see him.

'St John.' Marcus's voice gave nothing away. But his posture was alert and the laughter was gone from his eyes.

'Marcus.' What was he expected to say in return? He could hardly welcome the man to his own house. 'I trust the trip was uneventful?'

Miranda filled the silence. 'No trip with children is ever uneventful. And you have not met ours, have you? Come, children, and meet your uncle.' She gestured the two forward, a boy of about five and a girl who, if his memory served, must be almost four.

He continued down the stairs and to them and stooped to take the boy's hand. 'How do you do, Johnny?'

The boy was every bit his father's son and pierced him with a gimlet eye. 'My name is John.'

'John, then. I'm your uncle St John. Our names are rather the same, aren't they?'

'No, they're not. My father says we are not the least bit alike and he is glad of it.'

'John!' His mother laid a warning hand on her son's shoulder. 'And this is little Charlotte.' She nudged her daughter forward.

St John bowed low to her, and produced a penny from his pocket, handing it to the girl. 'Fair Charlotte, I am charmed to meet you.'

She smiled back at him and mumbled, 'Thank you, uncle.'

'You're welcome.'

'Where's mine?' Little John was glaring at him with a miniature of Marcus's commanding stare, and pointing to the penny.

'John…' Miranda warned again.

St John smiled back at him. 'Still in my pocket, Johnny. And your father is right, you are much more like him than me.' He produced the penny and handed it to the boy. 'Some time, when he is not watching, bring me the penny and I'll tell you stories of your father, when he was little.'

Marcus took a step forward, closer to his son, and St John could almost hear the frost forming.

'You've been remiss in the child's education, Marcus. Has he discovered how to get down to the kitchen and steal sweets without Cook noticing?'

Miranda shot him a warning glance, but little John was now looking at him with thinly veiled curiosity.

'There is a way. I learned it from your father, and you shall learn it from me. And don't tell your mother or she'll give us both a hiding.'

He could feel Marcus relaxing.

What did you think I'd tell him, Marcus? I am not so bad as all that.

The children retreated to cling to the skirts of the governess, or so St John thought. As he looked up, he realised he was mistaken. The style was simple, but the blue wool of the travelling dress was too fine for a servant. And the face of the woman looking down at the children with such obvious affection was shockingly familiar.

'Miss Canville?' Her presence had caught him off guard. He had known she would be with the family. But he had been expecting the desperate girl who had come to his rooms.

The fashionable young woman who stood before him was hardly recognisable. There was no hint of hardship in her. Her lovely face was untroubled, her smile peaceful. He felt himself relaxing as he gazed on her, as one might when enjoying a fine spring day. She looked deceptively innocent, with her hair caught in a modest knot and the children tangling in her skirts, but the look in her wide blue eyes when she gazed at him was anything but maternal.

'Captain Radwell. How good to see you again.'

'And you, miss.' He offered a belated bow. 'Are you faring well with my brother and his family?'

'Certainly better than I fared with you.' He was readying an apology when he noticed the slight quirk of her lips. She had him off balance again, and was enjoying it.

'Well. That is good to hear.' It was embarrassing, but he was suddenly at a loss for anything to say.

'The duke and duchess have been most kind to me. Thank you for placing me in their company.'

He nodded. 'Your servant, miss.' And then he remembered that he was only there to be a threat to her virtue. 'When it comes to something like that, at least,' he added and managed what he hoped was a leer.

And she laughed. There was no hint of embarrassed modesty, nor was it the knowing giggle of a mistress. She had laughed at him as though she knew his measure and did not believe his threats.

This was most irritating. Five years ago he could raise a blush on the cheek of any young thing, with much less effort than that. But after a drugging and a kidnapping that should have left her faint with terror, Esme Canville was laughing at him. His reputation as a danger to womankind was in need of polishing.

And then he remembered that he was no longer attempting to maintain the gloss on his infamy. He should be hoping it would fade into tarnished obscurity. But he would never manage to scare her into the arms of another man if she found his attentions a source of amusement.

He glanced to Miranda for help, but she was busy seeing to the children, and Marcus was his old pompous self, shouting orders to the servants in a right good humour. They were distracted and retreating down different hallways, too caught up in the business of homecoming to notice him.

And suddenly he was alone with Miss Canville.

She looked at him expectantly. 'It seems they have

quite forgotten me. But that is rather easy to do, I suppose.'

'Oh, no. I find you most memorable, and I am a very good judge of these things.'

Damn. That had sounded positively sincere and in no way dangerous.

She should have responded by blushing prettily. Instead, she cocked her head slightly to one side, considering him, and then said, 'I suppose you must be, for you have quite a reputation as a lady's man. But tell me, Captain Radwell—how many women do you find memorable? In round numbers, I mean.'

He sputtered. 'Miss Canville, that is a most impertinent question.'

'I suppose it is, but I am, as you've pointed out, just a green girl. I can hardly be expected to know what to say to a man of your reputation. You claim I am memorable, but if you find all women you meet to be memorable, then your last comment is more a tribute to your good memory than it is to any great beauty or virtue on my part.'

He smiled, despite himself. 'Let us just say that I have trouble forgetting women who come to my rooms in the evening making such suggestions as you did.'

Again, she considered before speaking. 'Well, that does narrow the field somewhat. But not to an extent where I might be truly flattered. There have been quite a few women who have done that, if the stories I hear are true.'

He could no longer contain his exasperation. 'Esme,

if you hear stories such as that, you are to pretend you haven't heard them and under no circumstances are you to repeat them back to me.'

'Just as you are not to address me by my given name without permission. And yet I could swear I just heard you use it.'

He stopped dead in his conversational tracks. She was correct. But just when had he begun thinking of her as Esme? 'That's as may be, Miss Canville—'

'Too late to redeem yourself, Captain Radwell. From now on, I must always be Esme to you.'

He sighed. 'Must you?'

She smiled. 'Yes, I must. And I will call you St John.'

'And I suppose it is too late to beg pardon and say that I merely forgot myself.'

'Scant moments ago, you confessed to an excellent memory. regarding me, at least. You remember my name, which is more than I expected. And if you can remember me, and forget yourself?' She smiled and he felt dazed by the flood of words. 'Then I think I will take that as a most singular compliment, indeed. And now, let us test your memory of the house. Perhaps you can give me a brief tour until my bags have found their way to my room.'

He shook off the effect of the smile and struggled to regain control of the conversation. 'It would not do for us to wander off alone. It is not proper for a young, un-married lady to be seen in the company of a notorious rake.'

'Then there would have to be someone to see us.'
She gestured around the room. 'In case you hadn't noticed, we are already alone. Hardly our fault, since it
is the rest of the family that has moved away.' She
slipped an arm through the crook of his elbow, and was
leading him down the corridor and away from the hall.

The feel of her arm in his was most pleasant, as was
the sensation of her standing at his side. She was neither too tall nor too short and when he looked down at
her, their eyes met with no unfortunate slouching or
craning of necks on either part. She fell easily in step
beside him as they walked, so that no adjustment of his
gait was necessary.

She smiled at him, and he smiled back, forgetting that
ease and comfort between them was never meant to be
the order of the day. That had not been the object in his
being here, but he was at a loss as to why he would care.
He was overcome with the feeling that he had fallen off
a dock somewhere and was being towed out to sea by the
current, further and further away from the safety of land.

'St John.' His brother's voice was as sharp as a rifle
crack, and it brought St John to his senses. As a bad
example to the girl, he was already a failure.

Marcus was standing in the doorway of the nearest
room, his eyes dark with a gathering storm.

St John withdrew his arm from the girl's and said
with as much composure as possible, 'And the first
stop on our tour is my brother's study. Marcus, you are
most remiss in treatment of your guests. Es…er…Miss
Canville does not know the direction of her room.'

'And she certainly does not need your help to find it.' Marcus glared at him, before turning and bowing to Esme. 'I'm sorry, Miss Canville, I cannot think what my wife is about, abandoning you like this. There must have been some problem with the children or the servants.'

As Marcus rang for the butler to take Esme to her room, St John noted to himself that the situation was indeed most strange. The children seemed quite all right when they were in the hall, as had the servants. And yet Miranda had gone away and left the two of them alone. Surely she did not expect him to seduce the girl in the first five minutes.

The butler was leading a somewhat wistful Esme toward the front stairs, and St John sighed with relief. Whatever her plan had been, he was most happy to see it effectively scotched. The girl moved much too fast for his taste. He turned in relief from her retreating form, only to be faced by the still-angry figure of the duke.

'We will speak in my study, St John. Please.'

St John recognised the word 'please' for what it was—merely a placeholder for the word 'now'. A command from the duke, masquerading as a request from a brother to set the family and servants at ease. Very well, then. After five years he was used to following orders and obeying commands. It would be no different here. He shrugged indifferently and strolled after his stiff-backed brother into the study. Flinging himself into a chair in front of the desk, he waited for Marcus to speak.

'If you are to be here, then we had best set down a code of conduct. I do not want this visit to degenerate, until it is even worse than the others.'

St John smiled. 'I doubt that would be possible. I've set the bar low enough to be hard set to find conduct that could crawl under it.'

Marcus ignored the comment and went on. 'If you wish to remain under my roof, I expect you to maintain a level of decency, and I have written down some rules to that effect.' Marcus reached into his pocket and pulled out a folded sheet of paper, and stared down at it.

'You've written them down?' St John craned his neck to get a glimpse of the paper, and Marcus angled it away so that he could not read. 'Well, how very like you, brother. So organised. God forbid we should leave anything to chance or memory. Is your pen ready? If the nib is trimmed and the ink handy, you can check off the points as we cover them.'

Marcus's eyes rose from the paper to pin him to his chair, but St John smiled back at him, trying and failing to force some trace of amusement into his brother. Then he waved his hand in dismissal. 'Read on, then. Let us get this done with.'

'First, you shall not harass the servants in any way: no chasing maids, no lingering below stairs, attempting to turn the staff to your will. No sneaking about the house like an intruder. You will enter and leave through the front doors, and if I tell you to be off, there will be no argument.'

St John examined his nails, indifferent to his brother's words.

'There will be no gambling, no whoring, no drinking.'

'Is that just in the house, or does it apply to the grounds, and the land surrounding? Because I know an inn just a few miles down the road...'

He looked up into his brother's glare. 'All right. I will have the deportment of a vicar, if you wish. But you'd best change the last to "no public drunkenness". I know the cellars in this house and I will not refuse a brandy, no matter what your list might demand.'

'Very well. Thirdly, you will not harass Miss Canville, or any of the other guests.'

'And what, exactly, is the definition of "harass"? If you wish me to break her heart, it is not as if I can avoid her totally.'

'Unwelcome attentions.'

'There again, you have me, Marcus. She made it quite plain that all my attentions were welcome, not that I chose to give them, mind you. This puts me in a damned difficult position.'

'One in which you have more experience than I, I am certain. You know from much practice where harmless flirtation ends and a true threat to honour begins. Do not cross the line. If she is as inexperienced as she appears—'

'There is no "if", Marcus. Of course she is inexperienced. The girl is a complete innocent.' His mouth snapped shut, as he caught his brother's searching ex-

pression. What did it matter what Marcus thought of
the girl's character? They would both be rid of her
soon enough. He began again. 'If she had any true
knowledge of the facts, she would not have made the
offer she did. And, yes, I probably do know more than
enough to destroy her heart while leaving her virtue intact. But I don't have to enjoy the situation. Your next
rule, please.'

Marcus looked almost sad, as he said the next
words, 'You will avoid prolonged contact with my wife
and children when I am not present. While the prospect of a truce between us pleases me, I find I cannot
bring myself to trust you with those I hold closest to
my heart. It is too late for you to be dear Uncle St John
to my children, or to pretend brotherly interest in Miranda. If I think you are attempting to ingratiate yourself into the household, I will remove you myself, by
force if necessary. Is that clear?'

St John bit back the desire to point out the difficulty
of removing him by force from anywhere he chose to
be. If the French army had not managed it… He took
a deep, steadying breath. 'Very well. It is no less than
I expected, or deserve, considering my past conduct…'
he took another breath '…for which, I apologise.'

The phrase hung in the air, surrounded by silence.

And what had he expected, really? To come back to
the house, say a few simple words and be greeted by
his brother with open arms? It was foolish beyond reason to think that he could turn back the clock and undo
any of it. And yet he had to try.

'I know that that is not sufficient. But it is all I can think to do. I will do my best to abide by the rules you have set down for me. You have my word, such as it is.'

And he held out his hand to his brother.

There was another long pause before Marcus took the offered hand in his own firm grasp. But there was no smile on his face and his eyes never wavered as they stared into St John's, searching his character.

Chapter Five

'This is the plan as I see it,' Miranda was biting the tip of her pencil, as she stared down at the paper in front of her.

Not for the first time, Esme wondered at the unusualness of the situation. The elegant woman in front of her was the last person Esme would have expected to take an interest in the problems of a nobody such as herself. And yet she seemed genuinely concerned.

Esme shifted in her chair by the morning-room fire, listening to the crisp rustle of her new gown. The clothing was another thing that Miranda had insisted upon. And matching accessories. When they'd left London, she'd had two trunks full of dresses, shoes, gloves, fans, bonnets and anything else she could think to ask for. And she was promised borrowed jewellery to suit any occasion, since Miranda had assured her that there was no want of such things at Haughleigh.

Miranda scanned her guest list again, as though

searching for a name. 'You need a husband, and you need him with expedience.'

Esme hesitated, afraid to offend her exalted new friend. 'On the contrary, I do not want or need a husband. I merely need to get rid of the one my father has chosen for me.'

'The quickest way to do that is to choose another. Preferably one so high born as to be impossible for your father to resist. What is the rank and income of the man to whom you are betrothed?'

'An Earl. Lord Halverston. I am unsure of his income, but he must be nearing eighty and is respected in the *ton*.' Esme shuddered, thinking at the vile stare from the carriage beneath her window.

'So I need to find you an earl, or better. Or someone without title, but with a fortune that no sane father could ignore. I can ask Marcus's advice on the income, for he knows anyone who matters in Parliament. And he should be young enough to suit you, but old enough to suit your father.' She glanced over the paper at Esme and began writing down names. 'I can think of several candidates in the area who might suit. And a plan of attack—'

'You make it sound as though it were a battle.'

Miranda smiled. 'But it is, my dear. It is. Or perhaps it is only a game. The gentlemen think that they have the upper hand in all things, but on this field they are consistently outmatched, should a woman truly choose to play. I will be throwing a series of parties and soirées, to entertain my new friend from the city.' She gestured in Esme's general direction with the pencil. 'It would be unspeakably rude to turn me down. And the gentlemen will think themselves quite safe, knowing that there is only one of you and…' she glanced down the paper '…three of them. Should there be matchmaking afoot, when the lot falls, it must surely fall on one of the other two.'

'And I am to choose between these three gentlemen?'

Miranda laughed. 'Three is a broad enough choice, I assure you. Any one would be fine. I would not steer you false. And we might not get all of them up to scratch. Meet them and choose the one who chooses you. Or someone else. If there is someone in attendance that you'd like better, then set your cap at him. There is no reason to limit yourself to my choices. If you need help in the matter, I will advise.'

Esme looked back doubtfully. 'That is all there is to it? I meet them and one of them is sure to offer?'

Miranda walked over and stood before her, drawing her out of her chair and to the pier-glass at the end of the room. 'I should quite think so. Look at yourself, Esme. You are lovely.'

'In borrowed finery,' Esme retorted.

'Not borrowed. Gifts. I have more than enough clothes, and I fancied a trip to the shops. It was most enjoyable to outfit you.'

'If you had more than enough, then your cast-offs would have been sufficient for me.'

'With your fair skin and hair? I should think not. You

would disappear in the colours that suit me, while I would look deplorable in the roses and pale blues that suit you so well.'

'But if most of the events are to be in the evening, surely it was not necessary to buy so many day dresses.'

'It pays to be prepared for any eventuality. One never knows who one might see during the day.'

And Esme's memory was flooded with a vision of St John, standing in the hall as she'd entered, and the look on his face when he'd seen her. She'd been warned to expect him, and apprised of Miranda's plans to use her début as an excuse to reconcile the brothers. But she'd thought that he'd be in bored attendance at some ball or other, or invited to the occasional family dinner. She hadn't dared hope that he'd be staying in the house with them, and waiting at the door for his brother's arrival.

The stunned look on his face as he'd seen her turned out properly was worth any amount of risk. As was his obvious discomposure at finding himself alone with her. It was doubtful that she'd be so lucky again, since Miranda showed every sign of being a diligent chaperon. She struggled to pay attention to Miranda's plans for the co-ordination of the Haughleigh jewelry with her new wardrobe.

'If we want these gentlemen to give you a second look, it helps to display you to your best advantage. Forgive me for saying it, but the clothing that your father allowed did not flatter you.'

'It was not intended to. It was serviceable, and inexpensive.' She could almost feel the coarse cloth against her skin, the heat of wool in summer, and the way the greys and browns hid the dirt as the shape hid her figure. She looked at her faint reflection in the window glass and saw a healthy glow to her skin and the curve of her bosom at the square neckline of the dress. 'My father would have found both these dresses and the person in them to be foolish beyond endurance. But I think I like them.'

'As will your suitors.' Miranda glanced down at the paper before her. 'Mr Webberly, not currently titled, but five and twenty and in line for his father's land. The Earl of Baxter, both titled and wealthy, and of an age that your father will approve: almost fifty. Not too old, I assure you. He is in excellent health and with a youthful demeanor. And Sir Anthony de Portnay Smythe.' She frowned. 'I am unsure of Tony's age or background. Perhaps he is not the wisest choice. But he is always a gentleman, and I must admit he is quite dashing. Should he fancy you enough to offer, he would be the one most likely to find a way through your father's disapproval.'

'And what of St John?' Esme tried not to appear too interested in the answer. 'Is he not single, and of an age to marry?'

Miranda looked searchingly into her eyes before saying, 'He is of an age, but not of an inclination. And it is as well for you that he has found some sense in these last five years, or we would not be talking now. He would have put you up in some *pied-a-terre* without benefit of clergy and then where would you be?'

Esme tried not to imagine where she might be, right now, if she were alone with St John, and the flush crept into her cheeks.

Miranda frowned. 'You must not romanticise the life of a courtesan, Esme. It is not glamorous. You would be jumping from the frying pan to the fire.'

'Perhaps.' But Esme had watched the look in St John's eyes change as he'd seen her in the hall. At first he'd scanned past, dismissing her as one of the servants. But his gaze had returned to her, when he'd noticed she was young and pretty, and there was an almost predatory gleam in the second appraisal. He'd liked what he was seeing. To be alone with a man who had that look in his eye would mean certain ruin.

But she remembered the shock and embarrassment that had followed the first roguish assessment, when St John's gaze had risen to her face and he had recognised her. And how quickly he'd looked away, only to glance back when he'd thought she wasn't looking. As though he had found his heart unexpectedly engaged.

Esme continued, 'And yet you said if I was to find someone I liked better, I should set my cap.'

Miranda looked stern, but Esme could detect the faint twinkle in her eyes. 'St John is much too wild, and shows no indication that he wishes to settle down. If you are still harbouring any foolish thoughts about becoming my brother-in-law's mistress, and if he shows any indication of the even more foolish idea of helping you to ruin, then I will do everything in my power to stop you both. Although it is of short duration, I value our friendship far too much, Esme, to allow you to do anything to jeopardise it. As St John's mistress, you would no longer be welcome in our home. I also value the bond of blood between my husband and his brother, and do not wish St John to destroy it by returning to his old ways.

'That said, if there is any chance that you can turn his head and bring him up to snuff on the subject of marriage and children—' she smiled '—then you would be doing this family a great favour and I would dearly love to call you sister. But, for now, I think it best to consider all possible candidates and not place all of the eggs in a basket so weak as St John's. Now let us go down to luncheon and show this list to my husband. Perhaps he can add other names.'

The dining room at Haughleigh was as splendid as all the other rooms, richly appointed in crimson silk and much too large for only three people. The servants had set the four places at an end of the great table, hoping to add intimacy, but without success. The duke sat at the head, which was no great surprise, with Miranda and Esme at either side. The place to Esme's left, which must have been laid for St John, was empty.

The luncheon was exceptional, but the discussion of Miranda's plans and potential guests who might suit Esme lacked the ease of their week in London. At first, Esme feared it might be caused by the expense of the parties, or the duke's discomfort of having her still with them, an uninvited guest. Many men would resent such an intrusion in their own home that they might tolerate for a week in London.

But then she felt the subtle shift in the air as another course was laid and removed from the empty chair next to hers. It was as though, even without being present in the room, St John was controlling the conversation. The duke would pause every so often during his own meal to glare at the untouched food on St John's plate. Then Miranda would make some off-hand remark, or ask a question, that would serve as a distraction to him until something else reminded him of his brother's absence. And then the pattern would repeat itself.

When the door finally opened, midway through the fish, all three heads snapped up to follow St John into the room. He took his chair without explanation and began to eat.

'You are late.' The duke was at his most commanding. There was no question but the tone demanded an explanation.

'I am sorry,' St John responded, sounding anything but. 'I did not realise that my prompt attendance at meals was mandatory. If there are other house rules you wish me to follow, perhaps you could write them down.'

'Only to see you flout them later.'

'No need to worry, brother. If I wish to flout any of your rules, I shall make sure that you are not there to see it, and thus it will not bother you.'

'Is that where you were, just now? Breaking house rules since you knew my probable location.'

'Actually, no. I was in my room, taking a nap.'

There was a tink of crystal as the stem of the duke's glass snapped in his hand. Wine spattered the tablecloth. Esme noticed the drop of blood forming in his palm before he curled his fingers into a fist and stuffed the hand into his jacket pocket. 'If you must talk at all, the least you could do is speak truth in two words out of three. First that fustian apology in my study, and now this. A nap in your room? Surely you can do better than that.'

St John glared back at him. 'It matters not what I say, since you construe all my words to be lies. I was taking a nap in my room. I was alone, to answer your next question.'

'If there had been a next question, I would not be asking it here,' the duke snapped.

'Of course not. You would be lecturing me in your study while brandishing an extensive list of things I mustn't do.'

'Can you not keep a civil tongue in your head, even at luncheon? And in front of ladies?'

'Another thing that was not on your list. Perhaps this would go easier, Marcus, if you would simply write down the things I am allowed to do. It would save my time and your ink and paper, since your list of "do's" will be considerably shorter than the "don't's".'

The duke rose from the table, too angry to respond, and stalked to the door, his uninjured hand outstretched. It struck the door palm first, springing the latch without bothering to turn the knob. Servants retreated and swirled behind him like the wake of a boat.

Miranda rose halfway out of her chair as if to follow, then glanced back at the two of them still at the table and sank back, returning to her meal as though nothing had happened.

St John said, with a hint of sadness, 'I think my brother is not so happy to see me as you'd hoped.'

Miranda took a bite of her food, not bothering to glance up again. Esme noted she was giving more than the necessary attention to chewing and swallowing, as though she needed time to marshal her emotions before speaking. At last she said, 'Perhaps if you did not provoke him so.'

St John sighed. 'Perhaps if he were not so easily provoked. I did not come here wishing to goad him. My earlier apology was sincere. I had hoped that prolonged contact would prove my intent. But that will be most difficult, since he cannot abide my company for more than a few moments at a time.'

Miranda's tone was chill. 'It is not as if he has no reason. I doubt that a simple apology will be the solution to the problem at hand.'

'But it will be a start. And despite what he may believe, I mean to follow his rules to the letter. Eventually, he will rage himself out, and then perhaps we can begin again.' St John looked down at his own plate, pushing it away untouched. 'But how long might it take for him to spend his anger? I had hoped…'

And then he looked up, smiling, and reached into his pocket. 'But maybe this will help.' He produced a velvet box and slid it across the table to his hostess.

'Something concrete to demonstrate my intentions. I had wanted to give this to you with Marcus here to witness. But Esme can assure him that my intentions in giving the gift were not dishonourable. I have debts that need settling if I am to prove to Marcus that I have changed.'

Miranda reached in front of her, snapped open the box, and recoiled as if it had been full of snakes. 'St John. How could you?' She covered her mouth with her hand and fled the room.

Esme got up and walked to the head of the table, examining the contents. 'Oh, St John, they are magnificent. But why—'

'Would my sister-in-law be so upset by the gift of an emerald necklace? I suspect my family has decided that the best way to deal with the past is to ignore it. It is an easy thing to pretend I do not exist when I am in Portugal, but much more difficult to do when I am in their presence, a constant reminder of the history between us. And this has upset her to the point of leaving us alone together. A very grave mistake, which I will now rectify.' He rose from the table as if to go.

'Wait. You cannot leave me here alone, and with only half the story.' She gripped his sleeve and tugged him back into the chair. 'What is it about the necklace that pains Miranda so?'

'The emeralds are very similar to ones that my sister-in-law once used to buy me off. A family heirloom, passed down through generations of Haughleighs. It should be gracing her neck, as it did my mother's and every other duchess of this house.' He grimaced. 'I used a pocketknife to pry the stones out and sold them, for drink and women. I treated it no better than dross. Came to my senses before the money ran out and used the last few gems to buy my commission.'

He held up the necklace and she took it from him, touching an empty setting at the centre.

'I sent the last remaining stone to Miranda for Christmas before I left for the war. That is the place for it. I kept the setting. I always meant to repay her.' He frowned down at the necklace. 'I saved every penny of my soldier's pay to buy new stones and have them reset. It is all I have left in the world. I was hoping to give it back and then we could be even. Better to start fresh with nothing than to live any longer with this debt. But it is still not enough. She is no more willing to accept it than my brother is to hear my apology.'

She placed the necklace back in its case. 'But what could you have done that was so horrible that your only brother will not forgive it?'

St John took a sip of wine. 'I seduced his wife.'

Esme's jaw dropped.

He held up a finger. 'Wives, actually.' Then shook his head. 'No. Wife would be more correct. His first wife, only. I attempted to seduce Miranda, but was unsuccessful.' His look was almost wistful. 'When she first came here, she was not the great beauty that she is now. But lovely all the same. And my foolish brother left her alone. I hated him, and I thought it would serve him right had he lost her.' He shook his head. 'I hope, if I did nothing else, I taught him to appreciate his wife.'

'And did you teach him to appreciate his first wife?' Esme's tone was sharper than she meant it to be.

'No. I loved her.' His eyes were so sad, and so distant, that she was sorry she'd rebuked him. He stared back at her, empty. 'As did Marcus, I think. And Bethany loved no one but herself. She played us against each other. And then she died. We were young, and foolish. I was particularly so. By the time she died, I was mad with wanting her and knowing I could never have her. It took years for the madness to fade. When it did, I was in the army, a thousand miles from home. I swore, if I lived to see England again, that I would make amends.'

Esme smiled encouragingly. 'I knew, when I looked at you, that you could not be the man my father said you were.'

St John smiled sadly back at her. 'Oh, no, darling. I am as bad and worse. Because I no longer attempt to steal my brother's wife does not mean I'm incapable of stealing from another man. Only more selective.'

Esme hinted, 'Then perhaps you ought to find a woman who is not already attached.'

'And let her attach herself to me? No, thank you.' His smile turned cynical. 'Or is this another attempt to achieve ruination? You still do not understand.' He leaned close to her and let his breath touch her cheek as he whispered in her ear. 'You think, because you see a moment's softness of heart, and because I do not strike women, no matter how much they deserve a good beating, that I am some kind of saviour? A dark angel, come to rescue you? Well, think again, little one. If you let me, I will take everything you offer.'

She closed her eyes so that he could not see the longing in them.

His tone turned·bitter. 'I will take from you things you do not know you have to give. And when you are empty and there is nothing left to take, I will be gone and you can go home to your father. Then you may look him in the eye if you are able, and explain to him why no decent man would ever want you. I have done it before, you know. There are worse sins on my con science than cuckolding my brother. Do not ask me to ruin another innocent, even if it is yourself. It is too much.' And he pushed away from the table, turned and walked from the room.

Chapter Six

Esme stood in the doorway of the ballroom at Haugh-leigh before her introduction to Devon society, fighting the urge to run. It would be most ungrateful of her to bolt from a party at which she was the honoured guest. It had been quite amazing to watch her new friend, Miranda, effortlessly organise dinner and a ball for more than a hundred people, creating guest lists and menus from notes of the many past balls she'd given, and sending the majority of preparations on ahead before they'd even left London.

It was to be a welcoming event for Esme, and a celebration of the duke and duchess's return to their estate. Miranda assured her that the neighbours would be happy to attend, and were likely to reciprocate with invitations of their own.

Esme tried to quell the trepidation she felt at the prospect. She'd had no Season of her own, and what parties she'd attended were small and rather dull. And she'd never been the centre of attention at any of them. But this night she was in the receiving line as the guests filed past, and Miranda had introduced them all, occasionally leaning towards her and whispering, 'Eligible' 'Very eligible' or 'Eligible and rich.' It got to the point where Esme could judge by the brightness of her friend's smile the income and suitability of any male guests that made their bows.

And she wished that it mattered. She truly did. Miranda was trying so hard, and Esme knew her prospects, and the urgency of the situation, if she wished to avoid the marriage that her father would choose for her. But she had always hoped, when she'd dreamed of the balls she was missing and suitors that she could never have, that her feelings would be engaged when it was time to choose a husband.

Perhaps that was the problem. She'd imagined herself doing the choosing, not waiting patiently to be chosen. Without Miranda's help, she might never have had any say in the matter at all. But in the end, it would be up to a gentleman to choose her. And now, having met the best that the neighborhood had to offer, she found herself wishing ardently that none would step forward.

'St John,' Miranda called out sharply, 'come here this instant and properly greet our guest. Because you are family, you may think you can slink past us and avoid the line. But the least you can do is make Esme welcome and thank your host before drinking our wine.'

St John rolled his eyes before saying with exaggerated courtesy, 'I am so sorry, your Grace, that living here most of my life led me to make myself at home.'

Esme could feel the duke stiffen and ready a response, and Miranda tensing at his side, ready to avert the conflict that she had created by calling St John to them.

And then she felt the tension dissipate, as St John's shoulders slumped in submission and he muttered, 'What am I about?' and began again. 'Of course, Miranda. You are right. I was being provoking and have no wish to spoil your evening with my behaviour. He turned to his brother, and said awkwardly, 'It really is quite splendid, to see the old house this way. For a moment, I was taken back to when we were boys and Mother held such parties here.' He scanned the room. 'Although I think your wife may have outdone her. Perhaps it is only that I am finally tall enough to see over the tables.' He leaned closer to Miranda. 'Did your husband tell you of all the times he led me here from the nursery, to steal cakes and lemonade? I was not always the scapegrace of the family. Marcus got up to his share of trouble and I was but a sweet and innocent child, following my brother's lead.'

The duke looked shocked, before admitting, 'He is right. I had forgotten it until now. But he is right in this. I always found the cakes we took from balls to be sweeter than the ones brought to the nursery to keep us out of the way. And as I remember it, it took very little effort to lead you astray.' He looked even more shocked and smiled as he said, 'It took no effort to lead you anywhere, for back then you followed me like a puppy on a leash.'

St John turned from the dazed duke. 'And, Miss Canville, is a formal greeting necessary? For I feel I know you quite well all ready.' He bowed low over her hand and then rose and looked into her eyes for a moment too long, until she could feel her cheeks beginning to colour. 'You are looking most splendid this evening.'

Of course he must say that to all the young ladies and so it meant little. But she had seen herself in the mirror, and tonight it was true. The rose silk of her gown suited her to perfection. Her hair was dressed with care and accented with real pearls borrowed from the duchess. And, best of all, the skin of her arms and throat was unmarked. She was as pure and beautiful as any of the ladies present.

It was good that she had failed in her original plan, for what would he have thought had she disrobed before him that first night, when the bruises were still fresh? No one chose fruit when the flesh was discoloured. They cast such aside. When choosing a woman it was probably no different.

She put those thoughts from her head and said, 'Thank you, sir.' And as she smiled back at him she felt the low fluttering in her stomach that seemed always present when St John was near. Or was likely to be near, or even mentioned in passing conversation.

It occurred to her that its absence accounted for the

strange dead feeling when meeting the other gentlemen of the neighborhood. They might be very nice, but they all suffered from the disadvantage of not being St John Radwell.

He was looking at her as if he saw nothing unusual in her behaviour. Perhaps her feelings did not show on her face.

'Yes,' he said, nodding in approval at her appearance. 'If you insist on looking so well when turned out for a ball, and looking at them with such fine eyes and that hopeful smile of yours, I imagine the eligible men in the room will be quite helpless to escape. I must thank the Lord that I am immune to your charms or I might find myself in a great deal of trouble.' And, after another half-bow, he turned and went in search of the wine.

Immune?

'I must say, St John is on his best behaviour this evening.' Miranda was smiling up at her husband.

As though she were some kind of pestilence. A disease.

'Yes,' the duke replied, 'that is rather a surprise. This is the first time in years that I've not had the desire to strangle him where he stood.'

Perhaps it was a transferable desire, for Esme quite felt the urge to strangle him herself.

'Of course,' Marcus remarked, 'the night is still young. He will most certainly have done something by midnight that causes the old rage to return. But he is right about my mother's parties. And the cakes. Why, when my father was alive…'

Esme's mind wandered from the discussion, as her eyes followed St John's retreating back through the room. How dare he? She was trouble, was she, now? And he felt himself lucky to be able to resist. Then he must hope that his luck would hold for she knew, with a sudden wave of resolve, that the only head she wanted to turn was on the impressively broad shoulders of Captain Radwell.

She set off into the whirl of the ball, intent on having the best time possible. She enjoyed herself with an almost spiteful enthusiasm. She positively glittered with the joy of being there. The dancing was divine, the company superb, and when she was lead into dinner on the arm of a frightened young man, she found the food to be beyond all imagining.

And was honest in her praise. It was the most delightful evening she'd ever spent, though perhaps the wine was ever so slightly bitter, and the pheasant flavourless, and the trifle less than moist, when she caught the occasional glimpse of St John entertaining his dinner companion at another table. The girl next to him looked flattered at the attention, and Esme thought she could hear the girl's silvery laughter as St John relayed some amusing story, and saw her faint blush in the candlelight as he leaned closer to her. Then, suddenly, the girl turned her face to Esme and stared at her with unexpected venom.

Esme pushed her own plate away with dessert unfinished. What could she have done to anger the girl, and deserve such a look? It chilled her to think that she had somehow made an enemy on her first public appearance. She shook off the feeling and attempted to focus on the conversation of the gentleman next to her.

She was trying, God knew, but why must it be so difficult? Mr Webberly was pleasant, honest and interested in her. He was not so much older than she, and, according to Miranda, he stood to inherit many acres of excellent farmland. Although his face was not as devilishly attractive as some people's in the room, it was open and honest and he would probably make someone an excellent husband.

And she hoped it was not to be her.

After dinner, he stood up with her, leading her slowly in a figure of the dance and handing her down the set. She tried to imagine him standing up to her father, or breaking with tradition to borrow a coach and spirit her off to Scotland. The picture would not form. She glanced back up the row, and saw Mr Webberley turning a local girl in the same steps, and looked again in shock. It was the pale girl who had been sitting with St John and who'd looked at her with such spite. And the man holding her hand could easily have been a total stranger to the one Esme had just danced with. His spine was straighter and his gaze more direct when he looked at the new girl.

She sighed in relief. It would be wrong to want him for herself. Not when someone else wanted and needed him more, and he wanted her in return. Esme had but to see that they spent the evening in each other's company, and she need never worry about his attentions again.

She shook her head. It was foolish to think of his attentions as unwanted. What she wanted was unimportant, it what she needed that mattered. An escape from the marriage set before her. One solution should be as good as another, and it would be much smarter to put her own wants and needs ahead of those of a complete stranger.

And then she looked down at the end of the set, to see St John lounging insolently against the wall, scorn for the young couple dancing together at the head. As her new partner took her hand and turned her, St John caught her eye, and she saw his mirth at her discomposure. He glanced from her to Webberley dancing at the head of the set and raised his glass in a mocking toast, as if to wish her well on the nuptials.

So many emotions rushed through her at once that it was hard to feel them all. There was shame at being caught husband-hunting, and embarrassment that he'd read her mind so easily from across the room. There was a moment's pride at the way his eyes had run over her before raising the glass. He'd looked at her as a woman, not as a girl, and something about the set of his shoulders had said that he could show her what she wanted to know better than the callow youth she was dancing with.

And there was a rush of all the things she did not feel when she looked at Webberley. It was not love, precisely. It was something stronger than love, but not so long lasting, a bone-deep desire to ignore what was good for her, to forget the future and revel in the present, spending every moment she could in the arms of St John Radwell.

The crush was intolerable. Even though she knew the room well, she could not help but feel that she was in a strange new world, now that the guests were here. When the next dance ended she crept to the ladies' retiring room to catch her breath.

Conversation stopped when she entered the room, and she wondered if there was some rule of conduct that she should be following of which she was not aware. But the ladies in the room crowded protectively around one of their own, and Esme immediately felt like the outsider.

It was the girl who had been dancing with Webberley. On close inspection, she was a little older than Esme, and she held herself awkwardly, as though she was no more at home in her surroundings than Esme was herself. There were obvious traces of tears on her cheeks that a friend was trying to conceal with powder.

Esme stepped forward without thinking and said, 'Is there something I can do to help? Should I get the duchess?'

The friend of the pale girl said coldly, 'I think you've done quite enough all ready.'

'Ann, please don't make it any more difficult.' The girl released a watery sigh, and Esme feared that the tears so recently stopped were likely to start again. 'Do not trouble her.'

Ann's eyes narrowed. 'No, why should I do anything to help you, if you will not help yourself?'

'I do not understand,' Esme said quietly. 'What is it that I am supposed to have done to your friend, when until scant hours ago I'd never laid eyes on her?'

'It is nothing.' The pale girl laid a hand on the arm of her friend, in an effort to silence her.

But Ann would not be quieted. 'Nothing but that there is a limited number of eligible men in the area. And the number of marriageable females has just increased by one.' Ann gave her a pointed look. 'We are from the country and you are from London. You are fashionable, pretty—worst of all, you are different. The gentlemen of the area have known us our whole lives. We cannot give them novelty. One of them is likely to offer for you. And this means one of us is to be disappointed. At the moment, it appears it may be Elizabeth. And, of course, this upsets her. But if you have plans in another direction, you might do us the courtesy of telling us so and setting her mind at rest. I have enough powder for all.'

Several sets of eyes stared at her in accusation, and she froze, searching her mind for the correct response. It had never occurred to her that there might be other schemes afoot at a gathering of this type. 'I have no designs on the gentlemen present,' she faltered.

'Oh, really? You have danced three dances with Mr Webberley, which is more than enough to incite comment.'

Had it been three? If so, they had made no impact upon her.

'I am sorry. I had not realised.' She attempted an encouraging smile that was not returned by the gathering in front of her. 'But now that I understand how things are, I will be more careful of the impression I give to the gentlemen of the area. If you will excuse me?' She backed hurriedly out of the room and returned to the ballroom.

She found Mr Webberley standing near the refreshments. He seemed to be looking for a face in the crowd; although he smiled in greeting to her, Esme could not help but think that it was not she he had been searching for.

She took the lemonade he offered with thanks and asked, 'Who is the tall girl you were dancing with earlier? The one in the unsuitable red dress?'

'Unsuitable? I find it most becoming.' There was a hint of censure in his voice. 'Her name is Miss Elizabeth Warrant.'

She smiled to herself at how quick the gentleman was to rush to the girl's defence. 'Well, red is hardly the thing so late in the summer. And it does not suit her. She would do better to choose something brighter.'

'Her family is not able to spend so extravagantly as some, with a new gown for every occasion. But I think she is turned out well, indeed.' His eyes were still scanning the dance floor.

Aha. She was definitely striking a nerve. 'I only wondered because she seemed so upset in the retiring room just now, as though she were hiding herself away. This is sometimes the case, when a woman does not think she looks her best. Or perhaps she is ill.' She said it lightly, as though it were not worth noting, but she noticed the man next to her pale.

'Elizabeth is ill? I am a neighbour to her family. If she is not well, perhaps retiring early would be best. But it would be a shame to spoil the evening for her sisters—'

'So you would offer to take her home yourself?' She finished his sentence and left him with no choice in the matter. 'Oh, would you? You are too kind, sir, to take such good care of a friend. Shall I see if she needs assistance, while you ready your carriage?'

'That would be best, I think.' She watched as Mr Webberley went in search of carriage and groom. He was secure in the knowledge that he had come up with the idea himself. It was too perfect.

Esme returned to the retiring room, shutting the door with a definitive snap behind her. 'Ann?'

The sour girl looked up at her with reproach and said nothing.

'Leave off helping your friend, for it would not do to have her looking too well. She is deathly ill and must return home at once.'

'I beg your pardon?' Elizabeth said, showing some spine for a change. 'I have no intention of leaving you to—'

'But you must. For I told Mr Webberley you are taken suddenly ill. He seemed most concerned. And please stop flushing. It is making you look far too healthy. Ann, do you have powder in a paler shade, perhaps? We need to kill the roses in those cheeks immediately.'

Ann recognised what was happening and smiled in satisfaction.

But Elizabeth said, 'I feel fine.'

'No, you do not,' Ann replied. 'You need to be taken home this instant.' She was furiously applying powder, and Elizabeth suddenly looked quite faint.

And yet the foolish girl insisted, 'I cannot go home. I do not wish to. My sisters would be so disappointed.'

'Which is why you must leave them here, to ride home with your parents. There will be other balls for you, but no night with a moon as fine as this one.'

There was still no light of comprehension in the eyes of the unfortunate Elizabeth.

Esme explained, 'If I do not miss my guess, Mr Webberley has found your parents and is even now explaining his intention to take you home in his carriage. Borrow a maid from Miranda if need be, preferably one who is a bit hard of hearing and a trifle blind. Or perhaps the rules of propriety can be bent, because of your weakened condition and Mr Webberley's position as a trusted family friend. Judging by the speed he rushed to your defence when I questioned him, and the look in his eyes when he thought you were ill, you need have no fear for your reputation as concerns Mr Webberly. He will guard it against all comers once he has proposed to you.'

'Oh, dear. I feel quite faint,' said Elizabeth.

'I hoped for nothing less. Use it to your advantage,' said Esme and turned to go. As the door shut behind her, she could hear Ann exhorting her friend to not be such a goose as to walk unsupported, but to take the man's arm and 'hold on 'til the last trump, if that was what it took'.

She smiled as she left the room and moved through the crowd at the door to the ballroom, satisfied with a job well done. But when she glanced down the stairs she thought she saw a familiar coat disappearing into the hall below.

St John. She tried to keep her heart from beating a little faster at the thought of him, though he seemed to be making every effort to avoid her for the evening. He had not danced a single dance with her, although she'd seen him stand up for several sets with others, including that wet hen, Elizabeth. And while she could swear that more than once she'd caught him watching her from across the room, he'd made no effort to speak to her.

Perhaps he meant to take a turn about the gardens, as many guests were doing. Suddenly, Esme longed for fresh air. She hurried down the steps and out the door.

Miranda had done a charming job of arranging the gardens for the ball. The paths were lit by tiny lanterns, and benches had been set for guests to enjoy the smell of the roses and the light of the full moon as it played on the surface of the ornamental pond. It was a beautiful night for a walk, although somewhat chilly. Esme rubbed the skin of her arms, wishing she'd thought to get a wrap before venturing from the house.

She passed several couples strolling arm in arm, and groups or people talking and laughing quietly, their clothes and hair silvery with moonlight. But there was no sign of St John, and she was getting quite far from the house. The path was no longer lit, and she suspected that this was a signal from Miranda that guests need go no further.

But she was not technically a guest, was she? She was a resident of the house, at least for now. And there was nothing to fear on the duke's estate. The full moon lit her way well enough. Perhaps just a little further…

'Looking for me?' St John's voice came out of the gloom behind her and she caught her breath.

'No. I mean, yes. Yes, I am. I wanted to…' The words froze in her throat.

'I'm sure you did, darling. Alone, in a dark garden, and so far away from the other guests. But I already told you, no. Did you think, once I saw you dressed in satin with stars in your eyes, that I might change my mind?' He strolled towards her. His movements were deliberate, with an almost animal grace, and his steps on the gravel of the path made no noise.

Was he different, or was it moonlight and champagne that made him seem so much more dangerous than he did during the day? She glared back at him, hoping that he would read her expression and ignore the shudder that travelled through her body as he taunted her. 'You really are the most odious man.'

He shrugged. 'As I've been trying to tell you, love.'

She tossed her head. 'It would serve you right if I found someone else.'

'Serve me?' He laughed. 'Alas, you'd not be the first missed opportunity, Esme. I will be wounded, but I shall survive. And it would be cutting off your nose to spite your face, when there are men in there who would have you honourably, to seek dishonour out of pique at me.'

It was her turn to laugh. 'They'll have me, will they? When they learn that there is no fortune that paid for these pretty clothes?'

'I'm sure many—'

'Then I fear, for all your debauchery, that you are much more naïve than I, St John. Without my father's consent, I have nothing. Of course, I can wait until I am of age, and I can do as I please if my father will allow me from the house. But how will I survive? I have no money, and no way to support myself. Again, I will have nothing. I do not fool myself so far as to believe I am such a great beauty that men will lose their hearts and all good sense. And it seems that many of the young ladies in the neighbourhood have plans for those same gentlemen that Miranda would choose for me. While they might find my company diverting, they will return to the familiar when it is time to offer marriage.'

She smiled back towards the house. 'I've already had to send Miranda's first candidate for my hand to assist a young lady who became most indisposed when she saw me monopolising him. If the gentleman has a lick of sense, he's making use of a trip in a closed carriage to convince the girl that she need fear nothing from me in regards to the disposition of his affection.'

'And if he has no sense?' St John asked in amusement.

'Then I believe the girl was being instructed, as I left her, in how to fake a swoon. If he cannot be moved to action when the moon is full and the woman he loves is near senseless in his arms, then I want no part of him either.'

There was a bark of laughter from St John. 'You set a trap for him so that he would marry someone else? Esme, darling, you do not understand husband-hunting at all.'

'It was for his own good, I assure you. Miranda meant well, but Mr Webberley was not intended for me. I could not very well have taken him away from the girl who loved him, and rejoiced in my success. It would have been wrong.' She turned away from him, looking out over the lawn, and wrapped her arms around her body, feeling the chill in the air. 'I should not have agreed to come here. It is folly to think that I will fit any better here than I might at home. Miranda should not be burdened with my problems.'

And the air warmed again as he stepped close behind her. 'While you continue to be a trial to me, Esme, you are no burden to my family. Miranda is overjoyed at having you. Now set your mind to rest and trust her to make you a match.'

'But I do not want them.' She hadn't meant to be so candid, but it was too late to call the words back.

'Not still dangling after me, are you? Little fool. I thought I'd made it plain enough. I can give you only one thing.'

She turned to face him, standing in the circle of his arms. 'Only the one thing I want. And yet you will not give it to me.'

She felt him tense, but he did not pull away. 'Offer to ruin you.' He stepped closer, then, and his arms slipped around her waist, pulling her close. 'To be here with me now is already your undoing, should someone find us.' He bent over her, and his lips brushed her hair. 'You should know better than to let a man take liberties with you, love, especially not a man such as myself. You are lucky that I have new-found self-restraint.' He put her from him and made to walk away.

'Self-restraint? You?' She remembered him, scolding his mistress loud enough for the whole street to hear. She could not help herself. She laughed. Then she stepped close to him again, tipping her head up to look into his face. 'Perhaps it is true. For all the stories I've heard told about you, St John, you cannot be as bad as people say.' Her voice fell to a whisper. 'Because you have me, alone in the dark. You can do as you will with me. And all you do is talk.'

He seized her and pulled her to him again. And then his fingers touched her chin, guiding her lips to meet his. He brushed lightly over her mouth, murmuring,

'And now I am done talking. Open your mouth, that I may kiss you better.'

She parted her lips in surprise, ready to ask him what he meant to do, when his mouth came down on hers and he showed her. His breath was in her mouth and then his tongue, filling her. He was stroking her with it, and his hand held her head so that there could be no escape.

Not that she could ever want to get away. She relaxed and let him take her mouth. Her body longed to be closer to his so she pressed against him, slipping her bare arms inside his coat and letting the warmth of his body take the chill away.

And it occurred to her in a haze of heat that what he was doing to her she could as easily do to him. And she slipped her tongue into his mouth, stroking in return.

He pushed her roughly away from him and dropped his hands to his sides. 'Just as I thought. Totally inexperienced.'

'H-have I done something wrong?' She reached to touch his sleeve and he brushed her hand away. 'Because I could learn…'

He snorted. 'If I wished to be a teacher, I imagine you could. But I would much prefer a woman who knows what she's about. To have to endure the fumblings of a green girl, to be gentle and careful of her pride and her delicacies? To initiate? When I want a virgin to bore me in bed, then I'll propose to one. But for now, Esme darling, my tastes require something that you cannot possibly offer me. Marry one of the young bucks in that ballroom. Take your pick of the crop. In a couple of years, when you are thoroughly tired of each other, then return to me with some experience and we shall do well together. But for now, will you just leave me in peace?'

She had been trembling from cold, but now it was shame that chilled her, and she turned and ran, back into the house, far, far away from the man behind her.

St John waited for the tide of animal lust that was rising in him to subside. She had clung to him, grinding her little body against him, and moaning softly into his mouth. And the feeling of her tongue as it had slipped past his teeth... It would have been so easy. He closed his eyes and spoke to the darkness. 'I trust you saw it all.'

He heard his brother step out from behind a nearby tree and on to the path beside him. 'Of course I did. You knew I was here. We walked out of the house together.'

'But you could have left us alone. Instead you stood in the dark and watched me kiss her. Are you a chaperon or a voyeur?'

He waited for an explosion from Marcus, but it did not come. 'I trusted you to do the thing we asked you to do and nothing more.'

St John glared at his brother, whose face was unreadable in the shadows of the garden. 'You trusted me...but not so much as to leave her alone with me. Thank you, brother, I know how much your trust is worth.'

There was tiredness in Marcus's voice when he

spoke. 'Considering our past, did you expect me to trust easily?'

St John sighed. 'I suppose I should not have expected you to trust at all. But I have done what Miranda asked, I think. I have broken her heart to the extent requested. Am I to be sent away?'

There was a long pause as he waited for Marcus to answer, and he steeled himself for the dismissal. It would not do to care too much in his brother's presence.

And then Marcus shrugged. 'As long as you don't bother the girl further, you may stay or go, as you please.'

St John stood very still, while considering the words. His brother did not care if he remained? Apathy was a far cry from the open animosity that he was accustomed to, or the rejection he expected. And before the girl had interrupted, they had been chatting in a way that was almost civil. Perhaps there was hope. 'Believe me, I have no intention of bothering the girl. And I sincerely hope that the girl is done bothering me.'

But somehow, he doubted that that was the case. She was likely to bother him very much, if he remained.

'You know my rules, and appear to be abiding by them,' Marcus said. 'Then do as you will.'

St John's mouth quirked into an ironic smile. 'By which you mean, I am to do as you will.'

'Is there some problem with that?'

'None that I know of. You had suggested nothing I didn't intend before arriving. I merely resented being told.' He forestalled his brother's retort. 'But not so much as to kick over the traces to annoy you. I am not five, Marcus. Nor even five and twenty. If you do not treat me as a spoiled child, I will promise not to behave as one.'

His brother's laugh came in a sharp bark, startling in the silence. 'Very well, then. Stay.' And the duke turned and walked towards the house, leaving St John alone in the darkness.

Chapter Seven

As always, breakfast at Haughleigh was superlative, and Esme reminded herself to count her blessings before partaking. While last night's ball had not been a triumph, it had been more enjoyable than any other she had experienced. Miranda had seen to it that she'd looked her best, and she had received compliments from many of the gentlemen she'd danced with. The music had been wonderful, as had the champagne and the dinner. She was the toast of the evening.

Of course, she had not become betrothed, as Miranda might have hoped, but that was a rather unrealistic goal for her first entry into local society, so Esme did not count it as important. Instead, she had done a good deed for Miss Warrant and effected an uneasy truce with the other eligible young ladies of the community. Surely this must count as a positive.

And she had received her first kiss. Her pulse quickened at the memory of it. It had been more than delightful, at first. The feel of his lips and his tongue and the strength of his body against hers was everything she had hoped it would be. If she could manage to forget the last moments, when St John had laughed and dismissed her, it would have been the most perfect night of her life.

She glanced across the table. St John looked like death warmed over. If he had not the decency to leave her alone, or the willingness to follow through with what he started, or at the very least the kindness to cry off without insulting her—she smiled to herself—then the least he could do was to look the morning after as he did now. Clearly an excess of drink had left him out of sorts, for his eyes were red and his hand trembled, and it appeared that the clink of glasses and the chink of the silver on china was almost more than he could bear.

She rattled her fork against her plate and watched in satisfaction as he winced and closed his eyes.

The duke was sorting through the post and passed a letter down the table to her. 'Miss Canville, your father, most likely enquiring after your health.'

'Thank you, your Grace.' She took the envelope and noted with satisfaction that there was no tremor in her own hands as she broke the seal.

My Darling Daughter, I trust this finds you in good health.

She felt her mouth go dry at the sound of her father's voice in her head, the innocent words dripping with venom.

She paused and took a sip of water before continuing to read.

It was, no doubt, some girlish fancy that led you from the house in the night. Do you dream of escape from the responsibilities placed upon you? I think the sooner you accept the truth, put such foolishness aside, and return home, the better and easier it shall be for both of us. You know I do not like to be kept waiting.

In her mind, a picture flashed of the last time she'd defied him. He had invited his friends to supper, and she had cried off from playing hostess because of a megrim. The menu had been prepared, and the library was set for cards after the meal. There had been no need for her to attend, since the group of elderly gentlemen who were her father's favourites rarely noticed her presence during the meal or missed her when she retired after it. But he had insisted that she come down to dinner. She ignored his repeated demands that she appear at the table, curled up on her bed with the headache pounding in her ears. What good would it do her to sit downstairs, dazed with pain, embarrassing him in front of his friends? Surely he must understand that this was better.

And at last he had come upstairs to get her. His voice through her bedroom door was reason itself. He would not raise it, lest someone hear and he might embarrass himself. 'Do not make this difficult, Esme. You know my anger grows with my impatience.'

She'd whispered, 'I am sorry. I am so sorry', knowing what would come. And then loud enough so that he could hear through the door, 'I'm sorry, Father. I do not feel well enough to attend you.'

His voice became more insistent. 'You will not escape punishment by waiting. And he'd begun to count. Slowly and evenly. 'One, two, three…'

Would it help to apologise again? Would it be any worse if he had to open the door and drag her from her room? She'd left her bed and stood next to the door, hand on the knob.

'Four, five, six…' His cane tapped impatiently on the floor in the corridor, keeping time with his voice.

She sat frozen in the spot, knowing that it was folly to wait, but still afraid to open the door.

'Seven, eight…'

And finally she'd broken through the fear and turned the knob. 'I am sorry, Papa. So sorry.'

And without another word, he'd pushed her back into the room and closed the door. He spun her to face the wall and she'd listened to him count along with the blows of the cane on her back and shoulders. He'd stopped when he reached eight and watched impassively as she slumped to the floor at his feet.

'Next time, I trust you will learn to come when you are called. You know I do not like to be kept waiting. Now, pull yourself together and come down to dinner. The guests are waiting.'

'Esme!' The voice was real and in the room with her, and startled her back into the present. She opened her eyes and was staring into the worried gaze of St John.

'Is there something the matter?'

'No. No, I am fine.'

'The look on your face…'

'Was no worse than the look on yours, I'm sure. You of all people should understand the results of too much wine and not enough sleep, and sympathise, rather than shouting at me.' She rubbed at her temple, soothing an imaginary megrim.

'Too much wine?' His eyes narrowed. 'When you left me last night in the garden, you seemed none the worse for it.'

'I'd had more than enough, I assure you,' she snapped.

'Really? And I thought you wanted more.'

She raised her hand to strike him and struggled to turn the gesture into something innocent before he noticed how he'd hurt her. But before she could regain control, St John had snatched the letter from off the table where she had dropped it.

'St John,' Miranda warned. 'Do not torment the girl.'

Esme looked across the table, and flushed with shame. She had forgotten that they were not alone. Miranda and the duke were staring at her in concern.

St John unfolded the letter. 'I apologise for the impertinence.' He glanced down at the note. 'I was afraid that there was something here that might have been upsetting.' He scanned over the words. 'That does not appear to be the case. It seems innocent enough.'

Miranda turned with controlled fury to her brother-in-law and said, 'All the same, it does not give you the right to read another's mail. Give her the letter and apologise this instant.'

'It is all right,' Esme said as placidly as possible. She returned to her breakfast, trying to pretend an appetite for the food in front of her. 'There was no harm done.'

St John was still looking at her; she could feel his eyes burning on her until she looked up to meet them. 'I think perhaps there was. I am sorry, Esme. I humbly apologise for any wrong I have done you.' He said it so slowly and with such emphasis that she suspected the words had nothing to do with the letter in his hand.

'It was nothing, really,' she murmured, staring back down at her plate.

She heard him fold the letter, and he slid it along the table, until it was in front of her again. She snatched it up and tucked it into her sleeve. 'Esme.' His voice was quiet, but insistent. 'Esme, look at me.'

She looked up.

His face was solemn, but encouraging. 'I am sorry, truly, that I have made you unhappy. If I were not sure that Miranda and my brother could find a better solution—' He stopped. 'No, even if they could not do better for you, I am not sure there is any way I could help. But whatever I do now, no matter how cruel it may seem, I do it because I want what is best for you.' And he laid his hand on hers and gave it a gentle squeeze.

She ignored the way her heart leapt when he touched her and said with her most obedient voice, 'Thank you, St John. I understand.'

She understood very well. She had found yet another man who was intent on doing what they thought 'best' for her, with little regard to what she might want for herself. But now that she had escaped from the tyranny of her father, it was only a matter of time before she set St John Radwell straight about what would be best for both of them.

She smiled down at her eggs and took another bite.

St John closed his eyes and watched the patterns of light and dark play on his eyelids as a breeze stirred the leaves above him. It was so pleasant to be sitting thus, under a tree in the garden, wondering whether a small nap might be possible and if it would help or hinder his appetite at lunch.

He should not get used to it. If he stayed too long at his brother's estate, Marcus would begin to wonder at his motives. It would not do to have to explain that his pockets were to let and he needed charity, yet again. The truth of the matter, that he could not afford to live elsewhere, would quite spoil the appearance he was trying to create that he was perfectly capable of surviving without help from the family.

The sunlight was warm on his upturned face. Good, English sunlight, he reminded himself. Not the cold and rain of Portugal in spring. No fears of battles past or still to come. And no sign of Esme Canville.

It was impossible to relax if he needed to maintain a constant defence against the girl. He had told her as politely as possible at breakfast that anything between them was an impossibility. And she had smiled her inscrutable smile and agreed with him so easily that he suspected she did not agree with him at all. If he was not careful, he would find himself in the awkward position of defending his honour from her unwanted advances.

The thought made him smile. Five years ago, when he had no honour to defend, life was simpler. He would have looked into those blue eyes of hers and fallen without a second thought. He imagined what it might have been like, and let himself drift away to thoughts of a sweet and willing Esme, and the sound of a single fly buzzing somewhere far above him.

But before he could lose himself in what had the makings of a very promising dream, he was roused to full consciousness by the sound of children's voices, distant, but growing nearer. A girl's hesitant quaver. The boy, firm and insistent.

He smiled. Ever Marcus's son, the next duke even in leading strings. He rose and walked toward the sound. It would not be a violation of Marcus's order, if he were to watch over them from a distance.

'We mustn't,' little Charlotte argued. 'Nurse doesn't know where we have gone. She will be cross.'

'Nurse will not miss us if we hurry, Lottie. What good is a trip to the country, if it only means more lessons in a different room? And you want to see the horses, don't you?' Young John was pulling her hand, but she refused to move.

There was a pause, as the girl considered. And then a hesitant, 'Yes.'

'Good. Then let us go to the stables.' John tugged again and they were in motion.

St John rolled his eyes. No nurse, and out for an adventure? Damn Marcus's rules. He'd be minus a nephew if he allowed the children to wander into trouble. He followed at a distance as the boy led the girl to the stables, jollying and then bullying her by turns to keep her moving.

St John breathed a sigh of relief when they neared the building, assuming that a groom would be along shortly to send them back to the house. But no adult arrived. He hesitated for a moment and then strode into the barn, after the children.

And his heart stuck in his throat to see them, standing beneath the head of a stallion, within an easy kick of the great, sharp hooves. The horse was eyeing them with suspicion, as the next duke explained to his sister that this would be his horse, once he had talked to Father.

St John stepped forward with care, in order not to startle the beast, and laid a hand on its neck, stepping between it and the children. 'It will not ever be your horse, lad, if your father catches you here without permission. Horses can be dangerous with people they do not know. I'm sure Marcus meant you to see them when he could show them to you properly.'

'He doesn't have time.' The boy pouted and St John gave him a stern look.

'Not today, perhaps, but he soon will, I'm sure.'

'He said that he and you would run away and have all sorts of adventures when you were little.'

So Marcus did remember their youth with fondness. He must be getting soft in his dotage, or children had clouded his view of the past. 'And did he tell you how much trouble we got into when we did? Proper punishment from your grandfather for stunts like this. We were boys, of course, and deserved what we got. But you would not want your little sister to pay for your wilfulness, would you?'

The boy looked doubtful.

'Or to see her stepped on by those great hooves, there, for standing too close?'

The boy looked very worried indeed now.

'I thought not. There'll be time enough for horses, and adventures, too, for this is to be your house and you'll be in it all summer and for many summers to come. Patience, my boy. You must learn to wait, not rush headlong into trouble, or your mother and father will be grey before their time. But no harm done today, and if you hurry, you can sneak back into the nursery before you're missed. Go through the kitchen garden and up the back stairs, and no one will see you. It is the way your father and I used, often enough. Now, go.'

The children hurried off, and he breathed a sigh of relief as he watched them nearing the house and going through the door.

'St John Radwell advocating patience and obedience? I never thought I'd see the likes of that.'

St John tensed at the sound of his brother's voice growing nearer. 'They are your children. You could have done it as easily as I.'

Marcus stepped into the stable and closed the door behind him. 'And missed that fine speech? Not for the world. I came in search of my missing children. You know boys and horses.'

St John nodded.

'But I never expected to find you here with them.' There was a trace of tension in Marcus's voice. 'I thought I told you to stay away from my family.'

'To avoid setting a bad example. I thought if I were to set a good one that the warning did not apply. And look at this animal.' He gave the stallion a gentle pat and it tossed its head and displayed a row of sharp teeth. 'I could not very well let them wander into danger, and then claim that I was following the letter of the law, could I?'

Marcus said softly, 'At one time, perhaps you could have. He is the heir, you know. He stands in your way.'

'To this land? Any desire I had for it is gone, along with many other youthful fancies. I'd only have made a mess of things had I found a way to them. This is better. The people are prosperous, the house well cared for. I've heard no more than the usual amount of nonsense out of the House of Lords, since you took a seat on the bench. The land and the title are yours, brother, and they appear to suit you. Enjoy them in good health.'

'You've truly changed, then?'

St John shook his head and soothed the horse. 'I never attempted fratricide, no matter how I threatened. I don't think, even then, I could have harmed a child, had there been one. I was never the threat that you thought I was, and never so dangerous as I wanted to be. If I have changed, it is because I'm wise enough to admit it.'

St John could almost feel the surprise emanating from his brother. 'And the other day, at luncheon?'

He sighed. 'I was taking a nap. In my room. Much as I was trying to do under a tree in the garden, when your whelps disturbed me on their way to see the horses.'

Marcus continued to quiz him. 'Is there a reason you do not sleep in your own bed at night, but must doze during the day? A guilty conscience, perhaps.'

'Would it surprise you to be right? I admit it. I cannot sleep, because I am afraid to close my eyes. Since Portugal, my dreams are rather more vivid than I might like.'

Marcus nodded his head in involuntary sympathy.

St John continued, 'I manage as best I can, with drugs at night and what rest I can steal during the day. I am sorry to be such a grave disappointment to you, but most days, my bothering the maids will mean nothing more than shouting at them for waking me.'

'You sound like an old man.'

He laughed softly. 'Perhaps. The war aged me, right enough. But I thought many nights as I lay there, knowing I would face death in the morning, what better place to come, should I survive, than back to my brother's home. For no matter how old and feeble I may become, you will always be older still. It makes me feel so much better.'

Marcus laughed and said, 'That is much more the sort of comment I expect from you, St John.'

He nodded. 'I am glad that I am finally living up to your expectations. And as requested, I will avoid your family, unless the situation is pressing, as it was today.'

'About that. Well.' Marcus cleared his throat. 'Perhaps it is not necessary to keep so strictly to the rules. If you wish to see the children, I see no reason why you cannot.'

'Your son is very like you, in looks and in manner.' He could tell he'd spoken right, for his brother seemed to swell with pride.

Marcus looked back toward the house. 'He will be difficult, I think, when he comes of age. Stubborn. Like his father.'

'Perhaps. But you will have a beautiful daughter to take your mind from your troubles. Very like her mother.'

At the mention of Miranda, Marcus said nothing, but the silence was cold air between them.

St John spoke again. 'Once, I was quite jealous of you on that count, Marcus. You cannot deny that you have a beautiful and charming wife. But time has softened me. Now, I merely envy you, and some day hope to be as fortunate. But I no longer begrudge you your happiness.'

He reached into the pocket of his coat and removed the box with the necklace. 'Here. Before you look inside, remember that pride runs as strong as stubbornness in our family. Take these back and do not refuse me. Give them to your daughter, when she is of age. May they be as fortunate a gift to her as they were to me.'

And, before his brother could respond, he turned and walked away.

Chapter Eight

He was trapped at another of Miranda's damn come-out balls for Esme, and St John gritted his teeth and counted the hours he had yet to remain social. There had been dinners and dances enough for a full London Season, whether at Haughleigh or some neighbour or other returning the invitation. Music and dancing kept him up most nights, and the constant teas and garden parties, with guests tramping through the house at all hours, left him unable to rest in daylight.

Without the laudanum, he could not seem to get through an untroubled night. And the lack of rest had left him out of sorts. He wanted nothing better than to sit by the fire to pass an evening, pretending to enjoy a book. Instead, he must remain dressed and upright, and out of the clutches of the Canville girl and any other neighbourhood chit with designs on him.

He had quite frightened away the other girls with a cool demeanour and a dark look. But Esme continued to be a thorn in his side. She had weathered rebuffs that should have sent her to her room in a flood of tears. Sharp words held no terror for her, coldness was ignored, and he rejected lechery as far too risky, since it was more likely to be met by eager curiosity than hysterics.

She continued to respond to everything with a patient smile and the occasional knowing glance that told him she trusted in his heart that he did not mean to hurt her.

And, damn it all, he did not mean it. It was all the more galling to know that she knew. He never should have apologised for the kiss in the garden. But she had sat beside him the next morning at breakfast, looking so unhappy and alone that he could not bear the sight. How was a man to enjoy his kippers with those sad blue eyes staring in his direction spoiling his appetite?

It had undone a good night's work in his efforts to dissuade Esme Canville. He had tried again and again since that night to turn her affections. Kissing in the garden had been a risk, even with Marcus standing guard over the girl. He'd come too close to losing control of himself. Better to keep a respectful distance and fill the void around him with enough sarcasm to repel every female in a five-mile radius.

An inexperienced girl should have been crushed, as all the others were. And an experienced one would have had the decency to pretend that his barbs had struck home, and perhaps to respond in kind.

But Esme remained a curious mixture of naïveté

and world-weariness, which both annoyed and intrigued him. It almost made him wish...

He shook himself firmly. He wished nothing, other than to be back in his rooms in London, away from damned balls, damned musicians and annoying young women. After a few days' peace and quiet and a good night's rest, he could find some other way to strengthen the fragile truce with his brother that did not involve forced courtesy, formal dress and dancing. If they communicated by mail, he could be back at the family table by Christmas.

He lounged against the wall, cultivating a pose of well-bred indolence, and watched the dancers spin by as his head pounded out a rhythm to match the musicians. There was Esme, floating past him in a whisper of satin and a flash of white teeth. Her pale hair was piled high on her head, smooth in front but with an elegant arrangement of braids in a crown set with tin rosebuds to contain the curls that cascaded down the back. The gold satin of her gown gave a warm glow to her skin and he saw hints of the delicate flesh through the tissue of her sleeves. The man who partnered her whispered something to her as they waited at the bottom of the set, and the diamond drops trembled from her ears as she laughed.

And St John waited for her glance to flash in his direction, searching for signs of jealousy or interest on his face as he watched her flirt with the man. She'd been watching him like a hawk at these events, looking for any sign of interest or weakness. The strain of watching her watch him, and maintaining his look of schooled uninterest took considerably more energy than the legitimate boredom he was accustomed to feeling.

But her glance did not come.

He felt naked, missing the feel of her eyes always on him. She was truly looking at her partner, and she smiled again.

She had spent too much time with the blighter she was now dancing with, for he'd seen them together for most of the evening. St John struggled to remember the man's name. Something effete. Possibly with a hyphen. No rank, no title, no family. Expensive clothes and no way to account for them. Good looking, of course, in the way that foolish women liked, but clearly pockets to let and up to no good. How many dances had they shared? He was not sure, but certainly it had been more that enough to cause gossip.

On the next turn, her partner's hand slipped to touch her body, momentarily caressing the curve of her waist.

Her eyes widened in surprise, but not in insult, and she did not pull away as the man pretended not to notice the liberty he had taken, so that it might appear accidental.

St John felt a dull pain in his hand and looked down to see his nails digging into the palm of his closed fist. He relaxed purposefully, and glared back at the dancers.

The music ended, and the man was leading Esme away from the crowd, past the refreshments and down the steps to the garden. St John felt the hairs on the back of his neck stand up. It was a dangerous situation. He scanned the room for his brother, who was playing host at the far end, oblivious to the danger Esme had placed herself in. What was Miranda after, letting Esme walk out with that man? The stranger was angling after an heiress, and she was too new to put him off.

And so it fell to St John to watch the girl's reputation for her. The irony was exquisite.

He followed them at a distance. The man had tucked her arm through the crook of his own, and she leaned into him, standing closer than St John felt was appropriate for two who had just met, one of whom was a green girl.

He watched the pair conversing.

The man's smile was ready enough, as he gazed down at Esme, but, from where he watched, St John thought he detected a certain predatory glint in the eyes, perhaps a hardness around the mouth, hidden behind the cynical smile. The man was no doubt assessing Esme's wealth, trying to draw her out about her father, and any possible settlement or allowance. And he must like what he heard, or he'd have moved on by now.

And Esme was gazing back at him, smile bright, head tipped up to catch his words, displaying her fine white throat to perfection. She was standing too close, in St John's opinion. Far too close. She might think it necessary to hear the conversation, but knowing her acquaintance as he thought he did, the man was speaking more softly, to draw her near.

Conniving bastard. His fist balled in his pocket, and he again forced it to relax. Then he signalled to his brother, gesturing him to his side.

Marcus pointed to himself in exaggerated surprise at the command and then strolled down the room to him. 'You summoned me? Are you not enjoying the evening?'

'It is a dead bore,' St John snapped. 'But then, these things always are.'

'Then your agitation is a sign of ennui.' Marcus had a self-satisfied smile on his face that was most irritating.

St John gestured in the direction of the interloper. 'I was just looking at the man there, chatting with Esme.'

'Smythe?' Marcus shrugged. 'He is new to the neighborhood and quite popular with the ladies. Miranda singled him out as a possibility.'

St John frowned. 'Well, you'd best nip that in the bud, if you wish to play at guardian.'

'And why do you think that?'

'Just look at him,' St John said, making no effort to hide his disgust.

Marcus was unimpressed. 'He seems an admirable match.'

'A fortune hunter, I'd wager.'

'Well, of course you'd wager. But you would lose. As far as I can ascertain, his reputation is impeccable.'

St John shook his head. 'Then you cannot be in possession of all the facts.'

Marcus chuckled. 'I have at least met the man. You are in possession of no facts at all.'

'But I can see what is before my eyes. The man is false coin.'

'And what business is it of yours?' Marcus was examining St John far more closely than he observed his guests.

'None, I suppose, other than that I want what is best for the girl.'

'You sound more like a jealous lover than a concerned friend,' Marcus said.

St John snorted. 'Don't be ridiculous. I feel responsible, that is all. To set my mind at rest, I need to know that the girl is going to a better place, should she choose not to go home.'

'Then you must trust the girl to know her own mind.'

'As far as I can tell, she has no mind at all. Pretty she may be, but the little hen-wit should not be allowed out without a keeper, Marcus.'

He smiled. 'She seems to like you well enough.'

'And if that isn't evidence, I know not what is.'

'As you will. But the girl is perfectly safe amongst my guests. If you wish her to dance with someone else, that is a matter between you and Esme.' And Marcus walked away, ignoring his protestations.

St John stayed to keep watch over the pair. Marcus was blind if he thought Esme safe with Smythe. The man was all flash. Just the sort to turn the head of a girl as naïve and unworldly as Esme. His coat was well cut, no doubt with the tailor's bill still in the pocket, along with numerous gambling debts and perhaps a *billet doux* from a mistress or some other man's wife.

St John knew the type well enough, having seen him in the mirror for years.

And there was Esme, smiling and nodding, gazing up into his face, leaning even closer.

Smythe leaned in as well, touching her hair again as he spoke into her ear. And then he clasped her hand warmly and brought it to his lips.

St John viewed the tender scene through a red haze, and watched as Esme turned and went back into the ballroom alone.

St John glared in Esme's direction and she caught his gaze as she passed him. Her chin came up a fraction of an inch, and her smile brightened. Her eyes were full of the devil.

St John waited until Esme lost herself in the crowd of the ballroom.

But Smythe remained in the garden, moving further away from the house.

St John followed at such a distance as to remain unnoticed. When they were clear of the other guests, and a good distance from the house, he caught up with the man and laid a hand on his shoulder. 'Smythe, is it?'

'I don't believe we've been formally introduced.' The man swung around easily to meet him, and favoured him with a cool stare.

'I think we can waive the formalities in this instance. You may now give to me what you took from

the young lady just now, and I'll see it safely returned
to her.'

'I have no idea…'

St John smiled. 'Don't you? Why not look in your
left breast pocket. You'll find a single diamond ear-
drop.'

'Oh. That.' The man waved his hand dismissively.
'I picked it up from the floor. I was going to restore it
to my host.'

'You picked it from the ear of the lady in question
when you were in intimate conversation, earlier. And
now, I suppose, you are about to tell me that you were
looking for my brother, the duke, in the garden? It really is far more likely, sir, that you meant to exit quietly with the diamond in your pocket. And that you took
one, not two, because one missing earring is an accident, while two are a theft.'

The man shrugged. 'I took one because it was all I
needed.' He reached into his pocket and tossed the earring back to St John. 'Your brother the duke? Then you
must be St John Radwell. I'd understood that you were
banned from the house because of your bad character.'

St John sneered. 'As is evidenced by your own presence here, my brother is none too particular about the
company he keeps. When he sent me away he was not
inviting common thieves to his parties.'

Smythe leaned against the tree behind him. 'That is
quite unfair. I am a most uncommon thief. Until now,
I was never caught. But, as they say, set a thief to catch
a thief.'

St John relaxed slightly. 'I have been called many things, drunkard, gambler, scoundrel, but never thief.'

'Perhaps not to your face. If we were to ask the husbands of some of the ladies you've entertained, they might use the term.'

St John shrugged. '*Touché*. Point to you, I think. If you are trying to goad me into a duel, you will not succeed.'

The man laughed. 'A duel? What a quaint notion. But I thought perhaps you meant to challenge me. For the honour of the girl, or perhaps your brother's house?'

'I let my brother protect his own house, although I'll thank you not to steal while under this roof.'

Smythe shrugged. 'I doubt I'd have much luck a second time, having been caught here once. You have but to put a word in the ear of your brother, and I'll be banned from the premises just as you were.'

St John sighed. 'How shall I put this so it is best understood? A duel would be troublesome, and messy. You would be dead on the grass in a matter of minutes, and I would be left to explain to all and sundry the reason for the quarrel. The whole thing would most likely spring back upon me and show me in a poor light.'

Smythe nodded.

St John continued, 'Your reputation must be exemplary, or my brother would not allow you in his home. You will turn out to have an aged mother, or a weeping sister, and I will be the duke's unloved, younger brother who has been nothing but trouble for years.

People will have no problem believing that I pushed you into it. So we shall not duel over this. The diamonds were borrowed, by the way, from the duchess. And my brother can afford many more to replace them, but I would not see Miss Canville distressed at the loss.'

Smythe snapped his fingers. 'So it is my interest in the girl that troubles you?'

'The girl.' St John sighed again. 'Let us say that I consider myself responsible for her welfare. And if I find that you have borrowed anything else that did not belong to you, or found any more of her lost items, if I see you hanging about her, making calf's eyes at her person, her non-existent dowry, or her borrowed jewellery, it will go hard for you. While I wish to avoid scandal, and would hesitate to call you out, I would have no trouble waylaying you on a dark street and slitting your throat from ear to ear. I could sleep with a clear conscience, knowing that the world is a slightly better place for my actions.'

Smythe smirked back at him. 'You do present a most persuasive argument.'

St John nodded. 'I thought you would find it so. Do you agree to my terms?'

'And if I do? It ends here?'

'I don't plan to go to the Runners, if that's what you mean. Or tattle to my brother. It matters not to me what method you use to seek damnation, or whether you do it from boredom or need. As long as you leave my brother and his guests alone. And the girl, of course. There is nothing there to interest you, in any case. She is quite poor and, from what I understand, already affianced to an earl.'

'The girl alone was quite interesting enough. The earrings were merely a distraction.' He saw the warning look in St John's eye and corrected himself. 'But alas, it would be unfair of me to trifle with such a charming young lady.'

'I am glad that we have reached this understanding. And you are leaving for the night.'

'Well, I had thought…perhaps one more dance.' Smythe gazed back toward the house.

'Let me clarify. That was a statement, not a question. I will give your apologies to your host, and to Miss Canville. Good evening.'

St John watched the man shrug and continue into the darkness in the general direction of the drive. Then he turned back towards the house.

When he entered the ballroom again, he saw Esme look toward the garden with interest. It annoyed him to see her eyes slide past him and search for another.

Be damned to all that. Now she was pretending she did not see him? He'd give her reason to take notice, if that was the game she wished to play. He strode forward purposefully and took her by the elbow, steering her in the direction of the stairs.

'St John? What is the meaning of this?'

'We must talk.'

'We can do that as well here as—'

'The devil we can,' he snapped.

'There is no need to resort to such language—'

'Since when have you cared?'

'Or physical violence.' She yanked her arm out of his grasp.

'Violence?' He hadn't gripped her arm too tightly, had he? 'I did not hurt you, did I? I assure you, there was no intention…' He touched her arm again to reassure himself, and then remembered himself and dropped his hands to his sides.

'Well, not violence,' she admitted. 'But you do not need to tow me like a barge. Merely ask me, and I will accompany you outside.'

'As you do any man who asks?' He could not keep the asperity out of his voice.

'What…? Oh, Mr Smythe.' She smiled, remembering him. 'We were gone for but a moment, surely. No one noticed.'

'I noticed. And I followed.'

She stared at him in amazement. 'You spied on us?'

'Us? Well, there will be no "us" with that particular man. I've seen to it.'

'You are seeing to my honour again, are you?' She was laughing at him again. He could see it in her eyes.

'Someone must.'

'And a fine one you would be to guard it. A fox in the henhouse, some might say.'

'Better me than Smythe. He was taking liberties.'

'He was a perfect gentleman and then kissed my hand, whereas, when you had me in the same spot, you kissed my lips and then insulted me.'

'A gentleman? Ha!' He could not resist a contemptuous laugh as he reached into his pocket for the earring.

'Yes. A gentleman. He was just explaining to me that, however much some parties might like to see us make a match, it would be quite impossible, as his heart was otherwise engaged. And when I told him I understood, he was so grateful he kissed my hand.'

'What utter nonsense.'

She was not laughing any more. Her temper broke over him. 'No, you are the one speaking nonsense. First you kiss me, then you send me away. You say you want me to find a match, but when a gentleman that I could fancy shows the slightest interest, you drag me away from the party and fill my head with lies. Perhaps you are like my father, and will only be satisfied when you see me unhappily married. What reason could Mr Smythe have had to tell me such? What could he hope to gain? And why is it so hard for you to believe, St John, that a man might be willing to resist temptation for even a moment, if he loved someone else. Perhaps your heart is as cold as you claim, for you always need see the worst in others.'

The words stung him, and his hand closed around the earring, before letting it drop back into his pocket. 'All right. I will concede that others might have motives that are honourable, and that I should not treat all so harshly. And if what you say is true…'

He could see the storm gathering behind her eyes again and rephrased, 'Of course what you say is true. I would have no reason to doubt it. You tell me that there is nothing between you, and so I will not worry further on the subject. But please, in the future, take care whom you are alone with. It would not do to be caught in the moonlight with too many young men.'

Esme rolled her eyes. 'Says the man who took me alone into the moonlight not once, but twice. Yes, St John, I will take care not to follow you, the next time you insist on speaking to me alone. And now, if I may go back to the ball?'

He could feel the heat rising in his face and ignored it. 'Very well. I think I have made the point well enough. Oh, and, Esme…'

She turned back to him. He reached into his pocket and produced the earring. 'You must have dropped this. I found it on the grass in the garden.'

Her hand flew to her ears and felt the lobe that was bare. 'Oh, dear.' She put a hand to her heaving bosom. 'Thank you, St John. I could not have lived had I needed to explain to Miranda that it was missing.'

And then she smiled, and the weight of her gratitude struck him like a physical force. For a moment her look held no mischief and her smile no calculation or hidden meaning. There was only relief, and thankfulness, and admiration. He was her hero for returning the diamond, even if the circumstances of its recovery were wrapped in pretty lies.

'Well, then, you needn't have worried. But I am glad that I could be of service to you. Most glad indeed.' He was fumbling to get the words out, staring down into those luminous blue eyes.

She took the drop from him, reaching to her ear. 'This is difficult to do without a mirror, perhaps I should—'

'Here, let me.' Why had he said it? She must have intended to go to the ladies' retiring room. It would have been the most proper course of action for them both. Instead, he took the thing back from her, and she stepped closer to him. A hint of her scent reached him as he bent over her, and he took a breath and held it, hoping she didn't feel the slight tremor in his hands as he touched her ear with one hand and replaced the jewel with the other.

And then it seemed only natural to leave the hand at the back of her head, as he leaned back to admire his work.

'St John?' Her head tilted in his hand, and her lips were ever so slightly closer to his, smiling expectantly.

It was maddening. How many women had he known? And how many had he known more intimately than this? His mind had never gone blank when they looked at him. His mouth had never gone dry when he'd spoken to them. His hands had never trembled to touch them.

He broke free of the spell, and jerked his hand away. 'I was just making sure that they are even. And secure. Everything is fine, now. Just fine.'

'Then you had best take me back to the ballroom, before someone notices our behaviour.'

'Yes. That would be best.'

Although he couldn't help feeling that the one person he least wanted to notice his behaviour was Esme Canville.

Chapter Nine

'St John, I wish to speak to you.' The duke's voice carried through the open door of his study and into the hall.

Damn. Six years ago, when he had been up to every kind of devilment, the study door had been shut tight and Marcus had left him with the run of the house. But now, when he wanted nothing more shocking than a nap in the garden and some peace and quiet, he could not get past the doorway unnoticed. The duke found any excuse to call him in.

He gritted his teeth and turned back to play obedient younger brother. 'What have I done now, your Grace? Come, tell me. I can tell by the set of your shoulders that I'm about to catch some type of hell. And, for once, I can't think of anything I might have done to deserve it.'

'You have done nothing objectionable, much as it surprises me to admit it. But I wish to ask your opinion of something.'

'My opinion?' St John said, in shock.

'Yes, you idiot. Despite what you may think, I value the views of others. And I cannot take this matter to Miranda, as you will soon see.' Marcus threw a stack of letters down on the desk and said, 'Read.'

St John sat in the chair before the desk and picked up a paper.

Your Grace,

As you are well aware, it's been weeks since my daughter has come to your home and I would think that by now there would have been an end to her little problem. It does not do to coddle the girl when she is in these moods, or to encourage her to disobedience...

St John looked up doubtfully. 'Well, I suppose there is some truth that you are encouraging her to be disobedient.'

'Only because you presented me with the problem. If you had not dropped her on my doorstep, she could have been as disobedient as she chose and it would never have come to my notice. Read this one.'

St John's eyebrows arched as he read. 'This seems to imply that you are holding her against her will. He's gone as far as he can, without being actually insulting, hasn't he?'

'Too far. The implication is definitely there.' Marcus's tone darkened and St John was pleased to see the duke's anger directed at someone other than himself.

'This is private correspondence. Canville is a nobody. Toss the letters in the fire and think no more about it.'

'But there is this one, where he's threatening to go to *The Times* and raise a scandal if we don't return his daughter.' Marcus slapped another letter down on the desk. 'The man is obviously mad, but I don't see what's to be done to keep him quiet. I have corresponded in return and think it will buy a little more time. But I've also spoken to my solicitors. If Canville chooses to press the issue, there is nothing for it but to return the girl to him. He is in the right. She is not of age and we cannot keep her here without his permission. I have no wish to disappoint my wife or see harm come to the girl, but we are running out of time in this matter.'

St John sighed. 'I am sorry that I brought this upon you. I wanted what was best for Esme, but was at a loss as to what that might be.'

Marcus shook his head. 'As am I. It might help if we knew more of her relations with her father. What was in the letter you took from her at breakfast?'

'It would be impolite of me to repeat it,' St John said.

'It was equally impolite of you to take it from her. Now be of some use and tell me the contents of the letter.'

'Nothing as inflammatory as his letters to you. He told her he was impatient for her return. She seemed upset, but I expect it had as much to do with my behaviour to her as with her father's. You watched me bring her near to tears at the ball.' He could not keep a hint of accusation out of his voice.

'Well, the girl will have to return home if we cannot find her a suitable match.' Marcus was looking at him with undue interest. 'I don't suppose you would have anything to say on that score.'

'I would say that it is an excellent idea and that you should proceed with it, post haste.'

'You know that is not what I mean.' Marcus paused. 'I watched you last night, and I wondered if you might be taking a more personal interest in her situation.'

St John looked at him in amazement. 'You allowed me here for the express purpose of being a bad example. I am sorry if I am not living down to your expectations. If I find it less than pleasant to toy with an innocent girl, without the reward of an actual seduction, or if I care when she walks out with an unprincipled rogue, it does not mean that I am considering matrimony.'

'But I have seen the way you look at Miss Canville. You hold her in regard, do you not?'

'As I do many other young ladies of the *ton*. I do not wish to marry them, either.'

As usual, Marcus ignored him and issued a command. 'You are three and thirty. It is time you marry someone.'

St John laughed. 'And since you have a female that needs marrying, you are ready to offer me up to fix the situation? I have news, your Grace. You are the one who needed to get an heir, not I. I am the younger son, and have not money, inclination, or any pressing desire to get myself leg-shackled, especially not to one as poor as myself. If you were offering an heiress, someone with twenty thousand a year and a house in town, then perhaps we could make a deal.'

Marcus reached into the desk drawer and produced
the jewellery box that St John had so recently given
him. He opened it and turned the emerald necklace out
onto the blotter where it glowed green in the afternoon
sunlight. 'There is more than enough here to make a
fresh start.'

'As well I know,' St John said with exasperation.
'Have you forgotten that I used it for that purpose once
before?'

'And yet you returned it to me, when you could
have used the price of it to establish yourself.' Marcus's
voice was low, but insistent. 'What you did was not
necessary.'

'For you, perhaps,' St John said.

'If you have no prospects, then it was foolish to
waste money on baubles, when you could set up a
household and have more than enough to spare. Or do
you plan to return to the service? If you do not wish to
stay in England and marry, than there is nothing dishonourable in a military career. Unless you received
some wound that would prevent you—'

'Marcus!' St John cut his brother off in mid-tirade.
He took a deep breath before continuing. 'First of all,
the necklace is not a bauble. When I took it from this
house, it was a treasured family heirloom. Since you
have the title and the rest of the entail, it might not seem
significant to you. But it was important to me that it
should be returned.

'I have no plans to return to the army. I am not
wounded in any way. Do not concern yourself on that

account. It is just that…' He should not have to share all the sordid details of his recent history with his brother. He was a grown man and did not need to justify his decisions. 'I will just say that it was time for me to leave the service. I left honourably and will not be going back.

'And lastly, as you point out, I am three and thirty. I am not the overgrown boy who left here five years ago. I am my own man, not one of your tenants, or a servant to be ordered about. I am sorry if my apparent lack of direction concerns you, but you must trust that I know my own mind and may have plans in place that cannot be discussed at this time. While I appreciate your concern for my future, I will not allow you to plan it for me, especially in such a way as to include Esme Canville.

'And now, if you will excuse me, I believe this interview is at an end. If you wish to turn me out of your house for my less-than-respectful attitude, so be it. But in the future, I would prefer that you refrain from meddling in my life, just as I have promised to stop interfering with yours. Good day, your Grace.'

And for the first time that he could remember, St John left his brother open mouthed and incapable of further argument.

Chapter Ten

St John stared into the fire in his room, trying to calm his restless spirit. He could no longer tell which he found more disturbing, the situation or the girl. Being back in the house and trying to navigate around his brother's whims took more than enough energy. But to add Esme into the equation? It was more than a sane man could bear.

At the ball the night before, she had *agreed* with him. And since, then she had been polite and co-operative. And once again he was left with the feeling that she meant to smile and nod at him and then do just as she pleased. Miranda's plan had seemed easy enough when he was to toy with her and walk away.

But when he walked away from a woman, she was supposed to collapse in despair, not turn and follow. He had never expected to find himself running ahead of her, as she pursued.

And she'd managed to catch him often enough since

she'd arrived at Haughleigh, only to smile her innocent smile and set him free. He'd have easily overmatched her, he assured himself, if he'd been able to rest. But the sleepless nights were catching up to him and the catnaps during the day were of no help. He needed rest.

He'd promised himself, once he came to Haughleigh, no more laudanum. And it had been easy enough when the family was still in London and could not see his odd hours and strange behaviours. He could sleep the day away without inciting comment.

But now there were expectations. Despite it all he must rest at some point or he'd find himself quite unable to manage the girl or his own family. If they did not find a match for Esme soon, the pressure from Marcus would increase. And then Miranda would join in as well. Some day he might wake from a nap to find himself walking from the altar, tenant for life with Esme before he knew what he'd done. And then he'd be responsible for her for a lifetime instead of a few weeks.

Certainly a small dose of the drug in his brandy would not hurt. It would mean an easy night and, come morning, a head that was sharp, if not exactly clear. He poured a glass of spirits and reached into his pocket for the phial. Toby had hidden the first one, for he did not approve of the habit and seemed happier thinking that the supply was cut. But Toby had not checked the pockets of St John's dressing gown.

He carefully measured a few drops into the glass, swirling the brandy to mix it. And as he raised the glass to his lips…he thought of Esme. How quickly the drug had taken her. And how pale she'd looked, lying on the sofa, lost to the world and to herself. He had done that to her, however inadvertently.

She'd not questioned him on it, not heaped him with the reproach he must truly deserve. Except for that moment when she'd mocked his lack of self-control.

She was right, of course, he had no self-control, but it did not matter. He needed sleep and for that he needed the drug. He raised the glass to his lips.

And in his mind, he saw the flash in Esme's eyes and the slight, contemptuous curl of her lip. She had looked inside him and seen his bravery for what it was, a sham.

She was a thousand times braver than he, willing to hazard anything when she'd come to him, if it meant escape from her father and marriage. Any man would be proud to have her, once he'd seen that blazing spirit. He half-raised the glass again, in toast to the girl, but the look of contempt hung before him and he could not bring the brandy to his lips.

He did not deserve her affection. He did not even desire to be worthy of it. But nor could he drink, knowing what her response must be should she find that the drug was his master and not merely his crutch.

He sighed and raised the glass again. 'To absent friends.' Then he splashed the brandy on to the fire, watching it flare and catching a faint whiff of the liquor before it sizzled and was gone.

He untied the belt to his gown, slipped it off and climbed between the cold and clammy sheets of his bed. Demons of the past be damned, he would rest to-night. He closed his eyes with no small amount of trepidation—and thought of Esme. Dear, sweet girl. As he imagined her now, she was smiling at him. Full of approval, but also full of mischief.

It was hard to imagine her face without the play-ful undercurrent of one who knew more than she was telling. It really was a shame that she was a young lady of virtue and not the demi-rep she wished him to make her. He could easily imagine the same smile, close beside him some night, her head on the pillow, her blonde hair tousled, her cheeks flushed with passion.

The Esme of his imagination was wicked in her abandon and more than willing to take his mind off the laudanum, should he but ask her to. If he reached for the drug, she would twine her fine white arms around him, drawing him back on to the bed to kiss him until he forgot everything but her.

She would do nothing of the kind, he reminded him-self. A decent young lady, such as herself, would be shocked at the suggestion, and horrified that he was making her the subject of his bedroom fancies.

But what harm could it do to think of her thus as long as he did not act upon his baser desires? He had told her often enough that he was not interested in a physical relationship. As long as he kept his thoughts and hands to himself, she need never know otherwise.

And he needed to find something that would help him to an untroubled rest. If he could not have the drug, then for a few sweet moments, before sleep took him, he would have his imaginary Esme, to do with as he pleased.

The voices came to him from a distance, as though through water. There was Esme's shocked cry of 'St John,' and a man's stifled curse.

And then the blow hit the side of his head and he staggered and fell.

It was strange. Instead of darkness as he lost consciousness, the opposite was true. There was light. A growing number of candles as the room brightened and swam into focus. It was a bedroom, he realised, but not his own. And for the first time he felt the chill air on his bare skin.

'Damn you, I said get up.' Marcus's voice was terse, and St John felt, rather than saw, the bedsheet thrown at his bare feet.

'So that you may knock me down again?' He lurched to his feet, shaking his head to clear it.

'Cover yourself.'

He was naked, and shivering. He scooped up the sheet and wrapped it hastily around his waist, and glanced across the room and into Esme's shocked face. She was huddled in the bed, knees drawn up and the coverlet pulled to her chin.

And then Marcus stepped between them and slapped him full in the face.

If any remnant of unconsciousness had remained, the slap cleared the fog. 'I can explain…' he began, then realised that, of course, he couldn't. Not in any way likely to be believed by his brother.

'You have abused my hospitality for the last time, St John.' His brother's voice was colder than he'd ever heard it, and there was murder in it. 'We will settle this at dawn, if you can find someone to second you.'

'I cannot fight you.' It was true. A duel would be a disaster for both of them. And Marcus could solve this so easily by banning him from the house yet again. 'This was an accident, I swear. It is not as it appears. If you will but listen—'

'I will not listen to you any more, as you twist the truth out of all proportion to gain my sympathy.' Marcus seized him by the shoulder and yanked him from the girl's room and into the corridor, letting him stumble over the sheet that hindered his legs to fall at the base of the opposite wall.

Marcus stared down at him, his lip curled in disgust. 'No, St John. I have listened too many times in the past. And this time, like a fool, I believed you. I thought you had changed. I trusted you.' Marcus shook his head in amazement. 'I trusted you not to dishonour the girl, and thought it was true that you wanted what was best for her. And then you attempted something even more despicable than I could have imagined of you.'

'You can't honestly believe that I meant to…' St John struggled to his feet.

'I will not let you use my home as a brothel, you contemptible wretch. This ends tomorrow, St John. At dawn. And do not think of leaving the house before that time, or I will chase you down and shoot you like a dog in the road.' And Marcus refused to speak another word, pulling a chair into the hall to sit as guard at Esme's door, leaving St John no recourse but to return to his room and await the morning.

There was a faint glow of the sun in the eastern sky, and the grass was still slick with dew. Footing would be less than ideal. But there was little breeze to affect the aim of a pistol shot, and the temperature was excellent for fencing. All in all, it was a better day for battle than many he'd had in Portugal. That he would need to face his brother on such a fine morning sickened him.

'This is a mistake,' St John tried again.

'Entirely yours. It is too late to apologise, St John, you must know that.' The anger was still there, but he could see the tiredness on Marcus's face. His brother looked old.

And Marcus did not understand what was about to happen. How could he? St John walked to the trembling footman who had been bullied into serving as his second when Toby had flatly refused to stand with him. Toby had looked him gravely in the eye and said, 'If you mean to kill a man, then at least do it for better reason than a woman's honour. I'd rather help you do murder than to listen to you talk about honour and then go and kill the duke, who never deserved it.'

Even his valet was ashamed to be seen with him. It was not as if the duel was by his choice. He'd tried apologies, both written and verbal, sending urgent notes to the duke via the servants. But Marcus would not budge.

St John had seriously considered running away. At least it would spare Marcus what would happen if they duelled. But it would mean running from Esme, and letting her think that he'd meant her harm. And there was the fact that, somewhere at the back of his mind, he would rather die here and now than to turn tail and avoid the fight. If he could not reconcile with his brother, then maybe it was best to admit the fact and end the quarrel in blood as Marcus had often threatened to do.

St John examined the weapons. As the challenged, he had the choice. He'd rejected pistols as too quick and inelegant to settle the age-old argument. There was no chance to change your mind, once you pulled the trigger.

But Marcus had brought the duelling swords that had hung over the mantel in the study since their grandfather's time. 'Do you remember these, Marcus? We used to play with them as boys.' He lifted his sword and gave an experimental swipe at the air. He felt the edge. The weapons had not been cared for. His sword was not as sharp as he would have liked, had he actually wanted to fight. It would not cut. But the point was true, God help him. He'd need to be careful.

'And Father gave us a whipping because they were not toys.' Marcus voice was distant, though they stood side by side.

'They still are not.' St John paced off the distance and watched as his brother picked up the other sword. He made one last attempt, before they began. 'I never meant harm to the girl, although you do not believe it.'

And now Marcus cut the air with his blade. 'You were naked and in her room. It does not matter if she invited you there.'

'Damn you, Marcus,' he snapped, finally angry enough to draw blood. 'If you care so much for the girl and her reputation, you will mind your tongue and take back what you just said. I was not there at her invitation. She had no fault in it. It was mischance. It was an embarrassing mistake, but if someone must pay for it, it will be me.'

'And if you care for the girl, there are other ways to salvage her reputation.' It was Marcus who saluted first and took his stance, which was stiff and unpractised.

'Planning to march me down the aisle of the chapel at sword point?' St John laughed. 'The Reverend Winslow would like that, I'm sure. When it comes to the sacrament of marriage, the Radwells can be counted on to entertain, if nothing else.'

'The thought had occurred to me. But her father might not consent. It would have to be Gretna Green for the pair of you. She would be willing, I'm sure. She has been mooning over you since before we came down from London. There is a carriage at the ready and a suitable head start could be arranged. Say the word and we can end this.'

'If I was willing. As I've told you before, I am not.

Not to save the girl's honour or my own. If you mean to kill me, Marcus, then get it over with. I am beyond tired of your empty threats.' He saluted in return and prepared for the attack. 'But is this fight for Esme, or Miranda, or Bethany?'

It was a low blow, but it had the desired effect. Marcus charged forward, unprepared, and St John was ready to parry the first cut and respond with a feint.

Marcus had regained his temper and knocked the blade out of the way with his own sword. 'Shall we say that it is for a lifetime of wrongs, committed by you against our family?'

'Fair enough. Will this settle it, then? When one of us lies dead?' St John reached with a lazy attack, and let Marcus parry and riposte watching the timing of his brother's action. The speed was almost such that he had to work to avoid it.

Almost, but not quite.

Marcus's breathing was ever so slightly laboured, when he said, 'I suspect that death will be the only thing likely to stop you from dishonouring yourself further.'

'How will *your* death stop me from doing anything?' St John engaged his brother's blade and pushed him back with a series of actions that were parried with difficulty.

'For that is how this will end, Marcus, if you insist on continuing. I do not fight to lose. I never have. And after several years on the Peninsula, you will find that I have no trouble stomaching what I am likely to do

today if you continue to threaten me.' He took control
of the blade again and forced Marcus back, as he parried three swift attacks, one after the other.

Marcus was tiring and his foot slipped in the grass.
St John ignored the advantage and paused, letting his
brother regain his balance. When Marcus found his
feet, he lunged forward and St John was deliberately
slow to parry. He waited for the impact of the blade and
the pain when it pierced his shoulder, but none came.
At the last minute the point of Marcus's sword swerved
to the side, slicing St John's shirt and leaving a scratch
on his arm.

He glanced down with indifference at the blood on
his own sleeve, and then up to his brother, who looked
as white as if the cut were in his own flesh. 'Clearly,
only one of us has the stomach to fight, if a little blood
frightens you so. But then, you aren't much better at
this than any other country farmer. I left a wide enough
opening, dear brother—why couldn't you have taken
it and run me through?'

'Don't think you can win my clemency by remind-
ing me of our parentage.'

St John laughed. 'Your clemency? I have not needed
that in a very long time. Now, fight if you mean to. I
grow weary of waiting.' He let the duke attack again,
and responded with an ineffectual parry, waiting for the
point to pierce his flesh. Again, Marcus changed direction at the last second and St John felt the sting of the
blade as it opened a shallow cut on his other arm.

He looked at it in disgust. 'There. I am wounded

again, and have had better scratches from the kitchen cat. Are you ready to call a halt, or must we continue?'

Marcus stepped back and took his guard again. 'Call a halt? As always, St John, you are trying to walk away in the middle of the fight, leaving me to deal with the consequences. If you cannot leave her alone, you must marry the girl. I am sick of your cowardice.'

St John felt the blood creeping into his face, and forced the rage into his gut to save for the fight. 'Now, Marcus, you are the one who has gone too far. You sit on your precious land with your lovely wife, and think that because you have money and power, and had the good luck to be born first, you have the right to decide my future. Then, when you lack the guts to run me through, you call me coward.' He attacked, then, again and again, forcing his brother to give ground. 'And now, I must finish this, since you cannot. If you do not kill me, you will not see another day. My apologies to your wife, and your children.'

He paused, and smiled at Marcus, giving him one last opportunity. 'But do not worry about them. When you are gone, I will love them as if they were my own.'

Marcus lunged again, wild and off balance, too angry to focus his attack, which went wide. And St John caught the blade with his own, and held it, driving the guards up and back into a blunt blow to the face. Marcus's nose streamed blood and he was dazed as St John knocked the weapon easily from his hand and brought his own point down and to the side so that he could close the distance between them. He struck Marcus across the throat with his forearm, and followed him to the ground.

His brother lay beneath him, struggling for air, St John's knee in his stomach and an elbow at his throat. And he saw the look of final recognition in Marcus's eyes, as he'd seen it in many other men on the battlefield, when he understood that he had lost and this was how it all would end. Then St John drew his sword arm to the right and let the dulled blade slide harmlessly across his brother's windpipe before tossing his weapon aside.

He rolled off his brother and collapsed on the grass beside him, closed his eyes and listened to Marcus retch and gasp for breath. The grass was cool and wet. The sun was not truly risen. How long had they been fighting? Scant minutes. But then, it did not take long to kill a man. He'd learned that well enough.

It would be good, to lie here and to not ever have to rise. Peaceful. He heard the first birds, waking in the trees. He could feel a slight chill as the shadow of his brother crossed his face. 'Can you finish it now, Marcus?'

The voice above him was hoarse. 'I cannot kill an unarmed man.'

St John laughed, and felt a tear on his own cheek. 'I can. At last, something I know I can do better than you. But I doubt I can kill you, even for calling me coward. And perhaps I am a coward, for I've been unable to summon the strength to kill myself. I'm sorry, big brother, but that is one more job you must do for me.' He leaned his face into the grass, smelling the greenness of it and the coolness against his fevered brow. 'It is so peaceful here. Let it end for me, now. Do what you meant to do. Please.'

Marcus's tone became more ragged still. 'Get up and fight, damn you.'

St John could feel himself beginning to tremble. 'I don't need you to damn me, Marcus. I've done that for myself. Bad when I left you, and worse when I returned. There was dishonour on my name, but now there is blood on my hands. So much blood. They made me a hero for it.' He laughed until his body shook 'And I can still hear the screaming. Without the laudanum, I cannot pass a still night. You've seen what happens without the drug. When I am in that state I do not know what I am doing. But I know what I'm capable of. And I must never inflict that on another. I am so tired. Of the drugs, and of life. Dear God, let it end.'

There was a noise that sounded almost like a sob, and he felt his brother drop to the grass beside him. And then Marcus lifted St John's head and slipped his rolled up coat beneath for a pillow.

'Rest. I will watch for you. You have nothing to fear.'

And for a moment he almost believed it.

He startled awake, some time later. The sun was higher in the sky and Marcus was leaning against a tree, a few feet away. He rolled on to one elbow, and asked, 'How long?'

'An hour. Maybe a little more.'

He stood up, and shook the wrinkles out of his brother's coat, handing it back to him. 'Thank you. That is more sleep than I've had for weeks.'

His brother shook his head. 'Finally, the duel I knew must come, that would settle things between us, once and for all. And in the middle of it, you fell asleep. My pride may never recover.'

'You were a formidable opponent.'

Marcus's smile was sad. 'You are not nearly so accomplished a liar as you used to be. You were more honest before, as we fought. I am a farmer, and you are a soldier. I was foolish to challenge you and am lucky to be alive.'

'I lied to goad you when I said you had aught to be afraid of from me. Whether you are living or dead, your house and your wife shall have nothing but my respect. I know I can never repair the wrongs I've done you, but I can at least leave you in peace and try not to make the present situation worse.'

'Leave? The devil you will. You've finally come home.' Marcus removed a flask from his pocket, and drank deeply. 'There is enough here for two, if you are interested.'

St John grinned at his brother. 'Thank you. I think I am.'

They waved the coach away and walked back towards the house, and St John felt lighter than he'd felt in ages. He searched his mind. That was not accurate. He could never remember feeling this way. He glanced over at his brother, walking wordlessly beside him. Without looking up, Marcus again offered him the flask. He was not alone. He took another drink. The brandy felt good, even on his empty stomach. The duke opened the door to the house and let him pass in first.

St John smiled as he saw Miranda before him.

His smile faded as she threw herself at him, striking at his face and chest, moaning tonelessly through her tears. And over her shoulder, he could see Esme, huddled on the stairs, also crying, but weak with relief.

Then Marcus stepped into the room after him. 'Lady wife, contain yourself, and unhand my brother.'

Miranda looked up from her tears at the sound of his voice, and rushed to him. 'We heard nothing, and when I saw St John, I thought you dead. Blood!' She sniffed. 'And brandy.' She shot an accusing look at St John, from the shelter of her husband's arms. 'What did you do to him?'

Marcus chuckled and mopped at his face with a linen handkerchief. 'Broke my nose and ruined my shirt, I think. But you will notice that he has two very nice cuts on his arms from me.'

'He could easily have killed me,' supplied St John, trying without success to be helpful. 'But he chose not to.'

From the stairs, Esme gasped.

'Overgrown boys. Playing with sharp sticks.' Miranda slapped at her husband in frustration, and then held him close, clinging around his neck. Which must hurt like the devil, St John reminded himself. He'd made no effort to be gentle with his brother when he'd choked him. There would be bruises tomorrow. He shot an apologetic look to Marcus, who rolled his eyes in response and jerked his head in the direction of the girl weeping on the stairs.

Esme was still trembling, and wet-cheeked as he strode up the stairs to her. He stopped short, a few steps below her and knelt at her feet. 'Miss Canville. I humbly apologise for invading your room last night. I can but beg your pardon, although it was an unforgivable offence.'

'I thought you were dead,' she whispered, unheeding. 'Or had murdered your brother. And that it was my fault.'

He looked up at her earnestly. 'This was but the culmination of an old quarrel. And we've never needed much excuse to fight.' He paused and corrected himself. 'Not that I consider my disrespect of you a small thing. On the contrary. I…I deserved…'

She shook her head. 'It is all right. If your brother had not discovered you, there would not have been a problem.'

'No problem?' He lowered his voice so as not to alert the couple in the foyer below them. 'Of course there was a problem. You had a naked man in your room.'

'But you were that naked man, St John. And I have nothing to fear from you. Besides…' she smiled '…I'd never seen a naked man before. It was very educational.'

After years in brothels and gaming hells, and five years in the army, St John was at a loss for the last time he'd blushed. But that was before he'd met Esme Canville. 'You should not have looked, and, even if you did, you should not mention the fact.'

'Really, St John. It's not as if I'm likely to comment upon it at dinner. And in truth you are very handsome, even more so without your clothes. You cannot pretend to be surprised that I should look at you if you came to me naked in the night.'

'I didn't come to you, you silly girl. Not intentionally, at least—I was not in possession of my senses.' He hung his head in embarrassment. 'Sometimes, in my sleep, I wander.'

She smiled. 'So, you mean to say, once you were relieved of the unnecessary restraints you place on yourself, you came to me?'

'I am sure it was not that way at all,' he sputtered, hoping she did not realise how close to the truth she'd come.

'And removed your clothing?'

'There was no clothing to remove. I never find it necessary, on warm nights.'

She leaned closer and whispered, 'Really? I had no idea. Is that common amongst men?'

He pulled away from her and ran a nervous hand through his hair. 'I pray to God you never find out what is common amongst men. You should be familiar with only one man: your husband.'

She shook her head in disbelief. 'And if I elect to

have none, I am to remain in chaste ignorance for my entire life?'

'Well—' he threw his hands into the air '—yes. You should.'

She smiled. 'Then I fear, thanks to you, it is too late for me already.'

'Thanks to me? Thanks to you, and your feather-brained attempts to destroy your honour, I could have died today, or killed my brother.'

She leaned close to him again, her eyes sparkling and intense. 'And that was my great regret. But masculine pride must take some blame for that situation. You admitted that to me before.

'And, as is typical of the male gender, you didn't spare a moment's thought to anyone else, when you found a reason to fight. Miranda and I sat for hours, afraid to speak, each knowing that the one's happiness at the outcome would mean the other's despair. When you walked into the door, I was shamed to find that I did not care that the duke might lay dead somewhere and that my only friend's heart was broken beyond repair. I was only glad that I could see you again and know that you lived.'

Before he could stop himself, he'd reached out and taken her hand. It was small and warm, and his breath caught in his throat as she twined her fingers with his. 'I am alive, and so is my brother. I promise, things are better between us than they have been for many years. I have you to thank for that. And I am grateful. But I do not wish to spoil the truce when it is so new, by abusing his hospitality. Please do not ask me to. I cannot give you what you want. No decent man would help you achieve dishonour with another. And I am certainly in no position to offer you better, as you would deserve.'

Her eyes shone with fresh tears, but he hardened his heart against them.

'I beg you, Esme, let Miranda find you a husband, or go home to the one your father has chosen for you. Once you are wed, you will be safe from your father and free of many of the restrictions you face now. Marry, Esme. Do it soon. And marry anyone but me.' And he pulled his hand away from hers and walked back down the stairs to his brother.

Chapter Eleven

Esme tossed in her bed, unable to sleep. The clock on the mantel was ticking more loudly than before. The sound of time passing was deafening her with its finality.

She punched her pillow and rolled to find a cooler spot. Her plan had lost all sense, at some point. She had hoped to find freedom by casting off her virtue, selling herself until she could find another way on. And then it had seemed possible that Miranda might find her a husband and she might never return home to her father's choice.

But that was not enough any more. She'd known, as she waited for the men to return from the duel, that she'd been foolish enough to fall in love. And with St John Radwell, of all people. If she'd woken one morning and made a plan to break her own heart, she could not have chosen better.

It was more than friendship between them. He

wanted her, as a man wanted a woman, no matter how much he might protest otherwise. He could not offer for her, as he kept insisting, and yet he wanted her all the same, or he would not have come to her room when sleep deprived him of inhibition.

She groaned and rolled again, pulling the pillow over her head. The man took the strangest time to find his honour, just when she needed him to be a cad. She doubted, should he take liberties with her, that he could manage to free himself from the obligation of marriage. It might have been true of the infamous rake that she'd heard so much about, but certainly not the man that she'd come to know.

St John held her at arm's length, meaning to protect her, no matter what that protection might cost to her chance at physical happiness. But if he would not have her, than some other man must, or she must return home. She could choose a loveless marriage, or life as a spinster in her father's house, doing penance for her mother's deceit.

She threw back the covers and planted her feet on the floor. There would be no sleep tonight. Not with the memory of St John, standing naked over her bed the night before. His skin had seemed golden in the moonlight, and she'd taken her fill of the sight of him before calling out to waken him from his trance.

Which, she supposed, proved her father right all along. A decent girl would have shrunk in horror, or perhaps screamed for help. At least she should have shielded her eyes from the sight. But she'd longed to touch, and to explore. And she'd hoped that he'd take just a few more steps and come into her bed to cover her body with his own.

It had been most disappointing when the duke had come to rescue her and spoiled everything.

And now, her thoughts of what might have been left her warm and restless in the cosiness of the room, and she longed to throw her nightdress aside and lie bare on the cool sheets, as he must do.

She stood up and moved away from the bed and the wild ideas rising in her mind. It was far too late to ring for a cup of tea, but perhaps a book from the library... The walk would cool her blood and a nice volume of sermons would cool her fevered brain. Sermons made her long for sleep in the chapel on Sundays. They would be just the trick now.

She crept down the hall to the stairs, the cold marble under her bare feet making her shiver. This was much better, listening to the night noises of the big house and feeling deliciously alone and at peace. She opened the door to the library and paused on the threshold, sensing the presence in the room before she saw him. Candles were lit and there was a crystal decanter of brandy on the small table beside the couch and a snifter already poured, although it gave no sign of having been touched. Above the back of the sofa, she saw the outline of St John's head with the firelight behind it, the warm glow giving a halo to his golden hair.

Without turning, he said, 'You might as well come in, Esme. The open door is making a draught.'

'How did you know…?'

'That it would be you?' He laughed softly. 'Who else would it be, cutting up my peace, keeping me awake nights?'

She stiffened. 'If I disturb you so, then I had best be going.'

'Don't be a goose. I smelled your perfume.' He glanced back at her, over his shoulder. 'And I can see my attempt at wit has failed. Never mind it. What brings you here, at this hour?'

'I should think that would be obvious. What would bring me to the library at this time of night?'

'You could not sleep and wished something to read.'

'But of course,' she said with more bitterness than necessary. 'And you have come for a brandy before bed.'

'This hour vary rarely finds me curled up with a good book, if that's what you're hinting at.'

She walked into the room and dropped into the chair next to the couch. 'While I am not allowed to curl up with anything else.'

He nodded. 'As it should be. You will not find me curling up with you, tonight, whatever I might have tried last night.'

'No,' she snapped. 'Never with me. Although you might at least pretend that the idea is not so repellent.'

His smile was sad, and there was a haunted look in his eyes that gave her pause. 'Do not think that, dear Esme. You are not in the least repellent. If you only knew…' He paused, as if lost in thought for a moment, then went on, the softness disappearing from his tone. 'As a matter of fact, I could quite enjoy you, my sweet, given half a chance. So young, so tender, so naïve. But I have given my word to my brother not to trouble the guests while I remain under his roof. So I must admire you from afar, and brood into the fire on what might have been.' He sighed, and it was mockery. 'I must exercise self-denial. It is a perversion that I've not yet experienced, to stare at you thus, with bare feet sticking out from under your nightdress, and use only my imagination.'

'Self-denial,' she scoffed. 'And that is why you've sneaked off to the library for a glass of drugged spirits.'

His head snapped up and the look in his eyes was sharp with pain and shame. And he grabbed the snifter in with an impulsive shudder and pitched it and its contents into the fire. The brandy made the flames flare blue, before they settled again, the light glinting off the shards of crystal on the hearthstone. His voice was harsh. 'There. Are you satisfied? There will be no drug tonight. Or sleep either, since if I doze I am likely to walk as I did last night, shaming myself and my family more than this filthy habit already does.'

She went to him, and reached out, but when her fingers touched his arm he drew back as though burned. 'Do not touch me, if you value your virtue.' He stalked back to the couch and collapsed into a seat, glaring past her, into the fire.

She walked to him and dropped to her knees on the

rug in front of him, blocking his view so he had no choice but to look at her.

'Well, then.' His tone was gruff. 'Are you still here? I thought I made it clear that your company was un-welcome.'

'No,' she whispered. 'You said that my touch was unwelcome. And so I will not touch you. But neither will I leave you alone while you need me.'

'Need you?' He sneered.

'You need someone, for I do not trust you to be alone. And I am the only one here. Would you prefer that I got the duke?'

'No.' His hand shot out and seized her gently by the wrist. He sighed and closed his eyes. 'Please. I would not wish him to see me this way. For the first time in our lives, he has begun to treat me as an equal, and not a constant source of disappointment. For him to find me now, unable to marshal my base needs for the lau-danum, would undo much.'

'Then let me help you.'

His eyes were open, and he was staring into hers with that sad smile again. 'I would if there were aught for you to do.'

'But there is.' She smiled. 'If you cannot sleep with-out the drug, then I will stay awake with you, until you are tired enough to go to bed. I can distract you.'

His mouth quirked and there was a long pause as his eyes travelled over her body. 'I have no doubt that you could be most diverting, but I believe I've made my po-sition on that quite clear.'

She was blushing. She could not help it, and she turned her face away from his so that he might not see it. She rose from the carpet and walked to the table near the window. 'No, silly. I am sure I saw some cards here, in the drawer of this table. Perhaps a few hands of something might pass the evening in an agreeable way. Whist?'

He rolled his eyes. 'Whist requires four persons. Be honest, now, Esme. What do you know of cards?'

'Very little. It is one of the many things that my father found too wicked for me to partake in.' She pulled the little card table close to where he was sitting and passed the deck to him. 'And so, you must teach me. I am afraid that I'm likely to be a rather slow pupil. It is lucky that you have all night.'

He smiled at her and shook his head. 'I am alone in the dark with a beautiful woman, she is barely dressed, and we have the whole night to spend together. And this vision kneels at my feet, offering to relieve my suffering. And then we play cards. Esme Canville, you must swear that no mention of this night will ever escape your lips. Never mind your precious virtue—my reputation as a danger to womankind will be utterly destroyed.'

He shuffled the deck and said, 'Very well. Cards it is. We will not bet, because it would hardly be fair of me with so inexperienced an opponent. Let us begin with a simple game of *Vingt-et-un*.'

When he sent her to bed, the clock was striking four, and she had begun to nod over her hand.

'Go back to your room, Esme. If you miss your beauty sleep, I do not wish to be held responsible for it.'

'And what of you?' He was very tired, but she could see the lines of strain in his face were not as pronounced as they had been.

'What of me?' His smile was wan. 'I will stay up for a time yet. The dawn is peaceful. I have reason to know. I have seen it often enough. When the first birds are singing, I find it easiest to rest.' He walked her to the door of the library, then stopped and impulsively seized her hand and brought her fingers to his lips. 'And thank you. You are right. It helped.'

She felt her heart soaring in her chest like the first singing bird. 'I will come again, tomorrow night.'

He shook his head. 'I should say no. I have a care for your reputation, girl, even if you do not. But I am so tired.'

She smiled. 'You should say no. But you won't. I cannot make you any less tired, but I can stay with you until this time passes. You have done much for me, bringing me here and giving me a taste of freedom and the friendship of your family. But I have done nothing for you but cause you grief. Let me do this one thing.'

'Very well.'

And he closed the door softly behind her as she found her way back to her room.

The next night found him pacing the library, restless as a caged animal. He would make several circuits of the room, then return to the couch, fearing that she would find him thus and interpret his nerves for weakness. But eventually the restlessness in his legs became too much and he was on his feet again.

It should not matter to him what she thought, for he should not be allowing her to sit with him. It was improper. Innocent enough as yet, but it would be far too tempting in his current condition to substitute one vice for another.

But it had felt so good to have her at his side the previous night that he had not noticed the hours slipping by. And she had been so eager to help him. He hadn't the strength or the desire to refuse.

The clock on the mantel struck twelve and he drummed his fingers on the table before him. It was later than last night. Perhaps she had seen sense and would not come. Or maybe she was so tired from the previous night that she had retired early and forgotten her promise to sit with him.

He had seen her, dozing in the family pew at chapel, and smiled as Miranda nudged the poor girl awake during the sermon, again and again. She needed her rest and it was wrong of him to wish otherwise.

But he found the prospect of an evening without her almost unbearable. After she'd left him at dawn, he'd remained in the library, and dozed fitfully as the sun had come up. Marcus had found him there, and kicked his boot to waken him, asking what he was about.

He'd begun to explain the insomnia, but had caught Marcus staring at the card table in front of the sofa. St

John had hastily laid a game of Patience and had avowed that it calmed his nerves, when he was restless at night.

Only to see Marcus glance to the second chair. His brother had given him a pointed look and remarked slowly and with emphasis, that cards were a harmless enough way to pass the wee hours, as long as one was careful what games one played. And then he'd said no more about it.

St John had been left with the impression that his brother guessed much more of the truth than he cared to admit. But if that was the case, then he'd been given tacit permission to meet with the girl unchaperoned.

Obviously, married life had softened his brother's heart, or his head.

He heard the door click and rushed back to the sofa to arrange himself in illusory comfort as the door opened and Esme entered. 'Here to spend the late hours with me, after all?'

'As I said I would be.' She took the seat across the table from him as he shuffled the cards.

'I thought perhaps you would not come.'

'Miranda came to my room to speak to me about my feelings on the gentlemen at our last ball. And to remind me of my duties to my honour. I think she is concerned that I am still too fond of you. I could hardly send her away because we had an assignation, could I?'

He felt a moment's alarm. 'This is not an assignation.'

She cocked her head to the side. 'Well, what would you prefer to call it? I am open to suggestions.'

'I would prefer not to call it anything at all. It is merely two people meeting, with a card table between them. The word assignation makes it sound…'

'Clandestine? Well, it is.'

'No. Intimate.'

'It is that as well, St John. Not physical intimacy, perhaps…'

'Not physical intimacy, at all.' He hurriedly dealt out a hand of piquet.

'I meant emotional intimacy. I dare say in a few short weeks you've got to know me better than any human being ever will.'

'Surely your husband—'

She fanned the cards he dealt her and tapped them on the table in annoyance. 'If and when I find one. The man my father has chosen was not intrigued enough to meet me before the betrothal. Am I to suspect this sudden interest in conversation will magically blossom on our wedding night?'

St John glanced down at her body and swallowed the lump in his throat. The lawn of her nightdress was not sheer, and the wrapper hid most of her body. Bet he was suddenly aware that there was very little between her smooth, pale skin and the night air, and that what garments she wore were loose and easily removed. He forced his eyes back to her face. 'No, I doubt that your husband, whcn you find him, will be in the mood for conversation once he has you alone.'

'And yet you have no trouble engaging me in discourse. Possibly because you made it abundantly clear, after the kiss in the garden, that I hold no interest for you.' She smiled back at him a little too brightly. 'And thus you are willing to speak to me as an equal and have come to know me better than any other human.'

'About that kiss—' His mouth snapped shut. The last thing he need do would be to tell her how pleasant it had been, or there would be no managing her.

'And what of it? I would rather not think overly long on it. I had been quite enjoying it, until you spoilt it. It was my first kiss, but of course you noticed that, as you pointed out my inexperience. I suppose one must start somewhere. I will no doubt do better, when I have opportunity to kiss again.' She rapped the deck on the table with her knuckles. 'Now look to your cards.'

She remembered the rules of the game well enough to beat him repeatedly. It might have helped if he'd been able to concentrate on the cards in his hand instead of the lips of his opponent, and the idea that she might have an opportunity to kiss again—nay, must kiss, if they meant to get her properly betrothed before sending her home—and when she did, the kiss would be with someone other than him. And if that had been her first kiss, she'd shown natural aptitude and a willingness to adapt to the needs of her partner.

Miranda must find her a suitable husband, and quickly. For Esme was right in one thing: it would be a waste to give such kisses to an old man, even for a fine fortune, an early widowhood and a chance to escape from her father.

She would lose her innocence in more ways than one on the first night, once she saw what it was she'd been yoked to. Her playful nature would change to cynicism. In no time, she would be as jaded as any of the ladies of the *ton*.

And she'd come dangling after him some night when her husband was away, just as he'd told her to. There would be no teasing conversations, no time for games at all. Just a hurried and vigorous joining before she returned to her home.

Until the next time the hunger grew in her and she came to him. And he would not turn her away. He sighed.

'Is there something the matter?' She looked up in puzzlement.

'No. Nothing. Really.'

She returned to her cards.

After she was married, her visits would be so different from this. And when they saw each other in daylight, she would be unwilling to meet his gaze. She would have no wish to talk or laugh with him. She would studiously avoid him so as not to cause gossip.

Of course, she was ignoring him now as well, all her focus on the cards, biting her lip in concentration. When she let it go, it had a bee-stung quality that begged attention, and she rubbed at it with the tip of her tongue...

And without warning, he threw the cards aside, and leaned across the small table, gripping her firmly by the shoulders and bringing his mouth down upon hers.

'Oh, St John. We mustn't.' She struggled but for a moment, before dropping the cards and clinging to the lapels of his coat.

He slipped his tongue into her mouth and tasted her between the words of protest. He could feel her body relax in his hands, surrendering to him as the kiss grew deeper.

When he moved his lips to her ear, she took in a breath and let out a great sigh. 'Well, we probably shouldn't. I think. Oh, dear.'

And then she ceased talking entirely and turned her mouth to his to let him kiss her again. With some hesitation, she began to kiss him back, slipping her tongue between his lips in tentative exploration. She paused, and he could feel her waiting for a repeat of the rebuke he had given her in the garden. And when it did not come she became more bold, nipping at his lip, and losing all fear as she took his mouth with her tongue.

He was at once happy with and frustrated by the table between them. It kept temptation in check to feel the wood pressing against his legs. But she was leaning over it, her robe brushing the discarded cards to the floor as she tried to get closer to him. She balanced a hip on its top, pivoting and reaching for him to wrap an arm around his neck.

It was dizzying to feel her so close, rubbing against his body, begging for more than he dared give. He released her shoulders, placed his palms flat on the table, and pressed down until his wrists hurt, denying the urge to stroke her hair and face, or to touch the breasts pressing against his chest.

There was a crack of splintering wood as a table leg gave way and tipped her off on to the floor and sent him stumbling after to lie in a heap beside her and the broken table on the Aubusson rug.

There was a horrible moment when she lay face down on the carpet making no sound at all, and he feared that she might be more broken than the poor table. And then she rolled on to her back, shaking with silent laughter.

And he rolled to her side, leaning on his elbow and watching her laugh. It was strange, he thought. She smiled often enough, but very rarely did he see her so overcome by mirth. The healthy flush in her cheeks and the twinkle in her eyes as she squeezed out tears of laughter was quite the most attractive thing he'd ever seen.

Finally, she managed to control herself sufficiently to speak. 'All right, St John. I must agree with you. You are a truly wicked man. For now I've broken my host's furniture while dallying in the library with you. What am I to tell Miranda?' She rolled to face him, plucking at his coat with her fingers.

'That is simple. You are to tell her absolutely nothing.' He rolled away from her and stood, brushing an imaginary fleck of dust off his trousers, and examined the table. 'See? The pins that held the leg have snapped, but it fits into the top like so.' He forced it back into a rough approximation of what it had been and smacked it sharply with the heel of his hand. Then he carried the temporarily intact table back to its place by the window, setting it down carefully so as not to disturb it. 'There. Almost as good as new.'

She looked doubtful of his repair. 'But the first time someone makes use of it…'

'Perhaps. Perhaps not. It will break, should they try to make love on it. I believe we have proved that right enough. But it should last a hand of cards, as long as the players are not too strenuous in their betting. And now, little one, I recommend that we steal away to bed, so that we may be as far away as possible from the scene of the crime, should it collapse before morning.' He offered her a hand off the floor and she rose gracefully, standing too close to him for common decency.

He took a cautious step back and led her to the door to the hall. 'Sly, my dear, but not sly enough. You will not tempt me into a repeat of that incident, no matter how appealing the idea might be.'

And then she smiled in triumph and he realised she was not going to deny it. 'At least now I know you were shamming in the garden the other day. You do not wish to be my teacher? Then, my darling St John, I will have to be the one who teaches you.'

And she turned without another word and walked away from him, down the darkened hall.

Chapter Twelve

'And you are sure the first two will not suit?' They were taking their breakfast tea in the morning room. Miranda was chewing on the end of her pen, but seemed strangely unconcerned by her lack of success as a matchmaker.

Esme nodded. 'Both are otherwise engaged, although I will admit to the smallest amount of regret when it comes to Mr Smythe.'

Miranda smiled. 'He is most appealing, I agree. Handsome, well dressed, and with gallant manners, although a bit of a rakehell. Rather like St John, don't you think?'

Esme choked on a crumb from the scone she'd been eating, and took a careful sip of tea. 'Really, I hadn't noticed. Unless you mean in the sense that they have both told me that an association with me would be impossible. But Mr Smythe, at least, had the grace to appear disappointed.'

'Hmm. Most unfortunate. About Mr Smythe, I mean. I would hate for you to pin your hopes on wringing an offer out of St John. He really can be the most contemptible villain.' But she was smiling as she said it, which seemed out of context. She continued, 'Although I suspect he would be a devoted husband. He is a hopeless romantic and thus is afraid of confessing affection lest his heart be broken.'

Or any more furniture.

Esme looked down to hide her laughter and toyed with her spoon, trailing it aimlessly around the cup of cooling tea. 'I suppose… He will be a fine match for someone, should he be so inclined.'

'Well, know that your father would never approve. I am sure he would find Lord Baxter much more suitable. Mature. Stable.'

Which made Lord Baxter sound quite boring, really. Miranda was clueless when it came to matchmaking. Esme said, 'I do not wish to choose a husband based on the wishes of my father. If I could find someone who wanted me, who I wanted as well, then I doubt my father's wishes would signify greatly to me. Truth be told, if the man cannot withstand my father's displeasure, then it matters not whether I want him, for my father's displeasure is the only factor in this plan that can be assured.'

She thought of the new letter she had received at breakfast. The words were not threatening, merely curt. Another insistence that she get over her megrims post haste and return home to meet her betrothed. But she could imagine the look on her father's face as he wrote them, and the tone he would use if he were speaking. The one that told her, without saying the words out loud, the painful consequences of inaction.

'Well, we shall see if my last candidate can fulfil your requirements.' Miranda smiled again. 'I was thinking something less formal this time. A card party, perhaps. Enough couples to make a few tables of four, some cheese and fruit. Simplicity itself.'

'Cards?' Esme thought of the game she'd just played so successfully with St John and felt a blush rising in her cheeks.

'You do play whist, do you not?'

'Badly.'

'Do not worry.' Miranda waved off her objections. 'We will practise before the event. A few rubbers in the library. You can partner with St John…'

'That would be…most interesting.' She tried to keep her tone neutral.

That evening, they sat around the same table that she and St John had used the previous evening. He was seated across from her and the duke and Miranda were on either side. The game went well enough and she played as best she was able, although it might have been easier to concentrate if she'd partnered with someone who had been less prone to inappropriate laughter.

After taking another trick, Miranda commented, 'Esme, you and St John play admirably together.'

'But not so well as to win the rubber,' Esme responded.

'Winning is not the most important thing,' Miranda insisted. 'What matters is pleasure in the game and an evening spent in good company. Your partner does not seem to mind losing, do you, St John?'

'Miranda, look to your cards,' the duke cautioned his wife.

'We are losing?' St John asked. 'I barely noticed. I was too busy admiring this table.' He tapped the top with his finger. 'Is it new?'

Esme tried to kick St John under the table, and was most embarrassed to see the duke flinch in response.

Marcus ignored the misplaced kick and answered his brother. 'This table and its mate have been in the library since we were children, as you should well remember. Stop talking nonsense and deal.'

'It is still sturdy, despite its age.' St John shook the table, which showed no sign of collapse.

Marcus snatched his wine glass from the table, before it spilled. 'St John, if you must destroy the furniture, please wait until I've finished my port.'

'Hear that, Esme? My brother has given me permission to destroy the furniture.' St John grinned at her and raised an eyebrow.

'No more port for you,' Marcus responded and combined the contents of St John's glass with his own.

'This table has a mate?' Esme glared across the table at St John.

'Didn't you notice? It is under the window in the library. At one time, there were three of them, but they are rather easily broken. Weak legs.' He rattled the table again.

'I think the third table is upstairs in the portrait gallery. St John, have you shown Esme the family portraits?' Miranda suggested.

'Or they could play cards,' suggested the duke and the group fell into comfortable silence, punctuated by the occasional snort of mirth from St John.

She stood before him later, when they were alone in the library, hands on hips. 'That was horrible of you, St John. Letting me continue for half the evening in fear that the game was likely to collapse out from under us, when all the while you knew it was a different table.'

'They are easy to tell apart, if you know them. There is a chip in the veneer of the one we broke.' He pointed to the table that he had set for their nightly game. 'This one is unmarked and perfectly safe.' He walked to the other side of the table and sat down.

She glanced across at him. The tiredness on his face was even more evident than the night before. At some point, he must give in and sleep, or die from fatigue. And the way he had moved when he saw her, it almost seemed that he was keeping the table between them, which was ridiculous. A man who had faced Napoleon should have nothing to fear from her.

'Shall we try to improve your game for tomorrow? We cannot play a real game with only two, but perhaps with practice you might learn to bet.' He reached for a glass and decanter on another small table near the couch, and poured himself a glass.

She stared at it in suspicion.

He smiled. 'Not drugged, I promise you. Only the port of which my brother was so protective. And with reason. It is excellent. Portuguese, as it should be. It would have been criminal of me to spill it. If you do not trust me, you may taste from my glass.' And he offered her his wine and poured another for himself.

The port was rich, and it warmed her blood, but she detected no trace of the drug that she had taken in London. She sat the glass down on the table. 'You are right. It is very good. But I should not finish it. So late in the evening, it will likely go to my head.'

He nodded. 'That is wise of you.'

She stared across the table at him, remembering his kiss and the feel of his arms around her, and did not want to be wise at all. She picked up her glass and took another sip of wine, letting the warmth build inside her. 'I suspect that, should a young lady alone in circumstances such as this have too much wine, certain men might be prone to take liberties.'

'Perhaps.' He set his own glass down.

'Of course, with me you will do nothing. Much as you are doing now.' She sighed and watched him as he watched the rise and fall of her bosom. Fire danced in his eyes when he looked at her, but he made no move to act. 'I am disappointed in you. You have a reputation as a dangerous man.'

'Well deserved. But that is in the past, I assure you. You are safe with me.'

'In the past? Tell me, then—what did you do in this illustrious past of yours?'

'I never plied a woman with port and made her fight for her virtue, if that is what you suspect.' He smiled, remembering. 'I did not favour the sort that would put up a struggle over something of that nature. The virtue of the ladies I favoured was long fled by the time I got them alone.'

'Oh, really? Were the ladies terribly wicked? And were you?' She tried not to sound eager for the story, but could not hide the curiosity in her voice.

He reached for his wine glass and filled it slowly. 'Not wicked. But they were not adverse to passing a pleasant afternoon picnicking alone with me in a certain secluded spot I know on my brother's property.'

'Is it pretty?' she asked.

'Very.'

'Then you must show me tomorrow.'

He glared at her. 'I most certainly will not. I would not take an innocent out into the woods without a chaperon. My brother would have my head for suggesting it. Any woman who shared a basket and a bottle with me on such an outing was already quite sure of what she wanted. And it wasn't jugged pheasant and fresh air.'

She looked disappointed. 'So you are not really a practised seducer because seduction was unnecessary?'

'I am a practised seducer because I enjoy it, love. When a man persuades a woman to spend a time in mutual pleasure, he should do it with grace and style, even if the conclusion is foregone.' He took a deep sip of the port, savouring it before swallowing.

'And what was your method?' She drummed her fingers on the table top. 'You are smiling again, and in the strangest way.' She waited for him to speak, and he did not. So she stared back at him, and felt the seconds grow long and the air grow heavy, and the oddest thoughts took shape in her head.

'First, I make sure I have the lady's full attention.' His voice was soft, and she felt herself leaning closer to him.

She drew back and broke the connection of their gaze, taking another sip of her own wine. 'And what happens after you have got their attention?'

'It depends on what they wish to happen.' He reached over and took the wine glass from her hand, and sipped from the spot where her lips had been.

A shudder went through her as she imagined the touch of his mouth on hers.

He smiled at the response.

She watched in silence as he held and warmed the wine in her glass in his cupped hand, his fingers caressing the bowl. At last he pinched the stem between his fingers.

She felt her nipples tighten in response. 'Oh, dear.'

He looked down at the outline of her breasts against the lawn of her nightrail and the subtle peaks forming.

As she felt his eyes upon her, the effect was becoming more pronounced.

When he spoke, his voice was mild and his face was all innocence. 'I really have no idea where I get such a reputation as a rake. It seems I need to say or do very little, and yet the ladies I am with have the most outlandish ideas. One minute I am enjoying a quiet lunch with a charming young widow, and the next, she is imploring me to drink champagne from her navel. I do not understand how it happens.'

'You do not have to oblige them,' she said, feeling the heat grow in her belly.

'But it would be churlish to deny such pleasant and accommodating ladies. And I quite enjoy champagne.' He was looking at her again over the rim of his wine glass with that curious intensity.

Her heart was pounding madly and the room was becoming warm. Her gown had seemed light before, but suddenly it was heavy and constricting and curiosity burned in her like the port. She took a gulp of her wine and reached for the ties of her gown. 'Would port work?'

'Would port work for what?' And then he saw the look in her eyes. 'Dear Lord, Esme. I meant that hypothetically. Or historically, perhaps. Not in the present tense. I was an idiot to mention it. It was only fatigue and one too many glasses of wine that persuaded me to mention it at all.'

She undid the bow at her throat and let the bodice gap. 'Oh, really? I think you discussed your method because you wanted me to hear it. You were willing to satisfy my curiosity, because you knew what I would do.' She reached for the next tie.

'Stop that, this instant, Esme.'

'I am not worried. We have been uninterrupted for two nights now. Tonight will be no different.'

'I will go to my room and leave you here alone,' he threatened.

'I seriously doubt that. You will not seduce me, for you wish me to seduce you to avoid the blame of it. Let us see if I am right, shall we?' She pulled slowly on the ribbon to let the bow unravel.

'Tie up your gown again and go to bed. I have had quite enough port for the evening, and you have had far too much.' He reached to take the glass from her, but she pulled away. It tipped and the wine spilled on to her, soaking the thin cotton of the gown. She could feel it clinging to her skin.

'Damn.' His gaze was frozen, staring at her breasts.

She looked down. The wine had rendered the fabric almost transparent. She could see the outline of her nipples clearly, as could he. 'Is there something the matter with them?'

'Perfect,' he muttered softly to himself. 'Absolutely perfect.'

'Really?' She relaxed. 'Well, that is good to know. But I certainly seem to have made a muddle of things. Perhaps I should go to my room and change.'

'Like hell you should.' He shoved the table out of the way and fell on his knees before her, pulling her forward so he could take her in his mouth, sucking her breasts through the wine-soaked fabric.

Her breath caught in her throat and she leaned her head forward to rest her cheek against his hair as he buried his face against her, his mouth searching for the opening of the gown to lick at her bare skin. The wine was chill on her, but his lips were warm, as were his hands as he parted the cloth and slipped the bodice to her waist. Then he pulled her out of her chair and laid her down on her back in the middle of the rug.

He stepped away from her, then, and she wondered what he meant to do. Then he reached for his port and lay down on the rug beside her. Slowly, he dipped his finger into the glass to catch a few drops and let them drip upon her breasts. Then he stroked her with his fingertips, massaging the wine into her nipples and drawing tiny circles on her body until her breasts ached for his lips. At last, his head dipped close and his mouth touched her and his tongue licked away the wine.

His teeth had caught a nipple and he was pulling gently on it, and she arched her back, hands clawing at the carpet. She reached to touch his hair, cradling his head as he moved to the other breast. She stared up at the ceiling above her and felt the world turning beneath her, spinning out of control. St John's hands travelled to her waist and held her fast as he sucked and bit and stroked until she was writhing beneath him, straining to be closer to him.

And then he stopped. He reached for his glass again and she held her breath as he poured it on to her belly.

He set the glass aside and lay upon her, covering her breasts with his hands and tracing a lazy pattern with his tongue on the flesh of her abdomen, before drinking the wine he had poured. Then he raised his head to look into her eyes.

And he froze. There was a sound at the door. He held out a hand, warning her without words to stay where she was, on the floor and out of sight. Then he jumped to his feet and resumed his seat on the sofa, snuffing a candle, and dimming the room as the door opened.

'Master St John?'

'What is it, Wilkins?'

'I did not realise that you were still awake. Will you be needing anything?'

'Nothing, thank you. I am fine here in the evenings and do not require your service.' St John paused. 'But wait.' He reached for the port decanter and a single glass and walked to the door to hand them to the butler. 'You can dispose of this for me before I drink it all. It does not do to be alone with one's thoughts and a full bottle.'

'Yes, sir.'

Esme heard the door close and remained on the floor, waiting for her heart to stop pounding in her chest. St John loomed over her, half-lost in shadows, half-lit by the dying fire. He offered her his hand, and helped her to her feet. He pulled her close and whispered, 'And now that *my* curiosity is satisfied, we must stop.'

'No,' she gasped.

'Yes,' he said. 'The butler is on his way to the servants' quarters with half a bottle and my blessing. You have more than enough time to return to your room undiscovered. But it was a near miss, all the same.' He pulled her nightrail back up on to her shoulders and began to do up the bows. 'I have taken grave liberties with you, but done you no permanent harm. We will stop before that is no longer true.

'Do not think you can tease me, Esme, and make me dance to your tune. Another man would not be half so patient with you as I have been and would have greedily taken more than what you were offering tonight.'

He tied the last of the ribbons and led her towards the door. 'But I want better for you than that. You deserve more than a few moments' happiness. You deserve a lifetime. And when you find the man that can give you that, it would kill me to think that I have ruined your chances by stealing from you what rightly belongs to him.'

He opened the door and looked out into the hall. There was a moment's hesitation before he sighed and said, 'And now you must go to bed before someone finds you here.' He pulled her close and gave her an innocent kiss on the lips. 'And to answer your question, yes. Port works quite as well as champagne.' Then he pushed her out into the hall and shut the door behind her.

Chapter Thirteen

The next afternoon was as Miranda had described. A modest gathering of tables for four, and Esme was to be partnered with the last gentleman on Miranda's list. She hid a yawn behind her hand. She was still only passable at whist, and, try as she might, she could not raise the enthusiasm to become better.

Of course, once one had played cards with St John, one was unlikely to be satisfied with tricks and trumps and playing for pennies. She could not help feeling that the game became much more interesting once one had put down the pasteboards and pushed the table out of the way.

Miranda had suggested a simple, sprigged muslin gown for her, and the pink rosebuds that covered it went well with the flush in her cheeks as she thought of the previous evening. She would be playing cards on the very spot where they had lain the night before.

And they might be playing on the very table where he had taught her how to kiss.

And she must not think of any of this again. Miranda had finished greeting her guests and hurried to her side, taking her hand in an encouraging squeeze. 'You look lovely today, Esme,' she said. 'Like a breath of spring. You are in fine colour as well. Are you excited at the prospect of meeting his lordship?'

'Yes. Of course, that is it.' Esme hoped her smile wasn't too dazed to be convincing. But in a moment's lapse, she had forgotten the reason she was there. This was to be her last chance at marriage. If Lord Baxter was the best that Devon had to offer, than she should do her best to appear suitable to him. Spinning fancies about St John when she should be concentrating on the man in front of her would be no help at all.

Miranda said, 'It is good to see you are looking forward to this. Men take notice when a girl is interested, and are flattered by it.' Miranda took her hand and led her across the room to meet her card partner.

'Miss Esme Canville, may I present Lord Baxter.' Miranda introduced them, and the gentleman bowed low over her hand. He was certainly gallant enough. The bow was deep and well formed. He was not as young as Webberly, or Smythe, but nowhere near as old as her father's choice for her. Baxter's hair was steel grey, and his face was lined, but not unhandsome. His eyes were not kind, but neither were they cruel.

He was not perfect, but he seemed the sort of man she could grow fond of, given time and opportunity.

She smiled back at him, polite and encouraging. 'I am honoured to meet you, sir. I understand we are to be partnered at cards this afternoon. I hope you will be patient with me, for I am new to the game of whist.'

'New to the game?' He dropped her hand. 'Then perhaps you would do well to partner someone as inexperienced as yourself. He looked at Miranda. 'Is there no other I could play with?'

Esme's heart sank.

Miranda was obviously nonplussed at having her seating arrangement questioned by a guest. It took a moment before her smile dropped back into place and she said, 'Why, no, Lord Baxter. I believe the tables are already set. Perhaps another time. But today I am most eager to have my friend in experienced hands as regards the game. And I was certain that you would be the best teacher for her.'

'Well, we can hardly expect to win, if we are unevenly matched.'

Miranda ignored his objection. 'Winning is hardly a consideration on such a pleasant afternoon as this. We are playing for amusement, and not high stakes, after all.'

'Winning not important? How like a woman to say such a thing.' Lord Baxter harrumphed. Esme had heard the noise from her father's friends, when there was mention of liberal government and difficulties with the lower classes, but had never expected to hear it from the lips of a potential suitor. She schooled her face into a neutral expression.

Miranda smiled and nodded, although there was a flash of irritation in her eyes. 'Yes, I suppose it is. But then, with children to raise and a household to run, we have little time for things as important as cards. You will be playing against the duke and myself. My husband has much the same problems with me as you will have with Esme. He finds it most trying. But it means we will be evenly matched.'

Esme thought Miranda must be as accomplished a liar as she was a card player to make the last statement sound convincing. She and the duke played as though they had a single mind between them. And now that Baxter had made her angry, Esme doubted that she would show the man mercy and lose to protect his ego.

Miranda led them to their table. Esme examined it. It seemed to be the one from the library, but it was hard to tell. Perhaps it was the mate. Several of the tables in the room looked alike, and the cloth covered the chip in the veneer. She must hope for the best. At an afternoon party there would be no reason for boisterous play. Things would be fine.

The game started well enough, but it seemed that she could not play with sufficient skill or speed to please her partner.

'Dammit, gel, you've lost the rubber for us again. If you cannot take the trick, then do not lead with such horrible cards.' He pounded the table for emphasis.

Esme cringed. And behind her, at a neighbouring table, she heard St John chuckle. 'I am sorry,' she said quietly to her partner. 'It was a terrible hand. It could not be helped.'

'A more experienced player can compensate for a

bad hand,' he grumbled. 'For the next, see to your cards and waste no more time gossiping.'

Since she had not spoken a word during the last hand, the charge was most unfair. She was preparing to tell him so when he gave several firm taps on the table with his finger.

Esme could swear that she felt a slight wobble, which subsided when the tapping ceased. Was that normal? Perhaps she was being over-dramatic.

Miranda shot her occasional worried glances, and whispered when they had a moment alone, 'I am so sorry. I had not remembered him in this way at all. Perhaps it is competition that brings out the worst in him. When I met him, he seemed a most retiring and polite gentleman. Please forget my suggestion that you might make a couple and let us do our best to get through the afternoon. Do not think that this is your last hope. We will find a different way.'

Esme breathed a sigh of relief. 'Do not trouble yourself about it.'

'But you looked so worried. If he distresses you so, you can move to another table.'

It was Lord Baxter that ought to move, given the fragility of the furniture. But how to offer that suggestion? Best not at all, Esme thought. 'No, I am fine.' She smiled with more confidence than she felt. 'Let us go back to the game.'

But St John was unable to let the matter rest. After a light refreshment, he convinced Marcus to trade tables and seated himself opposite Miranda, nodding to the two ladies. 'I have convinced my brother to give over your company for the afternoon, dear Miranda.' His eyes twinkled as he said it.

'And Marcus approved?' she asked with a trace of suspicion.

'We discussed it, and thought it was best that there be a change.' His weight shifted ever so slightly in Esme's direction. 'It is better not to let tables become too unmatched. I am too weak for the play over there. Marcus has far more skill at cards then I. He suggested that you partner me, although I must admit that I have not the patience for whist.'

Esme waited to see if lightning would strike, or the ground would open and swallow them, for all the outrageous comments passed as fact in an effort to gull Baxter into enjoying the foursome. She was tempted to point out that St John was an excellent card player. She had seen it herself. And he had professed a great love for this particular game. But then she remembered that they'd had no such discussion during their one evening of family play. It had been one of their nights together when he'd shared the information, so she could not possibly know it.

Lord Baxter was looking in frustration at the table of experienced players where he felt he belonged. Then he glared at St John. 'A man who cannot handle his cards is not much of a man, in my opinion.'

Esme noticed a steely glint in St John's eye at the insult, and watched it fade to innocuous good humour, when his lordship slapped the table top with his hand.

'Unlucky at cards, lucky at love,' countered St John. 'May fortune favour you in the next hand.'

'I fear we shall need it,' muttered Esme, trying not to smile.

'Ehhh?'

'Nothing, sir. I was merely seconding Captain Radwell's wish.'

St John dealt a hand and proceeded to play so ineptly that even Esme could best him. And when she won he congratulated her with excessive courtesy. She wondered if it would still be considered ungentlemanly to cheat at cards, when one were deliberately losing?

But apparently the Earl did not care from what source his win came. He stomped his feet and pounded the table in glee as he took the winning trick.

The table gave a decided lurch to the left and Esme braced it with her knee, amazed that no one else seemed to notice, although she suspected St John's smile as he lost had nothing to do with the game. And his eyes danced with mirth as he suggested another rubber.

Lord Baxter grinned like a predator. 'You don't know when to let well enough alone, do you, boy? Best leave the field, if you cannot handle the play.' He paused as if changing the subject. 'I understand you are just back from the Peninsula. Has the war ended, then?'

St John was silent for a moment, and Esme stifled her own desire to comment. But to have a woman answer for him as Baxter taunted him as a coward would only make things worse. She held her breath, waiting for the response.

St John blinked, and said with innocence, 'No. The war is most decidedly not over, at least not for those of us who have actually seen battle. But I have faith that the gentlemen still serving there can settle Boney without my help.' And then he said quietly, but in a tone that could not be disobeyed, 'Deal the cards, sir.'

Baxter stiffened and he dealt quickly, turning his attention to his hand.

Play began in earnest. St John raised his eyes from his cards and looked to Miranda and she smiled back. They were in communion as they took trick after trick. Esme felt a surge of jealousy, for it was clear that speech was unnecessary for them to be in harmony. She found herself wondering what had happened in the past that made them so sure of each other now, since Miranda played almost as well with St John as she did her husband.

Esme glanced to her own partner. He played as if he did not know she was there, and yet berated her each time they lost a point, slapping his palm upon the table for emphasis. He was boorish and horrible and all the things she wished not to see at breakfast every morning for the rest of her life. And she slid her leg away from its bracing position against the leg of the table and resigned herself to the inevitable.

It was clear that they would lose, and St John grew more courteous and pleasant, even as Lord Baxter grew more irate.

And, as Miranda reached to take the final trick to win the rubber, Baxter's hand came down upon the table and it collapsed, spilling cards in all directions and landing the contents of Baxter's wineglass into his own lap.

'I...I...I...' Baxter looked in horror at the ravages of the game.

Miranda raised her hand and servants appeared and spirited away the mess on the floor. She looked up at Baxter and said, with a brittle smile, 'That was most edifying.'

'Best two out of three?' St John asked.

And Esme kicked him smartly in the shin, not caring that there was no table to cover the action.

That night she came down to the library as she had for the previous three, to find St John in his usual chair in front of the fire, a book lying neglected on the floor beside him.

He rolled his eyes at her and picked up the book, trying to make it appear to her that she was an interruption. 'I had hoped, after last night, you would have sense enough not to come. It is too great a risk for you to meet with me.'

She sat down on a chair near the couch. 'Perhaps I am not here for you at all, and only came to the library to look for a book. That is a harmless enough impulse, is it not? And I am successful in my quest, for there are many books here, including the one you have chosen. What is it, please?'

He rubbed a hand over his face. 'I have no idea. I picked it at random and have read no further than the first page.'

'Well, then, I shall certainly not choose that one.' She stared at him in appraisal. He looked even more tired than he had the previous evening.

He sighed and said, 'My eyes can barely focus on the words, and yet when I close them, I do not sleep. This must end soon, or I shall.'

'Then do not waste breath trying to send me away. You cannot lose me so easily, St John. While I know you still suffer, I will not leave you. Do you wish me to read to you?'

He closed his eyes and shook his head.

'Well, is there some other way you might like to pass the time?'

He opened his eyes again, staring at her in disbelief, but said nothing.

'I would suggest cards,' said Esme, 'but I think I have had quite enough of them for one day. I have never been so mortified in my life. What you did to Lord Baxter was most unfair.'

St John drew himself up to sit straighter on the couch. 'On the contrary, what he was doing to you was most unfair. I observed you from across the room. You appeared to be most uncomfortable, and there was that great oaf, hounding you over missing tricks.'

'It was nothing,' she insisted.

'To you, perhaps. But I cannot abide those men that treat cards as though they were life and death, but talk of battle as though it were a card game. And bullying a woman over a game? He was beyond insulting. At one time, I'd have called a man out over less than that. If I thought that I could puncture him with a sword and let out some of his ill humour today, I'd have seriously considered it.'

He smiled at her. 'But the method I chose was better. If the man insisted on making an ass of himself with his boorish behaviour, he needed the barest nudge from me to do so in a way that everyone could enjoy.'

'You made it quite impossible for him to court me in the future,' she said. 'He would never dare show his face here, after the scene this afternoon.'

St John snorted. 'As if you would wish him to. Do not tell me you harboured a deep-seated affection for the man, based on the way he criticised your card play.'

She frowned. 'What I might wish for is not the point, St John. He might be the last hope for me, here in Devon. In my current situation, I cannot afford to be too selective.'

'Well, be more selective than that. I do not care if he is the last man in Devon, or the last man on earth, Esme. You should not tie yourself to him. Better to go back to the old man your father has selected. He will at least have the decency to die soon, and leave you a widow. But Baxter was most robust as he pounded on the furniture. I think we could count on him being a healthy boor for several more decades. He was not for you.'

She stalked to the window and stared out over the

darkened garden. 'You don't understand at all, St John. It should have been my right to make that decision, not yours. I could have managed with Baxter, given the chance.'

'And been miserable for the rest of his life, or yours.' St John had come up behind her and laid a brotherly hand upon her arm. 'He was not a good match for you, Esme. You did not suit. You are a treasure, a gift to be cherished. And when you give yourself, it should be to a man who is worthy, not a lout like Baxter.'

She shook off his touch and stared intently into the darkness, willing away the tears of frustration that she felt forming in her eyes. 'For all your experience with them, St John Radwell, you know nothing of what it means to be a woman. You talk as if I may have my choice of any available man, and then you think you can decide for me whom I will choose. You call me treasure, but then suggest I must go home to let my father auction away my gifts without my consent.

'You refuse to see the truth. I am no more special than a hundred other girls. And I am running out of options. If I wish to marry, and live honourably, as you insist I must, then when a man offers for me, any man at all, my answer must be yes, because there may be no second chance. Whether I get any pleasure from my choice is immaterial.'

His voice was sad when he spoke again. 'Very well. Perhaps I do not understand. But if you mean to marry without passion or love, then you should know that there are pleasures still within your control.'

He stepped behind her and wrapped his arms around her body; after a moment's hesitation, she let herself relax into him and be held. She'd have thought it a comforting gesture, if not for the rising heat inside her that proved her reaction to him was not one of solace.

He let his hands rise to her shoulders and trail down her arms to take her hands in his, meshing their fingers together. And then slowly, he led her hands upward to wrap around herself and touch her own shoulders. She could feel the warmth of his body behind her, and his breath against her hair, and the smoothness of her own skin where she was touching herself above the neckline of her nightrail. And then, he was leading her again. Lower, smoothing her hands over her body to cup her own breasts.

She gasped in shock, unsure of what he expected of her, and felt the thrill of the weight in her hands, gasping again as his hands contracted and made her squeeze, gently. Then he was leading her fingertips to her nipples, guiding her until she was massaging in gentle circles.

Her breath quickened as the feelings rippled through her, and she heard his breath quicken as well, and felt the occasional phantom touch of his fingers, still locked between her own.

And then he took one hand and led it down over her belly, pulling her body tight to his. Their fingers were flexing and twisting together and she felt the cool breeze against her skin when the hem of her gown began to rise as he worked with her to bunch the cloth in her hands.

And suddenly, her hand was beneath her gown, and he was stroking with her along the smooth expanse of thigh, up and up, until she reached the place between her own legs.

She tried to pull her hand away, sure for a moment that there must be something very wrong of her to want this, but he was squeezing with her other hand at her breast, and she was absently rolling the nipple between her own fingers. As the warmth spread through her blood, it was hard to care what caused it, or to worry about the right or wrong of it. She only knew that she wanted more of what she was feeling and that St John would show her how to get it. So she relaxed again and let him guide her.

He bore down with the lower hand, and she very quickly discovered things about her own body that she'd either never known, or had done her best to ignore. The slick wetness of it, the secret folds, the way it became more and more sensitive as she stroked.

He was rocking gently with her, and she could hear his breath coming fast behind her, and felt his teeth grazing her neck, then her shoulders. His body was hard against her, and it seemed that she was not the only one enjoying the touches of her own body, that somehow he could feel her pleasure as well as she.

Their hands were pushing harder and deeper against her, swirling and rubbing and stroking, and letting the fingertips delve…

Inside? Yes, inside, oh, yes, definitely there. She was kneading eagerly at her own nipple and she heard his breath in her ear, matching her gasps and felt his lips against her throat.

The feelings rolled through her like building surf and broke suddenly and the newness of it and the shock of pleasure took her and she sagged against him, spent, her legs no longer able to support her.

His arms were around her, keeping her safe. And then he stooped to catch her behind the knees and lifted her in his arms to carry her to the divan. It had been so wonderful that she could hardly speak. But there was more, she was sure, and she wanted it all, and wanted it from St John more than any other man.

He sat beside her where she lay, looking into her eyes and his expression was an amazed sadness. When his lips came down to touch hers, he covered her mouth and she opened it, letting her tongue stroke his. She bit at his lower lip, and was surprised to hear him moan. His hands were rough against her, now pulling her close and stroking her back and her legs, catching her hips and holding them tight. And she followed his example and touched him, feeling the broad shoulders through the linen of his shirt, and the hard muscles of his chest and his back, and the tight, smooth wool of his breeches.

He jerked as if shocked, and pulled away from her, and she reached for him again. But he was murmuring, 'No. No. No.' It was almost a laugh, and almost a groan of pain. She could not tell which. 'No, dearest. Not to-night. Not ever.'

He tried to pull away from her and she clung to him, trying to draw him back.

'No. I cannot, I must not, and I will not.' He was backing towards the door now, shaking his finger and smiling at her. 'You are like absinthe, my dear, like the laudanum. Small and sweet, and intoxicating. I could lose my soul in you. And lose my mind in pleasure and wild fancies without you. Do not tempt me to it, just now when I am trying to be good.'

She rolled to face him, and watched him watch her as her nightdress shifted to reveal her bare breasts in the moonlight. And for a moment, she thought he would come back to her, as he took a step, against his will, to be closer to her.

But then he turned again and grabbed the door handle with conviction, yanking it open and stepping decisively into the hall.

She sighed. 'Well, tell me, at least, that I am helping you to sleep.'

He laughed, bitterly. 'If you only understood. Sleep is the last thing on my mind. And now, Esme, this must end between us. I will play no more games in the night with you. I am too fatigued. I can no longer trust myself in your presence, or fool myself, as I did after last night, that it will be cards and conversation if we meet again unchaperoned. Come to the library tomorrow, if you wish, but you will be here alone.' And he blew her a kiss and closed the door.

Chapter Fourteen

She came down to breakfast the next morning, trying to ignore the thoughts forming in her head, the overwhelming fear that she was out of options, out of ideas, and out of time.

And there was another letter, sitting beside her plate.

She broke the seal with trepidation and read the words quickly, before St John came down to the table and took it from her.

Daughter,

The time for foolish games and procrastination has ended. We both know that you are not ill, unless one wishes to count sick to death of respecting one's parent. Or perhaps too pained by a decent life to continue in it.

You have spent quite enough time with your fancy new friends to cure a host of imaginary

*ills. You have four and twenty hours to find your
health, or I will come to Devon and find it for
you.*

*I have enclosed passage for you on the mail
coach and will be there to meet it tomorrow evening.*

*If I do not find you there, rest assured that I
will find you wherever you may be. I will drag
you home by the hair if I must, if that is what it
takes to prevent you following in the footsteps of
your mother.*
Your loving Father

She folded the paper quickly and stuck it into the
sleeve of her dress as St John came to sit beside her. He
smiled warmly at her as he helped himself to eggs and
toast. 'Good morning, Esme, and a fine morning it is.'

She stared at him as though he were mad. Fine
morning, when she would have to go home? He
couldn't know, of course. But she couldn't very well
show him the letter. It would only make him angry with
her father. And there was a limit to what anyone could
do about her father. 'I suppose it is,' she replied.

He tapped the table next to his plate. 'Seems sturdy
enough.' He picked up his fork.

'St John,' Miranda said in a warning tone.

'I am just being cautious. I have seen evidence that
the nearness of Miss Canville might lead an otherwise
calm man to destroy the furniture. Sitting as close as I
am now, I am merely assuring myself that, should I be

overcome by passion during breakfast, the table can withstand me.'

'Oh, for pity's sake,' Esme snapped. 'Do not quiz me again about yesterday. I have never been so embarrassed in my life.'

He smiled at her. 'And why would you feel any responsibility for what happened to Lord Baxter?'

'Why, you know full well that—' She stopped just short of announcing the truth in front of the family with their morning tea. 'Lord Baxter was there to meet me. This would never have happened if not for my visit.'

'I'm sure he would have done some such thing at another gathering. The only difference would be that you would not have been present to witness it.' He forked up more eggs before saying, 'Where did you find the old goat, Miranda, and whatever made you think he was fit for our Esme?'

'*Our* Esme, is it now?' Miranda cocked her head. 'Very well, then. I chose Lord Baxter as suitable for *our* Esme because of his exemplary behaviour on Sundays at chapel. He seemed most solicitous, if a trifle dull. How was I to know it was the exception and not the rule?'

'Well, good riddance to him. I am glad he revealed his true nature before wasting any more of our time. But I believe Esme has quite run through her first supply of eligible men, Miranda. She is the most spendthrift in courting them. You must find her another.'

'Must I, now?' Miranda pushed away from her own plate and folded her arms across her chest. 'Let me apprise you of the situation. There are none left to choose from. Any name I can think of is either unsuitable or already on the way to the altar.'

St John gave his full attention to buttering his toast and said, 'Look in London, then. I am sure you will find someone, if you try.'

Miranda spoke with unnecessary clarity, 'If we take her to London, then we will have to return her to her father's house, for there is no way the ruse of her illness will hold. I cannot very well parade her in Vauxhall, while telling her father she is too ill to leave her bed.'

'You will think of something, dear sister, for you are prodigiously clever. I have the greatest confidence in you.'

Miranda's eyes narrowed. 'If all it takes is cleverness, then perhaps you could apply yourself to the task. Surely you know of someone suitable. Perhaps someone who has already met her and who seems to greatly enjoy her company. Someone who at three and thirty needs to settle down, and find a wife.'

St John stared at his plate, refusing to look at her, and said slowly, 'I know of no one suitable. Would that I did. But I do not. I say this because I hold Miss Canville in the highest esteem. I wish that it were otherwise, that there was some way I could help in this. But it is quite impossible.'

'Would you both please stop talking around me as though I am not present?' Esme snapped. 'I know what you are trying to do, Miranda, and I thank you for it, however misguided it may be. Just as I could see from the beginning that it was hopeless. You knew before we started that those gentlemen would not suit, did you not? And you hoped that, eventually, St John would come round. But we are out of time. And he does not want me. How many times must he say it? I swear I am as tired of hearing it as he is of repeating himself.' The envelope scratched at her arm and she twisted one hand against her sleeve, wringing the fabric nervously. 'Now, if you will excuse me, I think I have had quite enough help from the both of you.' And she turned and exited the room with what dignity she had left.

'Esme.'

She hurried down the corridor toward the back door to the kitchen garden, almost running in an effort to escape the voice behind her.

But his strides were longer than hers, and he was gaining ground. 'Esme. Stop this instant. I wish to speak to you.'

She wiped at the tears in her eyes with her sleeve and heard the paper rustling beneath, a continual reminder of what she must do now that there were no choices left to her.

'And I do not wish to speak to you, St John. Now please leave me in peace.'

'Then you do not need to speak to me, but you need to listen. I will not have you running from the table to cry in the garden over the likes of me. You will at least let me explain. I doubt it will hurt any less, but you must understand my reasons for not offering for you.'

'They are clear enough, for you have told me repeatedly. I am green, I am naïve, I am far too boring for a man as worldly as yourself.'

He laid a finger across her lips. 'Do not put words in my mouth. There is nothing wrong with you, my dear. If, by some miracle, I could be a different man, I would marry you in an instant, and I would want you to be just as you are, strong and clever and more than a match for me.'

'Then you do love me,' she whispered. 'I know you do. And you cannot help but know how I feel about you, for I've taken no pains to hide it.'

He turned away so she could not see his face. 'What I may or may not feel for you or any other woman, and what you think you feel for me, is immaterial to this discussion.'

'That is always the way of things, is it not? What I want, what I need, what I feel, is immaterial. I am a possession to be handed from place to place. Your needs and my father's are of the utmost importance, and when you hurt me, you will salve your conscience with the fact that it was for my own good.'

He wheeled on her. 'When I hurt you, which I most assuredly will, it will not be for want of trying to avoid the fact. I am attempting to make this as painless as possible, for both of us.'

'Then you are failing, St John,' she snapped. 'For I ache at the thought of leaving you.'

'But you are not leaving me, Esme. We will think on it, and in a day or two we will find an answer. You may be heartsick now, but you are alive to feel it, unlike the other women I have loved. And heartache is not a physical malady. You will survive. But you will not trap me into marriage with melodrama.'

'Of course not. When I behave thus, it is giving in to girlish hysterics. You are the only one permitted to wallow in melodrama, while I put on a brave face and go home to my husband.'

'That is the most ridiculous—'

'Show me the scars, St John. The physical wounds that pain you so that you must hide in your room with your laudanum.'

'I am not hiding.'

'Of course you are. The brave war hero, and his unsteady nerves, who allows me to humiliate myself before him, but will not take my love or my body. He would much prefer my pity.'

'You came to me. I did not ask for your pity, or your love.'

'But you are lucky to have it. You need me, St John, whether you admit it or not. To prove to you that you are not the base seducer that you wish people to believe you, or so low and villainous as to be undeserving of a woman's love.'

'Do not think, Miss Canville, that I am some empty vessel, waiting to be filled with your foolish romantic notions. I do not need you, or any other. I am fine as I am.'

'Liar.'

'You do not know me.'

'I do.'

He flinched as the words stung him and said, 'Because you cannot see a mark on my body, that does not mean that I am not marked within.' He strode away from her down the garden path and muttered, 'You cannot know what it was like.'

'Then tell me.'

He sighed and turned back to her, dropping on to a nearby bench. 'You will give me no peace, until you have had it all, will you? Very well. Perhaps the truth will be the best way to shake you off. It goes back to long before the war. Do you understand why I had to go away?'

'There was a falling out between you and the duke.' She looked away delicately.

'I told you more than that, did I not? He sent me away because I would not leave his wife alone. But it goes back even further then that. I was young and foolish and I loved. I can hardly be faulted for it, can I? And I was reckless, as you wish me to be now. I did not want to wait, and talked the girl into a haystack and out of her clothes. Maybe it was too easy. Perhaps she loved me and I was the first. Perhaps she was merely bored and I was one of many.

'But when she found she was with child, she could not find me, and I lost her to a better man.'

'With child?' murmured Esme.

'With child.' His smile was cold. 'My feelings were less than sympathetic to my brother after his first wife died, and he less than sympathetic towards me for being fooled into marrying her when she carried my child. When he married Miranda, I tried and failed to take her from him. I went away and time passed, and I found another love while in Portugal.'

He sighed. 'She was a beauty, that was certain. And innocent in a way that my first love was not. And I was not about to make the same mistake again. I courted her properly and her father respected my suit. In Portugal...' he held his head higher at the thought '...I was the gentleman I never was in England. And I had the love of a great lady. Maria was not just my equal, but my superior in birth. She'd have been a countess, had she been English. She loved me, and thought me heroic, and I tried to live up to her ideals. I worshipped her, and I vowed not to make the mistakes of my youth. I never touched her, I swear. I barely dared to kiss her hand.'

The pain in his eyes was unbearable, and Esme sat beside him and took his hand in hers.

He shook off her touch. 'When we met, there was a proper chaperon, a duenna, present at all times. But to be allowed to spend time in her presence was enough for me. And I swore that after the war was settled, and her country free, I would return for her, and make an honourable offer.

'Her father favoured my suit, even knowing that I was the poor younger brother. He respected me. He trusted me.' St John laughed bitterly. 'It was hard to choose the bigger fool between us. If I'd been the man she thought I was, I'd have insisted that she come away with me. I'd have written to Marcus and begged him to take her and keep her safe until I could come home. But I was too proud to ask for help and too eager to please her father, and I did nothing.

'The war parted us, but I thought her safe, inside the walls of the city. But when the time came to take Badajoz…' His eyes were blank at the memory of it, and his face was a mask of pain and exhaustion.

Esme sat in silence beside him. She ached to do something, anything that would help him, but dared not stop him.

'I tried to get word to her before the siege began, but the French were holding the gates and the letters did not get through. Her family had a place in the country, and she needed to get away before the war came to her. But her father thought it safer to be behind the walls, with the protection of the French, than to be in the country alone and at the mercy of any soldier, English or French, who might happen by.

'It took so long, and so many men died. The walls were almost impenetrable, but finally we broke through.'

This time, when she offered her hand he took it, and held it in a painful grip as he continued the story.

'The men wanted their revenge. There was no controlling what happened, once it started. It was like a madness running through them. They wanted to punish the town for not opening the gates. But it was not the French they punished. It was old men and women and children. It went on for two days, before we officers were able to take control again. And I looked for her all that time. Her house was empty. Burned to the ground. I found her father, wandering mad in the street, but he could tell me nothing.'

St John sat, shaking in the morning air. 'And at last I found her. At the base of the wall. Her servants were weeping over the body. The soldiers had come. Our soldiers. And they'd beaten her father, and burned the house. And taken her.'

There were tears in his eyes.

'And her damned honour would not permit her to live with the shame of it. She thought I could not love her. That I could not forgive things that were no fault of hers. And she'd thrown herself off the wall.

'She was right in one thing. I could not forgive what happened. Not my men, who I could not control. Not myself, for letting it happen. My love of her had been the end of her, just as it had Bethany.'

'It was not your love that killed her,' Esme argued.

'Nor could it save her. In the end, it mattered not whether I was reckless or cautious, respectful or a rogue. They are dead and I am still here. My brother hated me, Maria's father cursed me for an English dog.'

He looked to her, stricken. 'Don't you understand? What can I offer you? What do I have left to give? I have no money. No home. My protection is worthless. I know not what fresh disaster I can bring down upon you, if you continue to pursue me. But I want no part in it. I cannot promise that your future will be happy, or free of pain. But at least I will know that I was not the cause of it, should some harm befall you.'

He looked away on the next words. 'I…I…care about you too much for that.'

'Liar,' she whispered. 'If you truly cared, you would not talk such nonsense. Let me tell you the truth of things, St John. Twice you loved, and twice you lost them. And once they were gone you punished yourself and everyone around you. You behaved so scandalously that your own brother drove you away. You found a new life and a career, only to walk away from it to hide in your rooms, drugged to insensibility.

'And now you are afraid that if you admit you love me, it will all happen again, but that this time you will not survive it. Do not tell me that what you are doing is in my best interests. It is nothing more than an effort on your part to protect your own heart. You think you would rather feel nothing at all than to be hurt again.'

He sat on the bench, shoulders slumped and head hung, refusing to meet her gaze. So she dropped to the ground and knelt at his feet, taking his hands in hers. 'I cannot promise that I will live for ever. No one does. But I seriously doubt that when I die it will be from love of you. I do not care that you have little to offer in the way of security. All I need is your arms about me, and I will be safe enough.'

And yet he said nothing. She waited for the words she longed to hear. Any sign that his resolve was weakening. But she received only silence in return.

She stood up and brushed a fallen leaf from the hem of her gown. 'Very well, then. If you insist on feeling nothing, than I must feel for both of us. Perhaps, when I am gone, you will see things differently. You will have gained little and lost much. And I hope that the next woman you love is more fortunate than I have been.'

He would not look up, but at last he spoke. 'There will be no next woman.'

'Do not be a fool. You had a mistress, and when there is money enough, you will have another. And some day you will decide you want an heir, and for that you will need a wife.' She was too angry at the thought even to cry.

His voice was without emotion. 'Perhaps what you say is true. But you do not understand men any better than I do women. I never said that I would live without the company of women. But I will not have to love them to get what I need from them.'

'Then I am happy that I failed to win you, St John,' she said. 'You are every bit as bad as I have heard. You could give a woman more happiness than I am ever likely to see. But your plan is to use them and give nothing of your heart in return.

'At last I agree with you. Marriage to you would be worse than the union my father has chosen for me. At least if I marry a stranger who wishes only to use my body for his pleasure, I'll have no foolish notion that I am doing it for love.'

As the tears started to fall, she turned and went back to the house.

This time, he did not follow.

Chapter Fifteen

Esme lay in her bed, hopeless of sleep. She had spent too many late nights in the company of St John, followed by sweet dreams of him and long luxurious mornings in bed. And now he expected her to give him up without protest and go back to her old life as though nothing had happened. Her mind might see his reasoning, but her body refused to be denied.

The clock struck eleven and she listened as another minute ticked away, counting out the seconds until tomorrow when she would do what she must and return home. It had been too long already and she could no longer impose upon the hospitality at Haughleigh, or face St John over breakfast, knowing that there was no future in it.

Perhaps Miranda could find another possibility for her in Devon. Perhaps not. But she dare not wait longer and have her father come to fetch her. Suppose he followed through on his threats and dragged her away by force in full view of her friends?

The horror of it overwhelmed her. If he succeeded, it would be bad enough, but if they tried to stop him there would be scandal. To the world, her father would manage to appear the wronged party, an elderly man who was only concerned with the welfare of his daughter. The Radwells' intentions in helping her at all would be suspect. And, as usual, no one would be interested in her version of events or allow her to choose her own future.

So she must accept the fact that her attempt to control her destiny had been an utter failure. She could not, try as she had, bring St John up to scratch to offer marriage or lower him sufficiently to take her as a mistress. He was content to let things stay as they were.

Of course it was all to his advantage, that their relationship was no closer. He professed to enjoy her company, but he wanted to pretend that what was happening between them did not matter, and what she saw when she looked into his eyes meant nothing, which made it all the more unbearable.

Surely he did not look thus at every woman he had dallied with. When they were in the garden, he had opened his heart before her. He had even wept. And he had almost confessed the depth of his feelings, but in the end he would not even allow her the consolation of hearing the words.

Very well. She would leave him, if that was what he wanted. But she would not go before taking from him all that he could give. St John owed her that at least, if he expected her to go home and marry Halverston. If there was to be no love in the marital act? She swallowed her fear. Then she must learn to use others as they wished to use her.

He had said he would not be in the library. Then he would be staying in a place he did not think she would dare to come. A decent young woman should not even know the location of a gentleman's bedroom because she would have no reason to visit it.

Esme had been filled with trepidation when she'd asked directions from the maid who cared for her room. Suppose the girl gossiped?

What did it matter? Tomorrow she must leave for London and would never see the house or its staff again. She had given the girl one sovereign for the information and another one to hold her tongue. And then she had crawled under the covers to wait until the house was asleep.

She swung her feet out of the bed and stood, afraid now that the moment had come. And then she untied the bodice of her nightrail and let it fall to the floor. She picked up her dressing gown and wrapped it tight around her. As the silk touched her naked skin it woke her body, and she felt the heat rising within her. The fear subsided, replaced by desire.

She took no light when she left her room, and walked silently down the corridor toward the wing on the other side of the house where she knew that there was one member of the family still awake. When she arrived at St John's room, she rested her ear against the door, listening for sounds within. All was quiet, but she could see a sliver of light under the door that showed candles were still lit.

She took a deep breath to renew her courage, grabbed hold of the door handle, turned, entered, and shut it quickly behind her.

At the sound of the opening door, St John had risen from his chair, tipping over the table next to him that held brandy and a book. He was in his own dressing gown, ready for bed, although she doubted he expected to sleep. His posture as he turned to face her was of a man ready to repel attack. But then he recognised her. She saw the joy on his face erased by pain and sadness and bone-deep fatigue. Without realizing it, he'd taken a step to be nearer to her, but then he got control of himself and stopped before coming closer.

'Go back to your room, Esme.'

'No. I will not let you send me away again. I know what I want, St John.' She held his gaze and reached behind her, turning the key in the lock of his door. 'Do not deny me.'

'But I must. You are mad to want it. And you must stop before it is too late. If you go now, no one need ever hear of this. But if I do as you ask, someone will find out, and there will be hell to pay for both of us. Go away, Esme, with your honour still intact.'

She reached for the knot of her dressing gown and undid it, letting the robe fall open and drop from her shoulders and to the floor.

'No.' But his voice shook as he said it, and he was

looking at her, all of her, standing bare in front of him. There was hunger in his eyes.

She could feel the beating of her own heart, as she waited for him to respond. It seemed forever before he moved, although she could hear his breathing, deep and unsteady as if he had run a great distance to stand before her and look at her body.

Then he closed the gap between them, snatched her dressing gown from the floor, seized her shoulder and turned her roughly towards the door to push her from the room.

She heard the gown slip from his fingers and the gasp as he saw her back.

Esme turned and reached for the robe, picking it up and wrapping it about her to cover the scars. 'There. You have seen. I'd hoped to hide them in darkness, or that it would not matter. It is not as if they show when I am clothed. They are low enough on my shoulders that no one need see, even in a ball gown. Miranda has assured me it is so. But if you can do nothing else, tell me truthfully, will it change things when my first lover sees my back?'

St John reached for her, and smoothed the robe down off her shoulders again, and she could feel his breath on her bare skin, as his hands followed the tracery of scars on her back and shoulders. His voice was ice. 'Who did this to you?'

'My father. It was the day my mother ran away. He came back from riding, and the crop was still in his hand when he discovered the note. He was so very angry, angrier than I'd ever seen him, and I asked him what the matter was.

'And he told me that my mother was a dirty whore, and that I would be no better, if I did not learn.' She closed her eyes, and could still hear the sound of the crop, cutting the air, and the lines of pain lancing across her back as it made contact with the flesh. 'When he was done, I ran to the attic and hid. It took several hours for the servants to find me. My governess was afraid of him, and did nothing. But she held my hands as the maids cleaned the wounds. They told me that the scarring might have been less if they'd tended to me sooner, but the blood had dried and my dress was stuck to the wounds. The cleaning and dressing hurt almost as much as the whipping.' She smiled sourly to herself. 'He learned, after that, to do things that did not leave a mark. An open hand may leave a bruise, but it heals quickly enough. A blow from a cane hurts, but it does not break the skin. And a fist does not need to strike hard to make the intent clear.'

'I will kill him.'

She shook her head. 'You will not. Because I do not see what good it would do either of us, at this late date, to have him dead and you in prison for it.'

He pulled her close to him, and wrapped his arms around her, cradling her against him, and she could feel the places where his own robe gaped and his skin touched hers. 'But I am afraid,' she said softly, 'that any man who sees the scars might think…' she swallowed hard and forced the words out '…that I must have done something to deserve the beating. I've heard it said, when a woman lies with a man the first time, that it is difficult. There will be pain, I know that. It cannot be helped. But perhaps, if there was a chance, if the man believed I was innocent…

'But if he has bought and paid for something without flaw, only to find it marked and spoiled…' She finished helplessly, 'There is nothing I can do.'

'There will be no pain.' His voice was a raw whisper in her ear. 'It is the breaking of the maidenhead you fear, and that happens but once. I will do that for you, but nothing else. Do not fool yourself into thinking that what we are about to do means more than that. I cannot marry you, Esme. And I will not offer you less than that. When the time comes, give yourself pleasure before your husband comes to you, so that you are relaxed and ready for him. Then let him do what he wants and trick him with a drop of blood on the sheets and a maidenly protestation of discomfort and fear. We men are easily gulled when we are aroused.' He reached to untie his own robe, and it dropped to the floor with hers, and she could feel the cold air on her skin, and warmth where he touched her, and his sex thick and hard, pressing against her from behind.

He turned her to him, and his lips found hers, his hands tangling in her hair. Her lips parted eagerly, and she sucked his tongue into her mouth, letting him thrust gently with it, before his mouth slid lower.

'You have nothing to fear, Esme. You are innocent. Soft and beautiful and perfect.' He took a nipple into his mouth, running his hands over her breasts and her belly, tracing the curves of her, and stroking over the scars on her back as if wiping away the memory of them.

Her breasts seemed to swell and grow hard, even as the rest of her felt soft and liquid and he was walking slowly forwards, taking her with him, backing her up until her knees hit the bed behind her. He pushed her gently down and she collapsed backward. Then he spread her legs and knelt on the floor between them, sliding his hands underneath her and pulling her body close to meet his mouth.

She bit her lip against the pleasure, trying to remember to brace for the pain that would soon come. But there was nothing but the moment, and the feel of his tongue exploring her, and the growing tension in her body as it slipped into her, before retreating to find her centre.

And then he'd replaced it with his fingers, thrusting slowly while his mouth worked magic. She clutched the sheet in her hands and hung on as though expecting the world to shake her loose, and his fingers stroked faster, until she thought she could stand no more. Then she lost herself in him, trembling and helpless as he pulled her up to lie on the bed and covered his body with her own.

And he whispered softly, 'One thrust, I swear. That is all you need and all I dare take. And the pain will be over and I will pleasure you again.' And she felt him, hard against her, pausing at the entrance to her body, before pushing inside of her. There was tightness, and a shock as he pushed home. He stopped and let her body adjust to the size of him and the magical feeling of being part of another person.

And then he was pulling away from her. She felt the friction of their bodies, and knew that one thrust was not enough for him to feel what she had felt from him. As he pulled away, she arched up to follow him, raking her nails along his back and pulling his hips back to hers.

He pulled away again, and again she followed, twining her legs around his and locking their bodies together, rocking herself against him until she felt him groan, and knew he was helpless to deny her or himself. She revelled in her ability to control him, even though he was bigger and stronger than she. And then he pushed her hips back down on the bed, and she let him come again and again into her, as her body learned to accommodate him, and she arched against him again, tightened her muscles as if she could keep him with her always instead of just one night. He shuddered and thrust harder, and then one last time, before collapsing into her and against her. And then he rolled off her body and lay beside her. Exhausted.

'Esme.' It was all he said, but he said it with such wonder, that the one word was enough. He was gazing at her through half-closed eyes, and as she watched he smiled and sighed, and then his eyes drifted shut and she felt his body relax into sleep beside her.

She lay for a moment, watching him sleep, and then

looked up into the canopy of the bed, feeling the aches in her body and the strange newness of it.

He would have to marry her now. Despite all his claims of wickedness, his sense of honour ran deep and true. He would not cast her off, now that they had lain together.

The thought gave her no pleasure. To be married to him should make her happier than anything in the world. But to know that he had done it because she had been foolish and selfish, and despite all his protestations that he'd no wish to marry, to know that now he would throw his own life aside and wed her to hide her dishonour?

He was trying so hard to change his reputation, but if he married in haste, there would be talk. Everyone would guess the reason for the wedding and would count the months before the first child was born, sure that it had been conceived on the wrong side of the blanket.

It was unbearable. She was no better for him than the other women he'd loved. His memory of them was clouded with guilt and regret. But they, at least, had had the good sense to die, and would not have to see the look in his eyes that she would see as he spent his life in atonement to her.

She laid her hand upon his shoulder, feeling the hard, smooth muscle of it. It was a good strong arm, and he'd protected her with it for as long as he'd been able.

But now it was her turn to protect him. From himself, if need be.

And she climbed out of her lover's bed and returned to her room to do what was best for both of them.

Chapter Sixteen

Through the linen of the sheet, St John could hear the clock chiming on the mantelpiece of his room. It seemed to go on and on, which was strange.

Ten, eleven, twelve.

That couldn't be. He could see, from the light filtering through the cloth, that it couldn't be midnight. Which would make it…

Noon?

He threw back the covers and stared at the clock. And the reality of the night before came swimming into view.

Esme.

He turned back to check the bed, and realised how ridiculous that must be. He'd known he was alone when he'd awakened, but was at a loss as to how or when it had happened. Had he really taken her last night, despite all his good intentions, common sense, and his oath to his brother?

There was a telltale spot of blood on the sheet next to him.

He ran a hand through his hair and swung his feet out of the bed. He was an idiot. Careless. Foolish. He had only himself to blame for the ruin of the poor girl.

He'd been tired, of course. Pushed beyond reason, and overcome by the girl's willingness and the sight of those scars on her back. And then the feel of her skin against his and the tightness of her body around him, and the way she'd clung to him like a vine. It had been madness to think that he could have taken just a taste of her and been able to stop before satisfying himself. It must have been the exhaustion that let him believe he could control what happened once she lying naked under him.

Which was no excuse this morning. He'd fallen asleep immediately after like some kind of lout, not even making sure that she'd found her way safely back to her room without discovery. Suppose she'd fallen asleep with him? The consequences...

Of course, it had not happened. The fact that he was still breathing was proof enough of that. Marcus would have shot him dead on the spot, not waiting for anything so formal as a challenge.

So the girl had gone back to her bed without his help. And he'd had the first good night's sleep in over a year. Twelve hours, free of drugs, and he was awake and clear headed, with an appetite for lunch. Strangely optimistic, for all the stupidity of the last few hours. And with an obvious plan before him and hope of a bright future.

He would dress and find Esme. He would pull her aside and offer for her, and if it didn't make her happy, then be damned to her feelings. They would be on their way to Scotland and married before lunch tomorrow, and there would be no more of this talk of the *demi-monde*, or other appropriate young men, or even her father's objections. If there was a problem later, he would appeal to Marcus to go to Canville and force the issue, in the way only a peer could. The man couldn't be such a fool as to refuse a connection with the Radwell family.

He sighed. It would not be as he'd intended, with a house and a fortune to offer her. There would be none of the safety and stability that she deserved. And the violation of her father's wishes, the breach of promise and sudden elopement, might stretch the patience of the regent beyond the breaking point.

There might be men more deserving of her. There surely were. Men who would never hurt her. Men who could be trusted to care for her better than he could.

But none of that mattered any more. He loved her. He had tried not to, he'd done everything in his power to avoid the fact, but still, he loved her with body and with mind. And so she would have to settle for him. A lifetime with Esme would give him more than enough chance to make it up to her. His heart was pounding with happiness at the thought of it.

He called for his valet and dressed hurriedly, trying not to smile back at the rumpled sheets. If Toby guessed the truth and had anything to say in the matter, he was wise enough to hold his tongue. Then St John raced down the steps to the dining room, in time to catch the footman who was clearing his unused plate.

'A little late this morning, St John? Or should I say afternoon?' Marcus tossed his napkin aside and pushed his own empty plate away.

'I was asleep.' St John said.

'I gathered. And you did not resort to...' He paused significantly.

'No. No, I didn't. The worst is over, I think. And I did not stir, once.'

Miranda was pretending not to know the meaning of the conversation, but he could see the obvious relief in the set of her back. 'We had hoped as much. Your valet was unable to rouse you, and Esme said that we should not trouble you. But she has left you a letter.'

'Letter? Whatever for?' He glanced around the table, suddenly aware that there was no sign of recent clearing away at Esme's usual place. The linen was free of crumbs, without so much as a wrinkle to show use. 'What she has to say to me couldn't wait until afternoon?'

'You don't know?' Miranda looked disgusted.

'Apparently not. Or I would not be inclined to say, "Know what?" Where is Esme and why is she writing me notes for lunch?'

Miranda looked puzzled. 'She said it was all settled between you. And that this was for the best. That you would agree, which I thought was rather harsh of you.' Miranda shot him another disapproving glance. 'Even if it is true. While I am happy for your recovery from your difficulties, it would have been nice of you to at least say goodbye, knowing as you did her tender feelings for you.'

'Say goodbye? Why would I have to say goodbye?'

Miranda was staring at him as if he'd gone mad, and even Marcus was looking at him as though he was some kind of idiot. His voice rose, despite his efforts to maintain his new-found calm. 'Dammit, woman, where is my Esme?'

'Your Esme, as you've decided to think of her now that she is gone, has returned to her father's house, as you have been encouraging her to do for weeks.' Miranda slapped an envelope down on the table in front of him. 'She left you this. And now, if you will excuse me, I'll leave you with a cold luncheon and what I hope are regrets.' Miranda swept out of the room on an icy cloud.

St John felt the growing dread as he looked at the letter in front of him, and his hands trembled as he seized the fish knife beside his plate and slit the seal.

Dearest St John,

For that is always how I will think of you. You are dearer to me than anyone and always will be, whether you would or no. And despite what you may claim, you have been my truest friend, and my love, and the only man in my life who has meant me no harm and has always tried to put my needs ahead of his own.

Despite your protestations, and your own lack

of faith in yourself, you are the strongest, and bravest man I've ever met, and you've taught me to be strong and brave as well.

And now, I must make hard decisions, and do what I hope will ultimately be best for both of us.

When I came to you on that night that seems so long ago, I thought I had no options, and no chance for happiness. I've come, with your help, to believe that this is not true.

I know I can't marry any of the men that I've met while here, no matter how honest they may be or how appropriate you may think them. And it is not because of what happened last night. Do not trouble yourself on that account.

The plain truth is: I do not love them. If they are honest and good, then they do not deserve a wife who cannot come to them with her virtue intact and her heart empty of love for another.

I love you, St John. Even if you do not want to read the words, you know that they are true. And now you are telling yourself that you took advantage of that last night.

Do not be such a ninny. It is most unattractive in you, and I will not hear it. If a woman waits until your mind is addled with fatigue and comes naked to your bedroom, refuses to leave, and clings to you, even as you try to pull away, than it is vanity on your part to claim any credit for the seduction.

You told me again last night that I was not to

expect marriage, or come crying to you for my lost virtue, after I'd carelessly thrown it away. And I do not and will not, for I have no regrets for what happened between us. This morning, I feel stronger than I have ever felt before, and at last see a way forward that might lead in time to happiness.

I am going home, St John, to my father and the marriage that he has arranged for me. My new husband may be everything I suspect. But as you have often pointed out, a married woman enjoys freedoms that a girl does not. Even at the worst, it will be better than remaining unmarried and in my father's house.

And as you have also pointed out to me, he is old. And rich as well. It looks quite horrible, as I write this, but marriage to the earl will not be a life sentence on my part.

I had thought, when I came to you, that a few years was the same as for ever. But now I believe that, if you are happy, as you have made me, one night can be for ever, and years of hardship will pale to scant moments when compared to it.

I can't, in good conscience, take a lover after I've given my hand to the earl. The secret of last night will be difficult enough to keep, although the lies will be a light burden when weighed against the moments that I will treasure in my heart for as long as I live, no matter what may come.

And I will probably be a rich widow in a few short years. I will now ask something so audacious that it will make all my previous behaviour look conventional. But could you wait for me, St John? It is not my place as a woman to ask it, but if there is anything in your heart for me, could you keep it safe until I am free to come to you?

I know it must pain you to let the world think you are marrying for money, and I cannot expect you to think of me if your heart is drawn to another, or to remain faithful to me, in any case. You have wants and needs of your own. But please, St John, please, wait for me, and, if you want me, come to me when I am free.

Whatever the future may bring, and whatever my body may do, I will never give my heart to another man and will always remain,

Your Esme

He stared at the words on the paper, as though he could will them to change.

'Not what you expected?' His brother's voice startled him from his reverie.

'How could I expect this? How could I know?'

'That the girl would leave?' His brother could not contain his sarcasm. 'You idiot. How could you expect anything else? It is what you wanted all along, what you yourself encouraged her to do.'

'No.' He cleared his throat nervously. 'I knew she should go. I just did not expect that it would be so hard to let her leave. If she had given me one more day, I would have offered…'

Marcus sighed. 'If she had given you one more day, then you would have wasted it as you have wasted all the others. Sunset would have come and you would have had some excuse to put it off until tomorrow, and tomorrow after that.'

'No.' His own voice was sharp. Too loud in his own ears. 'Today would have been different. Everything is different, now.'

'Don't be a fool. Of course it isn't.'

He looked up, and his brother met his gaze.

Marcus sucked in his breath. 'Dear God. Tell me you didn't do what I suspect you did. Under my roof, while the girl was in my care. Tell me you did not break your promise to me.'

St John looked at the plate before him and the food held no appeal. 'I can tell you whatever you wish, but I had hoped to try the truth for a change. Last night— it is as bad as you suspect. Perhaps worse. I have nothing to say in my own defence except that I tried to avoid it. And when it happened, it was for love and not mere conquest. And then I fell asleep. If the girl were standing before us now, I would offer for her in a heartbeat.'

'But she is not. She has gone back to London, to the man her father has chosen for her.'

St John felt his throat tighten. Wealth and position. It was not the first time that a woman had chosen them rather than him.

He could offer her love, of course, but she must have

realised what it would mean to be the wife of a pensioned soldier. And now, of all times, after weeks of wheeling and conniving and trying to break his will on the matter of marriage, she was being practical and taking him at his word. Now that she'd won, and got what she wanted from him, she'd decided she wanted the money as well. And she was offering to keep him, once she was rid of her troublesome husband.

His fist closed on the letter, and he crushed the sweet words in his hand. 'Very well, then. She is probably right in any case. I cannot ask her to live on love, and I certainly cannot compete with the match her father has arranged.'

Marcus snorted in disgust. 'Coward. You could go to her now, and she would come away with you. So all your talk of love and offers was nonsense.'

He sneered back at Marcus. 'And I suppose you would allow me to live off you, with a wife and children in the bargain?'

'I could afford it, you know.' Marcus considered.

St John shook his head. 'But I could not. Allow me some pride, at least, to want to be able to support a wife before taking one.'

'Well, you are right in that. It is easier to manage with an income. Old Halverston can certainly afford the keeping of her, but surely—'

There was a subtle clearing of throat as the butler entered. Marcus looked up, as the man stooped to murmur something. He shot St John a confused look. 'Were you expecting news from London?'

'No. Not really. I—'

'There is a footman, in Prinny's livery, at my door. And looking for you. Before we go out in the hall, do I want to know what you've done and how much it's likely to cost me, or were you going to leave it as a surprise?'

St John shook his head and rose, as if still sleepwalking, to go to greet the servant. And the probable truth of it seeped through to him, leaving him numb with the shock.

The footman was there, bowing stiffly and offering the letter, signed with the royal seal, St John took it, and thanked him, and assured him that there was no reply, but that he would be leaving for London shortly and would wait upon the regent at his convenience.

His hands trembled as he cracked the seal and read the contents of the letter.

'Well, what the devil is going on? Do you mean to keep us all in the dark?' Marcus was shouting at him, and he heard it through the fog in his head. It sounded very much like the Marcus of old, which was pleasantly familiar. He passed the letter to his brother, and sank on to the nearest bench.

'What nonsense is this? Miranda, read these words and tell me that I am going mad. The Earl of Stanton is dead without heir and my little brother has been named successor to the title. For meritorious service to the crown and uncommon bravery in the face of the enemy.'

Miranda snatched the letter from his hand and there was a squeal of delight.

'Am I to call him Stanton, now? Captain was bad enough. But his lordship? There'll be no end to it, I'm sure.' There was a fierce joy in Marcus's words and St John felt a cuff to the head before his brother's arm wrapped around his neck. 'Wake up, Johnny. Do not stand there like an idiot. Your problems are solved. There is pen and paper in the study. Write to Esme and tell her to cry off. Write to her father with a better offer. You are Halverston's equal now in title and land. His superior, if I remember the Stanton entail. If you are serious in your feelings for her, let us take the news to London.'

St John reached into his pocket and withdrew the letter from Esme, smoothing the crumpled paper. He refolded it carefully and tucked it into the pocket over his heart. Title, wealth, reputation, and security. He could lay them all at her feet, along with his heart, and she need never worry again.

'Toby!' he bellowed in a voice that carried through the house. 'Pack my bags. I'm going to London to get a wife.'

Chapter Seventeen

St John stared out over the crowd in the rented rooms that Esme's father had chosen for her betrothal party, searching for any sign of his beloved. Surely even her father would not leave the girl locked in her room for the celebration.

In the week they'd been apart, St John had written her daily, informing her of his intentions. If Esme received his letters at all, she either chose not to answer or was not allowed to. He assumed it was the latter. He had to, or lose his sanity. Surely, after the heartfelt letter she had written him, she could not chose Halverston.

Letters to her from Miranda went unanswered as well. Marcus's correspondence to the father could not be ignored, but it was answered with brevity. The girl was well and most grateful for their help, but she would be needing it no longer.

At last, St John received a similar missive from Canville, denying his suit and informing him that Miss Esme Canville was otherwise betrothed and viewed his attention as harassment. Any further letters from him would be returned unopened and he must cease all attempts at communication, for they were unwelcome.

It pained him to read the words, and they left the continual, nagging fear that they were based in truth, and not merely the ruse of her irate father.

St John's worst fear was that an attempt to visit Esme might only lead to her punishment. He vowed to stay well out of sight of Canville, and had vacated his rooms across the street from the home. Instead, he had taken discreet residence in the Stanton town house, awaiting the formal announcement of his title. It was more luxurious than he'd anticipated, almost as fine as the Haughleigh residence. But despite a full staff it felt empty to St John because it lacked the chance to stare out the window and catch a glimpse of the woman he loved.

Canville had wasted no time, once he had Esme back under his control. Marcus had seen the official announcement in *The Times*, shortly after their arrival in London. The banns had been read once, already. There were but two weeks left before St John lost her to Halverston.

Not lost, he reminded himself. She would be his, in any case. honour be damned, he would haul her from the church on her wedding day if need be and take her away to the continent. Never mind the scandal.

But Marcus had assured him that it would not be

necessary. They would gain entrance to the betrothal party, where it would be difficult to put them off without public embarrassment. The duke would intercede with Canville, and St John could explain things to Esme. All would be settled.

St John had his doubts that things could be handled so easily, but admitted it was the best course of action. Canville might slam the door of his home in their face, but it had always amazed him how many other doors opened without question for the Duke of Haughleigh.

St John watched his brother explaining their situation to the hired footman at the door of the hall. The Radwells were friends of the family. Clearly, their invitation had been lost in the post. Such a burden to have to deal with the mistakes of others. But what could one do?

St John tried not to grin and spoil the effect. Marcus was making it up out of whole cloth, and following it all with a look of noble disdain, turning to irritation as the servants hesitated. When he suggested that they get Mr Canville and explain the reason for denying entrance to a peer, the footmen wilted before him. Marcus waved aside their offer to announce him.

They proceeded down the stairs toward the receiving line and St John made to rush forward, only to have Marcus lay a steadying hand on his arm. 'No need to hurry, Johnny. Remember, we are trying not to call attention. The father is at the base of the stairs. Leave him to me. I think it wise that you keep to the far side and avoid the line entirely. Stay out of sight if you can. Your

objective is on the dance floor, with her betrothed.'
Marcus sniffed. 'The poor girl.'

They stared down at the couple dancing below them.
The floor was nearly empty. The guests that showed any
interest in the music looked on in disapproval as the
guests of honour waltzed before them. Had they no
blood left in their veins? Who could find it so terrible
that a couple soon to be married might wish to dance
in each other's arms?

St John erased the man from the couple below and
thought only of the girl. Some day soon, he would
have Esme, and then every dance would be a waltz.

The couple turned so that St John could see her
face. Dear God, when he was hers he hoped that she
did not look thus. She was staring into the eyes of her
husband-to-be, and seemed to all the world like a bird
trapped by a snake.

St John glanced at the man with her. Every bit as old
as she had said. And strangely familiar. The name Halverston was not known to him. But had he met the
man? When and where? If it had been during those last
months before he'd gone to Portugal, it was quite possible that they were acquainted. He recalled little more
about most of that time than the drink and the blue-dev-
ils that followed it.

St John searched the man's face, and found it stern,
but not unkind. What had he said, to make her so frightened? And why, when he looked at the man, did he feel
a chill?

The music had ended, and the earl linked his arm

in Esme's, taking her toward the balcony at the end of the room.

St John went down the stairs and pushed his way through the crush, following a distance behind. Esme had been right to be concerned about her future. There was not a face under fifty in the crowd, and most were much older than that. Had she no friends her own age, no confidants to explain her situation? He had hoped all along that it was some girlish exaggeration that had brought her to him. Merely a spirit burning too bright that her father had sought to break with violence.

But it was worse than that. She had known what she must return to, and had thrown herself at him with all her might, seeking all the pleasure she could in their brief time together. To leave`Haughleigh must have been like returning to the tomb.

But she needn't worry any more. He would take her from this place tonight and all would be well. He had but to wait until she was alone and spirit her away. If he could catch her eye, signal her in some way…

But her gaze was only for the man beside her. As it should be, only two weeks from the altar. And yet, all wrong. He knew from experience what Esme should look like, if she were in love. If she were happy. The woman before him was blank and empty.

Drugged? Could it be? Or merely frightened? When he talked to her, he would know.

Halverston had taken her on to the balcony and into the moonlight, and other couples gave them a wide berth, allowing the earl to steal a few moments alone with his supposed beloved. The last of the guests came back into the ballroom, and pulled the door shut behind him with a sly smile, leaving Halverston alone with Esme.

There was no way he could step out on the balcony and interrupt, without inciting comment. It would be best to wait. St John stood only a few feet from them, hand pressed against the glass in the door, watching. He had an excellent view of the couple, but was obscured from them by the potted palms that decorated the balcony. He would have ample warning, when they came back toward the door, and could step to the side and accost Esme as they passed.

If he could bear to watch as the earl stood with the woman he loved in the moonlight. It would only be a few more moments he reminded himself. And what was to fear from Halverston, really? The man was old and frail and wanted an heir. He was choosing youth and vigour, and hoping for the best. He was of very little threat to a woman with as much life and strength as Esme. He would be fortunate to lose her, for she would lead him a merry chase should he win her, the poor old fool. St John watched them.

The earl spoke to her, and at first she did not seem to hear. She stared out over the balcony at the pavement below, seeming lost to the man next to her.

Her lack of attention seemed to annoy him, for he caught her by the shoulders and turned her gently to face him, speaking directly to her.

She was attending, and her eyes went wide with fright, before fading to blankness again.

And the old man pulled her close to him in an embrace. They were caught in profile in the moonlight, youth and age together. The earl spoke urgently into the girl's ear and there was the flare of fear in her eyes again, before she shut them tight, as though if she could not see she would also be unable to hear.

And St John watched as the earl's hand dropped from her shoulder to her hip, first smoothing the fabric of her skirt, then caressing, then urgently kneading the curved flesh, holding her tight against him, so that she could feel him and know what he meant to do with her.

Esme shuddered in revulsion.

And suddenly, he remembered where he'd seen Halverston. It was no common brothel, but the kind of house where a man need not use his right name. Where if he had enough gold to offer, he could indulge his darkest whims without fear of retribution.

And the girls there had been afraid of him.

Blood was pounding in his ears as St John seized the door handle, ready to charge on to the balcony and pitch the man over it, should it prove necessary.

And then strong hands fell upon his shoulders and yanked him back into the room.

'What is the meaning of this?' He made as if to shake them off, but the servants that held him were not to be dissuaded.

'Let me go this instant.' People in the crowd were

beginning to notice. And the two burly footmen that held him were hurrying him out a side door.

'Let me go, you bas—'

A fist connected with his gut, and the man still holding him pushed him down the stairs and into the street.

He knelt on the cobbles, struggling to get his wind back, and heard the voice of his brother above him.

'That did not go as well as one might have hoped. But at least I was allowed to walk out on my own two legs, so I shouldn't complain.'

'Rank hath its privileges,' St John gasped.

'Apparently.'

He glared up at his brother, who was staring back at him in bemusement. 'Help me up, your Grace. We need to be going.'

'You have another plan?'

St John nodded. 'Esme will be mine before the week ends. But first, we must go to a brothel.'

St John stared intently at the opposite wall, devoting his full attention to a watercolour of an undraped and attractive female rather than the more shocking scene in front of him. The sight of his brother the duke, relaxing on a red velvet divan and chatting with the madam in a notorious house of ill fame, was disconcerting. Marcus must recognise the sort of place they'd come to, and yet he acted as though this visit was no different than lunch with the vicar.

St John checked himself. The man was two score, and had no doubt visited a brothel at some point in his life. But somehow, he'd never believed that his proper, older brother had tasted of life's vices, preferring to imagine him celibate.

And yet Marcus seemed quite at home, but it was the ladies who were discomfited. There was no small amount of giggling in corners, and pointing, and whispers behind hands about the rank of their new visitor. But when the duke's eyes met theirs, they shrank from him in awe.

He must learn the trick of it, the effortless dominion that Marcus achieved over his surroundings wherever he might be.

He looked back at the girls in the room, who had greeted him with all the warmth and eagerness that he wished to feel from Esme.

The madam gazed from him to his brother with knowing eyes, and refilled their wine glasses. 'If not entertainment, then what have you come for, Johnny? Or am I to call you Captain Radwell, now?'

He cleared his throat, embarrassed at the familiarity of her greeting. 'You will soon be calling me Lord Stanton, although the news is not yet public.'

He was surprised to notice her reaction, as her posture improved and her gaze became less forward.

'But that is neither here nor there for one of such old acquaintance, Annie. I am here seeking information only.'

'You ought to know that nothing in this house is free, your lordship.' She'd dropped easily into using the new title and there was a hint of subservience in her voice.

'If you wish money, name your price. But I think you'll have payment enough when I tell you what I want, and what I mean to do with what you give me. I offer you a chance to settle an old score. Your clients sometimes talk in moments of intimacy, do they not? Lord knows, I often said things I wouldn't care repeated.'

She seemed indignant at the suggestion. 'But we do not share this information. You know us as whores, sir. But that does not mean we are spies or blackmailers.'

He smiled back at her. 'Nor have you been able to use what you've learned to your advantage, I suspect. Whereas, if someone like myself, or perhaps my brother, were to find facts damaging to say, perhaps, the Earl of Halverston—you call him Eddie, when he is here, I believe—we would be able to take the information to the proper authorities.'

'And why the sudden interest in Halverston?' But her eyes were glittering with something other than avarice.

'On my last visit to your establishment, I had the misfortune to meet him. I heard the cries of the girl he had been with and saw the marks upon her body.'

'It has been five years,' the madam reminded him.

'But I have not forgotten. The change in my status puts me on equal footing with the old lecher. And the reconciliation with my brother puts me slightly ahead. The fact that Halverston is betrothed to a young lady who I hold in esteem—well, that outweighs the first two reasons, for I will gladly tear the black heart from

his body before I let him have her. But if there is a way
to administer justice quickly, quietly, and legally? All
the better. You will lose his custom, of course, but I
wager you'll be glad to see it gone.'

She relaxed into the cushions beside the duke and
signalled a girl to bring them another bottle of wine.
'You are right in your suspicions. He is like—you will
forgive me, your lordship—the French pox. Impossible to get rid of, and growing steadily worse.' She
glanced up at the girl holding the wine. 'Please ask
Emily to join us.'

They sipped their drinks in silence; and shortly after,
a girl entered and sat with head bowed at the end of the
couch. She was pale and blonde and St John's stomach rolled as he noticed her marked resemblance to
Esme.

Annie announced, 'Gentlemen, this is a favourite of
Lord Halverston. Emily, these gentlemen would like
your help.'

'Friends of Halverston?' Her eyes darted up to meet
theirs, and she looked from one to the other in suspicion and growing anxiety. Her voice was steady as she
said, 'Certainly, anything you gentlemen may wish.'
But her expression said otherwise.

'You have nothing to fear, my dear. We will not be
going upstairs. What we need can be settled in this
room, and you will be paid handsomely for your time,
if you are truthful.'

She nodded.

'You are intimately acquainted with Halverston?'

Her laugh was bitter. 'There is no one else who is more so, because no one else will have him. I have been assured that I need do nothing else, if I can keep him happy and away from the rest of the girls, and there is a bonus in it for me. When the old bastard dies, and I hope and pray daily that he does so before finishing me, I'll have enough money to start a house of my own, or retire to a more respectable trade.'

St John struggled to control a shudder of revulsion, and he could feel his brother leaning forward in concern for the girl. 'We will take you from here today, if you wish, and give you all the money you need to start anew.'

She looked at them appraisingly. 'That would leave him with no distraction. And who would he turn to then? I might save myself, only to see his tyranny inflicted upon some other poor girl. Gentlemen, do not have a care for me. If you are so great and good, if you have any feelings for the welfare of those such as myself, then kill the monster.'

St John reached a comforting hand to the girl, then, fearing it would be misconstrued, let it fall back into his lap. 'We were hoping you could help us in some way. Has he ever spoken of anything, any wrong done outside this house, that we might use against him?'

She nodded. 'Because no one cares for the wrongs done inside these walls.'

St John flinched at the words, but shook his head. 'If there is nothing else, then I assure you, he will die for this. I will kill him myself. He is too old to call out,

and the world will see it as assassination, and not justice. But if there is something that we could make into
a public scandal…'

'Then you can be rid of him and remain free of his
murder. And I will be rid of him as well.' The smile
spread slowly across her face. 'Go to his house, your
lordships. There is a drawer in his desk, the contents
of which will be most interesting to you. He trades with
the French. Many things. Brandy, silks, currency.'

Marcus shook his head. 'Many nobles engage in
black-market trade. This is hardly news. Their patriot-
ism wears thin, it seems, when they realise that a pro-
tracted war will separate them from French brandy.'

'But there are other secrets that will interest you,
your Grace. Years of debauchery have left his estates
depleted and it is more expensive to appear rich than
to quietly husband what wealth you have. And to feed
his appetites here is no small thing. Much of what he
wishes to do, when alone and above stairs…' A cloud
passed over the girl's face, and she shook her head as
if to clear the memories. Then she smiled a cold, brittle smile. 'As with any service, when things are difficult or dangerous, they often cost more. He has
squandered his wealth, and now he must find ways to
refill the coffers. He is none too particular about how
he does it.

'Halverston has friends in the War Office. He is in
a position to overhear many things, the names of
spies, troop movements. Information that can be
slipped to his French contacts, in exchange for

money and comforts. And when he finds a man in power who is prone to sins of the flesh, he encourages the perversions and then turns them against the sinner, who must buy his silence with money or secrets.'

St John's lip curled in revulsion. 'A spy for the French. And a blackmailer.'

'Yes,' Emily said. 'And he brags about it to me, knowing that there is no one I can tell. Is it not bad enough that I must give myself to the old lecher, and be used to debase his friends? To know that I am paid for with French gold is even worse. There is a safe in his study, where he keeps papers that he wishes to copy, and the names of his contacts in England and in France. If you have those, you have him.'

'Then we must find a way into his household, to get them. A safe, you say? This will be devilishly difficult.' Marcus was puzzling over the situation, when St John began to smile.

'Difficult for us, perhaps. But I think I know of a solution.' He touched the girl lightly on the arm. 'Emily, we will need to know that the earl is to be away from home, so that we are free to operate. I hesitate to ask…'

She smiled the same hard smile as she had before, and tossed her head. 'If you swear to me that it will mean an end to him. Then you shall hear from me when he is to visit, and I will do whatever is necessary to hold him here.'

He leaned forward and kissed the girl lightly on the head. 'You have my eternal gratitude, Emily.' Even as he said it, he realised how little that was worth. 'And what protection I can offer.'

He could see the calculation in her eye, and the knowing look that passed amongst the girls.

St John cleared his throat. 'I do not know how best to phrase this offer, since I've never done such before...'

There was another flurry of silent communication in the room, and several giggles expressing doubts that he was inexperienced in offering a *carte-blanche*.

'But I wish to take you from this place and offer you a residence. I would be willing to meet all expenses. And in exchange...'

Emily's lips quirked in a knowing smile.

'You would be required to look out of the window.'

The smile slipped from her face and was replaced with confusion.

'And tell me what you see, of course. By letter. It's probably best that I stay as far away as possible. But if you could report on the girl in the room across the street. If you saw her. To know that she's all right. It would mean so much.'

There was a stunned silence from the girls in the room. And Emily repeated, 'You are offering to keep me, your lordship?'

He mumbled, 'Well, not as such...'

'And all you wish is that I look out of a window.'

'And let me know about the girl across the street. You can go today, if you like, to inspect the apartments. They are yours as long as you need them.'

And she laughed. It was the first sincere sound he'd heard in the house since arriving there.

'Would you like more tea, Miss Esme?'

'No. Thank you, Meg. Really. I am fine.'

'Something else, then? A bit more bread, perhaps? Consommé? For dessert, there are some cakes that cook says used to be your favourite.'

Esme pushed the food around on her plate and tried to look satisfied. 'No. I've had enough, really.'

The maid looked worried and whispered. 'You've got to eat more, miss. You're not taking enough to keep a sparrow alive.'

Esme looked up at her helplessly. 'I know. Tomorrow, perhaps. Today, I am not feeling well.'

Meg nodded in sympathy. 'I know just the thing. Herb tea. Some camomile to help you sleep and black haw to ease the discomfort. You'll feel right enough in a day or two. I'll bring it right back.'

Esme watched the girl as she walked to the door of the bedroom and through. She heard the decided click of the lock once Meg was in the hall. There had been a hesitation before the bolt had shot home. She was sure of it. It was Meg's duty to lock the door, 'to keep Esme from any more foolish wandering' as her father had put it. There was some small comfort in knowing that Meg did not enjoy her job.

She stared out the window to the apartment across the street. Empty, or so it appeared. What good it would do her to see him, she did not know. One more glimpse and she wouldn't be able to carry through with what needed doing, if she was ever to get out of this bedroom. She must walk down the aisle free of tears and hesitation, and to go to her new husband willingly.

She must force herself to think of Halverston thus. Husband. Even fortified with several glasses of wine, she could hardly bear his touch on the dance floor. And then he had taken her out on to the balcony and confirmed her worst fears. He had whispered poison into her ears as his hands had strayed over her body, with the party guests only a few feet away.

Halverston would die soon, she assured herself. And she would be free of him, and her father.

But it would be better if she did not see St John until after the deed was done, and she had become used to her new life.

She looked across the street at the empty rooms. If he was not in the room across the street, he must be staying in the apartments of his mistress. The thought sickened her.

And she scolded herself for her missish sensibilities. He would have other women. She was sure of it. She should take comfort in the fact that he cared enough for her feelings not to flaunt the other women under her very balcony. If he could wait the few weeks until she was married and out of this house, before staging any more public scenes, that would have to be enough.

It was foolish of her to hope that he would return to his rooms alone, pining to be near her. Foolish to be thinking of him at all. He had promised her nothing, other than to help her avoid pain. And she had given herself to him, so the chase was over. His interest was probably waning with each passing day. It had been idiotic to write him the letter, and she had no doubt proven herself to be the green girl he had accused her of being. He had never claimed to be anything other than a rogue. And such a man as that did not spare feelings for the girls he'd dishonoured. They did as they pleased and be damned to everyone else.

She had hoped that she might be increasing, which would solve some problems, but create others. She could merely have announced it to her betrothed before the wedding, and marriage would have been impossible. But there was a chance that her father would have beaten her, if he found out, and it would not have been good for the baby. Still, she would have had a bit of St John with her, and that would be something.

And then she could have gone to him, with an heir in her belly and he would have had to…

No. She squeezed her eyes tight against the fantasy. That dream was just as likely to end with a look of disgust on his face at being saddled with the expense of a bastard. He could not afford a wife. What would he want with a child? And suppose he married her and their union was marked with coldness and bitterness because she had trapped him into it?

But that point had been moot. She was not now or ever likely to carry St John's child, and the aching misery inside her could not be cured with black haw tea.

A light flickered in the window across the street and,

unable to help herself, she snuffed the candles in her room, plunging it into darkness, and stepped out on to her balcony in the chill night air and crouched behind the balustrade, hoping to catch a glimpse of the man she loved.

A footman was lighting tapers in the room she knew from her single visit to be the sitting room. He was pulling back Holland covers and hurriedly laying a fire. She looked closer.

It was the man that St John had called Toby. If his servants were there, then the rooms were still his. The wind brushed lightly against the hair on her bare arms and she felt a shiver of excitement.

The door to the room opened and she held her breath.

A girl entered. Not much older than herself. And alone. Her dress was satin and had been fine once, if a trifle gaudy. It had the appearance of long use and it fit her ill.

She looked hesitantly around the room, unsure of her new surroundings. She stroked the crystal decanter that rested on the tray next to the table and poured herself a glass of what appeared to be sherry. Then she settled down on the couch, drawing her legs up under her. She sipped the wine and smiled.

It was a look of total and almost sexual satisfaction. The look of someone who had seen harsher times, but was content with her present circumstances.

Esme felt the panic rising in her, and hurried back into her room.

Her worst fears were manifest. St John had found another.

Chapter Eighteen

Anthony de Portnay Smythe lounged in the back of a rather unsavory pub in an even more unsavoury inn of London, enjoying a mediocre whisky. Its flavour was rendered much more subtle by the knowledge that he had purchased it with ill-gotten gains.

His fence was examining the sack of jewels collected from the latest week's work. A gold signet from a rather repellent young marquis. A diamond necklace and matching earbobs from a dowager with a penchant for gossip and gin, and a set of emerald studs from a barrister in Kent who had been more successful at the gaming tables than in court. The last had been devilishly tricky to get, since the only open window to the house was on the third floor.

'Fifty quid.' Edgar the fence was being difficult again, but Tony was having none of it.

'They're worth a hundred.'

'And I'm giving you fifty. The signet's got to be

melted down. It's worth nothing as a ring with that crest on it. Any fool will know where it came from.'

'But the gold is good. And it's heavy.' Tony stroked the necklace beside it. 'And look at those stones. They're worth ninety, all by themselves.'

'If I could sell them.' Edgar pointed to the emeralds. 'One of the studs is missing. Sixty.'

'I was in a hurry. I fell out of the damn window getting back. No time to count them. Seventy-five.'

'Done.' Edgar scooped the jewels off the table and into his pocket, and dropped the money on the table without counting it.

Tony sorted through the coins. The money had been counted out before they'd started to argue. That old bastard. Edgar had known they'd end at seventy five, but he'd haggled anyway.

It was embarrassing to be so predictable.

Edgar moved away, and they studiously ignored each other as though the meeting had never taken place. There were similar people performing similar transactions at nearby tables, and Tony ignored them as well, preparing to drink the rest of his whisky in peace.

Tony enjoyed his visits to the Blade and Scabbard. It was the only place in London he knew where a man was guaranteed absolute privacy, no matter the size of the crowd. Since no one wished to be seen there, one did one's fellow patrons the courtesy of not seeing them. Despite the busy tables around him, Tony might as well have been drinking alone in his rooms.

A shadow fell across the table. And there was a

scrape of chairs as two men drew seats on either side of him and the illusion was shattered.

'Good day, Smythe.' St John Radwell on one side and his brother the duke on the other. Tony allowed himself to feel alarm, but took care not to let it register on his face. The jig was most decidedly up.

'Good day? I suppose. I hadn't really noticed. Not much for the daylight hours, myself. Well, gentlemen, it's been charming. Now, if you'll excuse me.' He gave them a cheerful smile and rose to go.

There was a hand on each shoulder, pressing him firmly back into his chair. His body met the wood with more force than was necessary. St John Radwell smiled back at him. 'Not just yet, I think. First we must have a little chat.'

'Well, we seem to have covered the weather. And that leaves me…' Tony considered '…nothing to say for myself. Not a thing.'

The duke's voice was a gruff rumble, with no trace of his brother's false warmth. 'If that was meant to excuse your stealing my wife's earrings, it was sorely inadequate.'

'No. An excuse would be something more like, "I did not know that they belonged to your wife when I took them", or "it was one earring, and not a pair", or "your brother stopped me, so really it was nothing at all."' Tony continued to smile and spread his empty hands to prove that he was no threat. If they meant to do him harm, then they must live with the fact that he was an unarmed man, and the devil take them for their brutality.

'I fail to see where attempted robbery in my house can be construed as nothing at all.' His attempt at levity was wasted on the duke, who gave no indication of possessing a sense of humour.

'Frankly, robbery is a bit out of my line as well. Burglary,' Tony corrected. 'That's the ticket, gentlemen. Burglary. I prefer that the owners of the swag not be present when I collect from them. Most times, the people I take from can spare the loss and deserve the theft. Miss Canville had done nothing to me, but I was sorely in need that night and meant to make do with the one jewel. If it's any consolation, it would have troubled my conscience had I succeeded and caused her distress. And I would have found a way to pay her back, when I was able.'

'Well, that makes it all better, then.' It was St John, speaking again, and his voice dripped sarcasm. Of course, Radwell had wanted to plant him a facer just for dancing with the girl. Stealing the earring had given him a better reason.

Tony took a moment to regret the whole evening at Haughleigh as a mistake, and then said, 'Well, is it off to the Runners, then? Or into the alley to teach me a lesson? Since I never took anything from you, an apology is all I can offer in reparation.'

'Not quite.' St John was now grinning at him in a most unpleasant way, and Tony remembered his threat. Perhaps a simple beating was not what they had in mind. To end the evening bleeding his last in a ditch somewhere was definitely not part of his plans.

He looked pointedly at Radwell, hoping to jog his memory. 'You said that we were quits if I left Haughleigh and the girl. And I have. I've stayed far away from both. On my...' he paused '...too late to swear on my honour. Upon my soul. I still have one, not that it's worth much to you.'

Radwell smiled. 'That is true. You have followed my instructions to the letter. But it appears that you have not reformed your character. My brother and I cannot very well look the other way, after seeing you trading in stolen goods tonight.'

'Of course you can,' Tony retorted. 'It is no business of yours. And frankly, gentlemen...' He looked around the room at the ragged band of cut-purses and criminals seated at the other tables '...it is in the best interest of your health to leave this place quickly and forget you saw me here.'

Radwell glanced around the room and snorted. 'If I believed that the men assembled in this room were capable of fighting as a unit, I might, just might, be concerned. But you know as well as I that they will scatter when the first body hits the floor. Their concern will be for their own necks, not yours. There is not a thing I can do to you, in plain sight of your fellows, that will incite comment or notice. And if I leave money on the table for the barmen, I won't even have to clean up the mess afterward.'

Tony let the words sink in. The body on the floor would be his and no one would care. He was alone and there were two of them.

It had always been so peaceful at the Blade and Scabbard. He had but to mind his own business and he could enjoy a quiet drink. And now Radwell and his brother had spoilt the ambiance.

He sighed. 'Very well, gentlemen. Do what you will. But if possible, leave me the strength to get home and enough money for a cab.' He closed his eyes and waited for the first blow.

'We are not here to administer punishment.' The duke was almost formal in his pronouncement and the new tone was less menacing than that of his brother. It was most pleasant to hear the voice of someone who did not particularly want to kill him because he'd flirted with Esme Canville. 'Get on with your suggestion, St John.'

Tony opened his eyes. Radwell was looking at him with cool speculation. 'I've seen your skills at pick-pocketing and sleight of hand. You took that earring, and Esme never felt it. Those talents will probably not be needed, although stealing the thing in the middle of a crowded ball bespeaks impressively steady nerves. And I've heard you, just now, talking about climbing in windows, so you must not be afraid of heights. Also useful.

'But how are you at opening safes?'

Dear God. To even admit such was folly. It had to be some sort of trap. If not, what were these men planning? Tony proceeded with caution. 'It depends upon the lock. There are picks that will open most locks, if the user has skill with them. But if it is a Bramah lock, then nothing will work. They are said to be un-pickable.'

'Then for your sake, I hope you have both the picks and the talent to use them. And that we are not dealing with this Bramah lock. Or that rumours are not true.'

They wanted him to open a safe. He stalled. 'Well, some time spent in observation of the premises will establish—'

The duke said, 'We have done all the observation that is necessary.'

Tony sighed. 'I meant observation by me.'

Radwell went on as if nothing had been said. 'A young lady of his acquaintance assures us the owner will be gone tonight until well after midnight. The safe is on the wall behind the desk. The servants do not appear to care overly about their master's well being, so detection is unlikely. They were stealing his brandy in clear sight of the windows, when we left.' Radwell grinned at him. 'As they say, there is no time like the present.'

'This is easy for you to say, since you will not be the one taking the risks.'

Radwell sneered. 'Nor are you, since we will be there to haul your miserable carcass out of danger, should a problem arise. The young woman distracting the earl is the only one hazarding her life this evening, and she assures us that she is up to the task, as long as we can finish the job tonight and arrange for her safe departure from her current place of employment.'

Which was all cryptic enough, so Tony ignored it.

'And what assurance do I have that you will be there waiting for me, should something go wrong?'

'You have our words,' the duke proclaimed, as though this should be enough.

'And if I do not help you?'

'Then you know what I will do to you.' Radwell looked almost gleeful at the prospect.

'Which shows me what your word is worth, since you promised once before to do nothing.'

Radwell shrugged. 'My word is not worth so much as my brother's. And desperate times breed desperate measures. Let us sweeten the pot. If you do not help us, you will have more trouble than you can ever imagine. But if you do, you have your freedom, our gratitude and the contents of my purse.'

Tony rolled his eyes. 'And I'll wager your purse is empty. I am not so green as all that. Try again.'

'The contents of my purse, then.' And the duke tossed a bag out on the table where it landed with a resounding clunk.

Tony undid the string and poured out the money inside. He would not have to work for a very long time. And the temptation of house-breaking and lock-picking with permission from the nobs was really too much to resist.

But suppose it was a Bramah?

Then he would pick it and have the great pleasure of bragging about the adventure later. He would be infamous. He returned the coins to their bag and slipped the lot into his pocket. 'Gentleman, we are in agreement. Tell me what I am to get, and point me to it.'

* * *

'Do you seriously think we can trust him?' Marcus looked doubtful, which St John found strangely annoying.

They sat in a carriage, across the street from the earl's town house, staring out the windows and up to the darkened rooms above.

'Not far, I should suspect. But that is not the same as not at all. We can trust him to do this one night's work. I saw the look in his eyes at the end. He is hooked fast as any fish by the sight of the money and the lure of the theft. He will open the safe, steal the papers and come back to show us he's done it. If the incident with Esme was any indication, he is very good at what he does, but does not dare to brag about it. I doubt he can resist the chance to let someone else see him at work, without fear of repercussion.'

'But what of blackmail?'

'To him, or to us? If this goes according to plan, there is nothing we need fear revealing. If it does not? All the risks are his, and we have but to deny the whole thing.'

Marcus arched a disapproving eyebrow.

'Or we can acknowledge him and our motivations. If the papers exist, as I'm sure they do, there is no one who will fault us for our rash actions. I doubt there is any behaviour that could touch the Duke of Haughleigh and his spotless reputation. While I?' He thought of the Regent and wondered if the ink had dried on the letters patent that assured his title. And he realised it did not matter. If he could have Esme, then he would kiss his own aspirations goodbye and not think twice. 'Well, if we are discovered, I doubt that scandal can do much to mar my record.'

As they watched, the window of the study opened, and a figure stepped out on to the narrow ledge, edged to the side and carefully shut the window behind him. Two stories above the pavement, Smythe walked to the corner of the building as easily as if he was on a city street in daylight, and hooked a leg around a bit of ornamental stonework, before starting his climb to the ground. He made the descent easily, dropped into the landscaping, and reappeared in a moment, straightening his clothing, and brushing the dust off his jacket. Then he strolled toward the carriage as though he had not a care in the world. He opened the door, took a seat across from them and pulled a packet of papers from a pocket of his coat. 'I believe this is what you were looking for, gentlemen. I stopped to read them to make sure. You had but to tell me the reason for this endeavour and I would have been a willing participant. I do not deny that I am a thief, but I am no traitor and would see those that are get the punishment they deserve.'

'And I suppose this means that you will be returning the money my brother gave you, since this was done for King and country.'

Smythe's expression was unreadable. 'I am a patriot, sir. Not a saint.'

St John had expected as much. 'And while you were in the safe, you did not help yourself to its other contents?'

Smythe grinned. 'It would have been a shame to waste the trip. There was very little there, truth to tell. Only the papers and this.' He pulled a small box from his pocket. 'I believe it is intended to be a wedding ring.' He revealed a heavy gold band, small enough to fit a lady's finger.

'Keep it, with my compliments on a job well done,' St John responded with satisfaction. 'He will not be needing it, in any case.'

Marcus was examining the papers, and looked up, giving a solemn nod. 'As bad as we'd hoped, and worse. These need to go to the Foreign Office, immediately.'

St John smiled. 'And I will wait for the earl to come home. We will have a discussion. It will be edifying for him, and most satisfactory for me.'

'And what of me?'

St John looked up at Smythe, and realised he'd all but forgotten the man was there.

'You, sir, are a paragon, and I will fight any man who says otherwise. I will be staying here to await the earl, but my brother will give you a ride to wherever you choose to go.'

Smythe looked doubtful. 'And that is all? No threats, no warnings to mend my ways?'

He grinned and clapped the man on the shoulder. 'I should think not. If I had anything else I needed taken, I should certainly keep you in mind. But if you are hoping to use me as a reference? Then I think that is an unlikely event. Let my brother drive you to your lodgings and I would hope that you forget this evening, just as I plan to forget your part in it.'

Smythe smiled and his body relaxed into the squabs, tucking the box of rings back into his coat. 'Very well, then. It has been a pleasure doing business with you, gentlemen.'

St John allowed himself to be presented and entered the study of the Earl of Halverston. Although he had never before been in the room, a week's covert observation of it left him with a sense of déjà vu.

'Good evening to you, sir, and to what might I owe the pleasure of this visit?' Halverston was a gracious host with a pleasant smile, and had not St John known better, he would have observed nothing more than the distinguished elder statesman and pillar of the community that others saw when they met the earl.

St John ignored the old earl's proffered hand and Halverston returned his appraising gaze. Halverston was more formidable than he'd remembered, although St John's memory of the man as he'd behaved in the brothel removed some of the gloss from the image of gentility before him now. This man might be old, but his fine clothes masked the frailty of his legs. His eyes were not clouded by drink, but cold and shrewd, no matter how warm the greeting he offered.

St John glanced back at the butler, lingering near the door. 'What I have to say is for your ears alone, my lord.'

The earl arched an eyebrow at the impertinence of it, but gestured the servant away, reaching for the decanter to pour a whisky for his guest, which St John left untouched on the desk.

'Very well. We are alone. And now, sir, speak your mind. Have you come here to reminiscence about old times together?' He smiled in a way that hinted at the knowledge of shared perversions, and St John felt his stomach churn at the thought that he might have been looking into his own eyes twenty years hence, had not he changed the direction of his life.

'No, I have not. Although I suppose I should thank you for the brief glimpse into hell that our meeting afforded me. It was sufficient to tell me that it would be better to let the French put a bullet in my brain, than to grow into a poxy old lecher. But that is tangential to the matter at hand. Certain papers have come into my possession. Things which the Foreign Office will be very interested in. Until tonight, they resided in the safe on the wall behind your desk.'

The Earl was doing his best to appear uninterested, but his voice was tense. 'And how might you know the contents and location of my safe?'

'You are indiscreet in so many ways, your lordship. Not the least of which was telling a poor abused girl of your schemes with the French.' He pointed to the tapestry on the wall where the safe was concealed. 'You might wish to check the contents, to verify what I am saying, and then we will continue our conversation.'

The Earl rose, and his movements were smooth and sure as he walked to the safe to open it. But the return trip to the desk seemed to have aged him by a score of years. 'What do you want from me?' The question was hoarse and feeble, and St John wondered if he was supposed to feel pity for the pitiless traitor before him.

'Alas, what I want cannot be. I would wring the life from your scrawny body for your treachery and your perversion, and because you stand for so much that is wrong in the world. But that would be murder, would it not? And pleasant though it might be, and capable though I am, it would not help me achieve my ends. So I am willing to settle for second best.'

He stared hard into Halverston's eyes and felt the other shrink in submission. 'Firstly, there will be no more trading secrets with the French. The papers are on their way to the necessary authorities, and they will decide what it is they wish to do with you. That is not my problem. But I doubt that any of it will appear in *The Times*, as that would be of no use to anyone. You will be much more useful to your country, if the discovery of your treason is not made public.'

There was a glitter of hope in the old man's eyes.

'That is, unless you do not abide by my other conditions. Second: there will be no more visits to a certain house of ill fame, to Emily or any other girl. If you have any misguided plans for vengeance, know that the girl is safely away, and under my protection. Any attempts at retribution, or a return to your old habit in some new location, will result in public revelation of the scandal. Is that understood?'

The earl nodded, but there was a flush to his cheeks that made St John suspect he was biting back his true feelings on the matter.

'And last, you are to cry off immediately from your engagement to a young lady of my acquaintance. Do not think that you can continue in the way you have been going, with a young wife to get an heir on. No girl of gentle birth should be forced to remain in your poisonous company, and certainly not Esme Canville. Do I make myself clear?'

'So I am to give up everything, my livelihood, my diversions, and my betrothed, or you will spread lies about me in the papers?'

'If you mean your treason, your perversion, and the poor girl who is being forced against her will to yoke herself to you? Then, yes, you must walk away from them all, or I shall tell the truth, your lordship, the total, unvarnished truth to anyone else who will listen. You have no choice in the matter.'

The earl laughed. 'Of course I have a choice. There is always another way, young man. Now get you gone from my study. For whatever I decide to do, I do not have to put up with your insufferably priggish presence for a moment longer.'

'Very well, then. I will be watching for the announcement of the end of your engagement. You have twenty-four hours. If you have not gone to *The Times*, I certainly shall.' He nodded and left the room.

St John walked towards the front door, signalling the footman for his hat and stick. He had not reached the exit before a single shot rang out from the direction of the study.

Chapter Nineteen

Esme felt her heart quicken in fear at the sound of the curses rising up the chimney from the room below. Her father was louder than he'd ever been, and she struggled to think if there was something she'd done to provoke it. She spoke only when spoken to, she never questioned his orders, no matter how outlandish they might be, and she responded promptly to all summons.

Except for the beating she had endured on homecoming, the last two weeks had been most uneventful. She had taken all meals in her rooms and had heard no objections from her father. At times it almost seemed he had forgotten her presence, although she was aware of him, moving about in his study beneath her. But now, it appeared that things were about to change.

She was on her hands and knees on the hearth in an instant, her ear up close to the flue of the cold fireplace, listening to the shouting in the study. It was impossible to tell what had upset her father so. There had been no visitors that she'd noticed from her prison window. Perhaps there was something in the post, or the papers. But he was now incoherent with rage and she doubted even if she had been in the same room with him she would have been able to ascertain the reason for it.

She heard the crashing of glass against the fireplace, which must have been the crystal decanters that stood on the corner of the desk. There were a series of loud thuds, which could only be the heavy, leather-bound books that lined the walls, striking the floor as he pulled them from their places.

There was a hesitant suggestion from the butler. An offer of port, or a whisky to calm the nerves, though it was still early in the day.

There came a shouted negative from her father and the slam of the door below her.

Which would mean one of two things. He was going out, or he was coming up. She stood, smoothing her dress and carefully wiping her face with a handkerchief. To appear untidy in his presence would only make the inevitable worse.

The door to her room sprang open, and she could see her maid, hesitating in the hallway behind her father.

'You.' The word was full of venom, and her father pointed at her with one hand, while gesturing wildly with the newspaper in his other hand.

She nodded politely. 'Yes, sir. I am still here.' She tried to keep the reproach from her voice.

'This is your doing, I don't doubt.'

'If it is anything to be found in today's paper, I do not see how I could be held responsible for it. I have not left this room in a fortnight.'

'Then you smuggled a message out with your maid,' he shouted. 'I am sure of it. And you've done something to upset him and this is the result.'

'Upset whom, sir? There have been no smuggled messages. I have no idea what you are speaking of.'

And he slapped her hard in the face with the paper, then held it before her eyes, pointing to an article on the front page.

'The Earl of Halverston is dead. By his own hand. What could have driven him to this, girl? I wonder.'

'I swear to you, sir, that I have no idea.' Her mind was racing. She would not have to marry him, then? But then she would remain with her father and there might be no chance of another offer or of escape.

He rattled the paper again and she flinched at the threat of a blow. Then he opened it so she could see the headline. 'In his study. A single gunshot. He was alone when it happened. But he had just received a visit from the brother of your former host.'

'St John?' The name had slipped out before she could stop it.

'And thus you betray yourself. Not Captain Radwell, like a decent girl would have called him. From you it is St John.' He was rolling the newspaper in his hands, and she watched with fascination as he formed it into a weapon. 'St John Radwell, who has been trying to gain entrance to this house since the day after your arrival here. What did you say to him? What did you let him do to you? And what does he have to do with this situation?'

'I have no idea. I swear.' She was backing away, and avoided part of the first blow, as it bounced harmlessly off her arm.

St John had been here.

'Don't lie to me, girl.' He stepped in and swung again, hitting her on the cheek. It was as hard as any slap, and her eye teared as her face began to swell.

'I am not lying. I don't know what happened. I swear it.' And she prayed it sounded convincing as the next blow struck her in the abdomen, doubling her over and leaving her gasping on the floor.

He stepped away then, and she felt Meg rush to her, supporting her as she regained her breath.

'And you.' Her father was turning to the maid now. She pulled herself upright and shook off Meg's protecting hands.

'She had nothing to do with it, sir. Whatever it is that you assume happened, it was my doing. All mine.'

'Very well. Then you can have her punishment as well as your own.' And he struck her again on the other cheek, with the back of his hand. He turned to Meg again, who was cringing behind her.

'Get your things and get out of this house. I do not permit disloyalty from my servants, and I will not let them come between me and the proper discipline of my daughter.' He strode from the room, leaving the quaking maid in his wake.

'Oh, miss,' she murmured. 'Oh, Miss Esme.'

Esme sighed. 'It's all right, Meg. Do not worry yourself. Here is what you are to do. When you leave here, go to the house across the street, to the rooms on the second floor. Tell the lady there that you are cast off without references, but that you would have mine if I could give it, and that I wish St John Radwell to find you a position with his brother or in his own household.'

'Oh, miss,' she said again. 'What of you?'

'I've managed before, Meg. I am not so soft as I appear. Now go, before my father sees you.'

The girl started towards the doorway. And then turned back to her. 'He'd have had to fire me for carelessness anyway, miss. For I'm always losing things. Keys, for instance. I have no idea what happened to the key to your room.' And she pressed the heavy brass key into Esme's palm and hugged her once before running from the room.

Esme went to the door and carefully locked it behind the retreating girl. It would do no good for her father to find her door open. She did not need an extra punishment. She needed to find the best way to use the resources at hand. She had the key. Which meant she could come and go as she pleased.

She would not be escaping the house through marriage, then. But, should she think of somewhere to go, she could at least get out of her room. With no money, she was little better than trapped. It had been foolish of her not to send a message with Meg. She could have begged for assistance from St John. Perhaps his visits meant nothing, but at least he had not forgotten her.

She knew of only one place that might take her in, should she leave the house in the dead of night, but it might have been easier, if the woman across the street had at least anticipated her coming.

Perhaps a signal of some kind. She walked to the window and looked out and into the rooms across the street, to see the lovely blonde woman rising nervously and turning to the door to greet someone. Surely Meg had not arrived so soon.

The girl was holding her own copy of *The Times* and seemed most agitated by something she saw there.

And then St John stepped into the room and went to the girl.

She dropped the newspaper to the floor and threw herself into his arms, hanging from his neck with her feet barely touching the floor, and she showered his face with kisses, as he smiled down at her.

The key slipped from Esme's fingers and dropped to the floor, forgotten. She would have no need of it now. The thought was vague and unfocused in her mind. She might be able to escape the house, but there was nowhere on earth she could go. Because the only alternative was far more painful than the thought of remaining where she was.

And, at last, the pain of her father's blows reached her, and she collapsed on the floor of her room in a ball of misery, and wept.

Chapter Twenty

St John chafed at the discomfort of his collar, which had been starched to a wooden level of stiffness, and the cravat, which was immaculate and knotted simply, although perhaps a trifle too tight. His coat was black superfine, his breeches the same, his hose silk, and his boots polished to mirror brightness.

He looked and felt like a well-dressed vicar.

He knocked on the door and waited patiently for the servant to admit him, dropping his new card on the silver salver presented to him. An earl. Would that be sufficient to impress Mr Canville? It was every bit as good as the title her father had secured for her. Better, actually, for his title was older, more respectable. The land was more productive. He'd been over it a hundred times in his mind, pointing out the advantages to himself.

Now all he had to do was prove himself to Esme's father.

The butler opened the door to him, and he could see the look of panic on the man's face, before his mask of imperturbability dropped again and he could inform milord that Mr Canville was not in.

'Then I shall wait.'

The butler cleared his throat. 'He does not wish to see you, my lord.'

'Stuff and nonsense.' St John waved the dismissal aside, while wedging his foot in the door as a pre-emptive measure. 'He was not in for Captain Radwell. But this is the first time the Earl of Stanton has visited. The title should at least get me over the threshold. Show me to the study, and call for Mr Canville. If he means to turn me off, he must do it to my face.'

The butler shrank before him like a retreating tide.

Hell and damnation, Marcus had taught him well. St John had assumed at first that having a title would be rather like being an officer. In the army, he had given orders and his men had followed. He could do so again as an earl. But his brother had explained that situations often demanded more diplomacy, as would the problem of Mr Canville. Then one simply had to pretend that the rules did not apply to one. Ignore. Dismiss. Proceed in good humour to do exactly what one wished, secure in the knowledge that the world revolved around one.

It had been most annoying, when his brother had used the technique upon him, and St John was happy to practice it fully on any who might oppose him now.

Mr Canville entered the drawing room, leaning

slightly on his stick, and greeted St John with a perfunctory nod.

St John watched the stick, with its twisted length and silver handle, and remembered the marks on Esme's back. His blood chilled, and then heated to a boil as he imagined grabbing the stick and using it on its owner.

He fought down the response and smiled placidly back at her father.

'And to what do I owe the pleasure of this visit, Lord Stanton?' Canville forced the title out through a tight smile, as if he had trouble crediting its validity.

The cheek of the man. Again St John's temper flared and he forced it down. It would not do to antagonise him. 'It is concerning your daughter, Miss Esme, sir. I became acquainted with her while visiting my brother's home this summer.'

Canville stared at him, unblinking.

St John continued. 'I was told that she had been betrothed, and that there was no hope for me. But the union will now be impossible, due to the unfortunate death of the earl. And I had hopes…'

'To court her, when the body of Lord Halverston is barely cold?'

'Not so soon, of course,' St John corrected. 'After a respectful time, if the lady is willing.'

'I could not think to give my daughter to one such as you, for the name St John Radwell is quite infamous.'

No more infamous than the old lecher you tied her

to before, you snake. 'No longer, sir, I assure you.' St John replied meekly. 'My brother the duke and I have reconciled. My time in the army had quite a transformative effect. I was awarded a peerage for my service to the crown.' *Which ought to be good enough for you, you tight old screw.* 'The title is old, and the land is fruitful.'

'There will be no settlement, if that's what you're after.'

'I did not expect one. It will hardly be necessary, for my income is ample and will be more than sufficient for both of us.'

'But there are others who would seek her hand.'

Already? 'I am sure that, given the chance to choose, she would receive my suit favourably.'

'Given the choice?' Canville's voice rose beyond the level of courtesy.

St John had put his foot in it and it was too late to back out.

Esme had been dozing and started awake as the book slipped from her lap and struck the floor. The dream had been most vivid this time and it was a shame that she had to wake and end it. It was a favourite of hers: the dream where St John came to the house and persuaded her father to let him take her away.

'I do not see what her choice has to do with anything. It is I who will dispose of her as I see fit.'

'Then I must assure you that my suit is superior to the others.'

The voices floated up through the chimney flue, faint but clear.

It could not be. What she thought she heard was the result of an overheated imagination combined with the last echoes of the dream. Wishful thinking and nothing more.

She hurried to the fireplace and fell to her knees on the hearth, brushing the remains of the previous night's fire to the side and pressing her check to the bricks along the back wall.

'I think you lack the necessary seasoning to make a good husband.' That was clearly the voice of her father. And he was talking marriage with someone.

She held her breath, waiting for the other man's response.

'But seasoning is something I can gain, with time.'

St John. She stuffed her fist into her mouth to keep from screaming the name aloud. He was in the house and he had come for her, just as he had in her dreams.

'Why should she wait when there are men already old enough?'

'I am three and thirty, titled and landed. I do not need to wait upon a better position, nor do I expect to mature, significantly.' She could hear the steel in St John's voice as he challenged her father. 'If you are waiting, perhaps, until I've lost some teeth, or my spine is not as straight? Then I shall wait as well, sir. We shall see who lasts the longest, myself, or the octogenarian you will no doubt choose as a fitting match to your daughter.'

'And wait you shall, for you will find, sir, that you can never meet my specifications for a fit husband for my only child. No amount of time, no money, no land can wipe away the stain of your past.'

'Much as nothing could stop Halverston from putting a bullet in his brain, when the truth would out.' She smiled as she heard St John's temper rising to equal her father's. 'You will find, sir, that I am of stronger stuff than Halverston. There is nothing I have done that I cannot bear to live with. My past is stained, but I have survived it and mean to make a better future.'

'And you may make your future alone, for you shall not have my daughter.'

That was that, then. Her father had refused him. There was a pause. Her heart sank as she waited to hear St John take his leave.

And then his voice came to her, cold with fury. 'You old fool, I've had your daughter right enough. For all I know my bastard is growing inside her now. Give her to another man, and I'll tell him so. You'll find it damned difficult to give her away after that.'

'Then I will give the foolish slut to no man at all. She can stay in her room and repent for the disgrace she's brought on this house.' Her father was shouting. She shivered, knowing what would happen once St John left her alone.

But his response was a battlefield shout that was so loud he could have been standing in the room with her. 'The devil she will. You've hit her, sir. I know you have, for I have spies watching the house. It is only my respect for Esme that keeps me from giving you the beating you deserve. I've tried the honourable course. I have been far more polite to you than you deserve. And yet you deny my offer?

'Very well. Perhaps I've finally found a man with less honour than myself. We will play the game by your rules, sir. I love her. She's mine. I will take her and to hell with you.'

Esme heard the door to the study slam open and footsteps striding into the hall. And then St John shouted, 'Esme! Where are you? Come down here this instant.'

She rattled ineffectually at the door, and then re-membered the key and pulled it from its hiding place, fumbling it into the lock.

'Esme! Damn it, woman! Come out of your room so that I may profess my feelings for you.' St John's command was easily loud enough to be heard in the street.

The key hit home, the lock turned and she fell into the hall as the door gave way in front of her.

And strong arms caught her before her body could hit the floor. He pulled her to her feet and his lips were at her ear, murmuring, 'You didn't think it would be so easy to get rid of me, I hope.'

'I was afraid to dream it.'

'And you have nothing to fear now.' He was pulling her down the hall with him.

She cringed against his shoulder as they approached her father.

'Stop it. Stop it this instant, Esme, and go back to your room. And you, Radwell, get out of this house.'

St John's grip on her waist tightened. 'My lord. I believe that is the correct form of address for an earl, *Mr* Canville.' He spoke the 'Mr' with a crisp emphasis that left no doubt as to who was the better man. 'And now, if you will excuse us.'

'I will not allow you to kidnap my daughter, Radwell.'

'And how do you mean to stop me?' St John laughed. 'Better men than you have tried and failed to kill me. Perhaps you intend to call the Runners. I'm sure they will settle this quietly enough, once they see my livery. Halverston proved to me right enough that the law is different for the landed. And now, it seems, I must prove it to you. Your daughter is nearly of age, sir. Soon there will be nothing you can do to hold her. Most men would think you a fool to try. But I mean to take her from this house today. By the time you can summon aid, we will be well beyond your reach. Face it, you have lost.'

He turned back to her, pulling her close. 'And as to you, minx. You wanted a say in your future. You are coming with me this minute, or not at all. No questions, no regrets and no time to pack a bag. Are you ready? Yes or no?'

And in full view of her father, she raised her head to St John's and kissed him full on his open lips. When he pulled away, the look in his eyes was dazed.

'Oh, aye. You are more than ready. But am I ready

for you is the question?' He swept her down the stairs and out the front door. Her father's railing faded in the distance as she looked into her lover's eyes.

They ran for the waiting coach, which was black and with a strange crest on the side. She glanced at it in puzzlement. 'What is that mark on the door?'

'Your new coat of arms, my lady, once we reach Scotland. I've heard Gretna Green is lovely this time of year. And it seems…' he looked up at the sky as though trying to remember '—it seems I have a hunting lodge not too far from there. I wonder what it looks like. We'll soon find out. I mean to honeymoon there.' He pulled her into the carriage behind him and shut the door.

He took her hand and linked it with his own. 'And I have other land as well. A nice piece of Cornwall, ceded to me for service to the crown. And there are jewels as well, fit for a countess, for that is what I will make of you.'

Her heart skipped once in her chest before she spoke. 'Jewels are unnecessary. I am only interested in the man, not the title.' She bit her lip, and spoke with artificial cheerfulness. 'But I really must insist, if you mean to marry me, that you not flaunt your mistress in my face. To install her across the street from me might be convenient for you, but it was most painful—'

He leaned forward and kissed her with a passion that made argument impossible. 'Halverston's ladybird, not mine. I set her there to watch over you. When she heard of his demise, she offered to show me the depth of her gratitude, but I told her that my soul had no mistress but you.' He stroked her face. 'She saw your father strike you. When she told me, it was as if I felt the blows.'

'They were nothing.' She planted a kiss in his palm. 'It is over and I need never see him again.' She smiled. 'I doubt he will relent and approve my marrying you.'

'Then perhaps I shall not bother with marriage. I could keep you, senseless with pleasure, until you are totally ruined and have no choice in the matter but to take me as husband. It's me or nothing for you, Esme.'

She shivered with pleasure. 'And what of your newly found reputation?'

He laughed. 'I had need of it when I wanted to be a gentleman. But I am a noble, now, in case you haven't heard. As an earl, I can be as dissolute as I please and there is very little that can be done about it.'

The carriage set off at a dizzying pace and she allowed herself to lunge forward and collapse against him. 'So I am to be kidnapped by a heartless libertine and forced to submit?'

He looked at her fondly. 'Not heartless, for I dare say I found my heart when I found you, Esme, my sweet. But the rest is accurate enough.'

'Oh, my.' She fanned herself theatrically. 'The thought leaves me quite faint.' And she reached slowly for the hooks at the back of her bodice. 'Perhaps if I loosen my garments, it will be possible to catch my breath.'

'Esme, do not dare. For you know what will happen to you, if you tempt me.' The warning was a low growl, but he smiled as he said it.

'Oh, dear.' She unhooked another hook. 'In broad daylight?' Her bodice was slipping down her arms and he lunged to pull the shades at the carriage windows.

'In a moving carriage? Repeatedly?'

'Repeatedly?' His wolfish smile had changed to a look of shock.

She steadied herself against the carriage seat and shifted to let the dress fall to the floor. 'Well, I am to be married, so if you mean to ruin me so totally, you'd best hurry. You are supposed to be terribly wicked, are you not?'

He paused to admire the scene, and then smiled and said, 'Wicked. Oh, yes. Terribly.' He was loosening his cravat.

'It is such a long, long way to Scotland.' She lay back on the squabs, one leg dangling and the other on the seat next to him and looped her hands through the leather strap above her head. 'And I am utterly helpless.'

'If you are the helpless one, then how is it that, since the first, you have been able to make me do whatever you wanted?' He tossed his jacket on to the floor beside her dress and reached to undo his shirt.

'Not true.' She smiled as she watched him struggling to remove his boots as the carriage rocked around them. 'I never got you to say that you loved me.'

He threw the second boot on the pile with the rest

of his clothing. 'Then you shall have your last wish. I love you, Esme. Allow me to demonstrate.'

And he did.

Welcome to cowboy country...

Turn the page for a sneak preview of
TEXAS BABY
by
Kathleen O'Brien
An exciting new title from Harlequin Superromance
for everyone who loves stories about the West.

Harlequin Superromance—
Where life and love weave together in
emotional and unforgettable ways.

CHAPTER ONE

CHASE TRANSFERRED his gaze to the road and identified a foreign spot on the horizon. A car. Almost half a mile away, where the straight, tree-lined drive met the public road. He could tell it was coming too fast, but judging the speed of a vehicle moving straight toward you was tricky.

It wasn't until it was about two hundred yards away that he realized the driver must be drunk…or crazy. Or both.

The guy was going maybe sixty. On a private drive, out here in ranch country, where kids or horses or tractors or stupid chickens might come darting out any minute, that was criminal. Chase straightened from his comfortable slouch and waved his hands.

"Slow down, you fool," he called out. He took the porch steps quickly and began walking fast down the driveway.

The car veered oddly, from one lane to another, then up onto the slight rise of the thick green spring grass. It just barely missed the fence.

"Slow down, damn it!"

He couldn't see the driver, and he didn't recognize this automobile. It was small and old, and couldn't have cost much even when it was new. It was probably white, but now it needed either a wash or a new paint job or both.

"Damn it, what's wrong with you?"

At the last minute, he had to jump away, because the idiot behind the wheel clearly wasn't going to turn to avoid a collision. He couldn't believe it. The car kept coming, finally slowing a little, but it was too late.

Still going about thirty miles an hour, it slammed into the large, white-brick pillar that marked the front boundaries of the house. The pillar wasn't going to give an inch, so the car had to. The front end folded up like a paper fan.

It seemed to take forever for the car to settle, as if the trauma happened in slow motion, reverberating from the front to the back of the car in ripples of destruction. The front windshield suddenly seemed to ice over with lethal bits of glassy frost. Then the side windows exploded.

The front driver's door wrenched open, as if the car wanted to expel its contents. Metal buckled hideously. Small pieces, like hubcaps and mirrors, skipped and ricocheted insanely across the oyster-shell driveway.

Finally, everything was still. Into the silence, a plume of steam shot up like a geyser, smelling of rust and heat. Its snake-like hiss almost smothered the low, agonized moan of the driver.

Chase's anger had disappeared. He didn't feel anything but a dull sense of disbelief. Things like this didn't happen in real life. Not in his life. Maybe the sun had actually put him to sleep....

But he was already kneeling beside the car. The driver was a woman. The frosty glass-ice of the windshield was dotted with small flecks of blood. She must have hit it with her head, because just below her hairline a red liquid was seeping out. He touched it. He tried to wipe it away before it reached her eyebrow, though, of course that made no sense at all. Her eyes were shut.

Was she conscious? Did he dare move her? Her dress was covered in glass, and the metal of the car was sticking out lethally in all the wrong places.

Then he remembered, with an intense relief, that every good medical man in the county was here, just behind the house, drinking his champagne. He found his phone and paged Trent.

The woman moaned again.

Alive, then. Thank God for that.

He saw Trent coming toward him, starting out at a lope, but quickly switching to a full run.

"Get Dr. Marchant," Chase called. "Don't bother with 911."

Trent didn't take long to assess the situation. A fraction of a second, and he began pulling out his cell phone and running toward the house.

The yelling seemed to have roused the woman. She opened her eyes. They were blue and clouded with pain and confusion.

"Chase," she said.

His breath stalled. His head pulled back. "What?"

Her only answer was another moan, and he wondered if he had imagined the word. He reached around her and put his arm behind her shoulders. She was tiny. Probably petite by nature, but surely way too thin. He could feel her shoulder blades pushing against her skin, as fragile as the wishbone in a turkey.

She seemed to have passed out, so he put his other arm under her knees and lifted her out. He tried to avoid the jagged metal, but her skirt caught on a piece and the tearing sound seemed to wake her again.

"No," she said. "Please."

"I'm just trying to help," he said. "It's going to be all right."

She seemed profoundly distressed. She wriggled in his arms, and she was so weak, like a broken bird. It made him feel too big and brutish. And intrusive. As if touching her this way, his bare hands against the warm skin behind her knees, were somehow a transgression.

He wished he could be more delicate. But he smelled gasoline, and he knew it wasn't safe to leave her here.

Finally he heard the sound of voices, as guests began to run around the side of the house, alerted by Trent. Dr. Marchant was at the front, racing toward them as if he were forty instead of seventy. Susannah was right behind him, her green dress floating around her trim legs.

"Please," the woman in his arms murmured again. She looked at him, the expression in her blue eyes lost and bewildered. He wondered if she might be on drugs. Hitting her head on the windshield might account for this unfocused, glazed look, but it couldn't explain the crazy driving.

"Please, put me down. Susannah… The wedding…"

Chase's arms tightened instinctively, and he froze in his tracks. She whimpered, and he realized he might be hurting her. "Say that again?"

"The wedding. I have to stop it."

* * * * *

Be sure to look for TEXAS BABY,
available September 11, 2007,
as well as other fantastic Superromance titles
available in September.

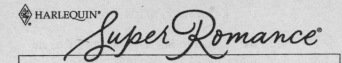

HARLEQUIN
Super Romance

Welcome to Cowboy Country...

TEXAS BABY
by *Kathleen O'Brien*

#1441

Chase Clayton doesn't know what to think.
A beautiful stranger has just crashed his
engagement party, demanding that he not
marry because she's pregnant with his baby.
But the kicker is—he's never seen her before.

Look for TEXAS BABY and other fantastic
Superromance titles on sale September 2007.

Available wherever books are sold.

HARLEQUIN
Super Romance

**Where life and love weave together
in emotional and unforgettable ways.**

HARLEQUIN®

Mediterranean NIGHTS™

Experience glamour, elegance, mystery and revenge aboard the high seas....

Coming in September 2007...

BREAKING ALL THE RULES

by

Marisa Carroll

Aboard the cruise ship *Alexandra's Dream* for some R & R, sports journalist Lola Sandler is surprised to spot pro-golfer Eric Lashman. Years after walking away from the pro circuit with no explanation to the public, Eric now finds himself teaching aboard a cruise ship.

Lola smells a career-making exposé... but their developing relationship may force her to make a difficult choice.

REQUEST YOUR FREE BOOKS!

 Harlequin® Historical
Historical Romantic Adventure!

2 FREE NOVELS PLUS 2 **FREE GIFTS!**

YES! Please send me 2 FREE Harlequin® Historical novels and my 2 FREE gifts. After receiving them, if I don't wish to receive any more books, I can return the shipping statement marked "cancel." If I don't cancel, I will receive 6 brand-new novels every month and be billed just $4.69 per book in the U.S., or $5.24 per book in Canada, plus 25¢ shipping and handling per book and applicable taxes, if any*. That's a savings of close to 15% off the cover price! I understand that accepting the 2 free books and gifts places me under no obligation to buy anything. I can always return a shipment and cancel at any time. Even if I never buy another book from Harlequin, the two free books and gifts are mine to keep forever.

246 HDN EEWW 349 HDN EEW9

Name	(PLEASE PRINT)	
Address		Apt. #
City	State/Prov.	Zip/Postal Code

Signature (if under 18, a parent or guardian must sign)

Mail to the **Harlequin Reader Service®:**
IN U.S.A.: P.O. Box 1867, Buffalo, NY 14240-1867
IN CANADA: P.O. Box 609, Fort Erie, Ontario L2A 5X3

Not valid to current Harlequin Historical subscribers.

Want to try two free books from another line?
Call 1-800-873-8635 or visit www.morefreebooks.com.

* Terms and prices subject to change without notice. NY residents add applicable sales tax. Canadian residents will be charged applicable provincial taxes and GST. This offer is limited to one order per household. All orders subject to approval. Credit or debit balances in a customer's account(s) may be offset by any other outstanding balance owed by or to the customer. Please allow 4 to 6 weeks for delivery.

Your Privacy: Harlequin is committed to protecting your privacy. Our Privacy Policy is available online at www.eHarlequin.com or upon request from the Reader Service. From time to time we make our lists of customers available to reputable firms who may have a product or service of interest to you. If you would prefer we not share your name and address, please check here. ☐

HH07

ATHENA FORCE

Heart-pounding romance and thrilling adventure.

Professional negotiator Lindsey Novak
is faced with her biggest challenge—to
buy back Teal Arnett, a young woman with
unique powers. In the process Lindsey
uncovers a devastating plot that involves
scientists from around the globe, and all of
them lead to one woman who is bent on
destroying Athena Academy...at any cost.

LOOK FOR

THE GOOD THIEF

by Judith Leon

*Available September
wherever you buy books.*

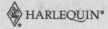

COMING NEXT MONTH FROM

HARLEQUIN®
HISTORICAL

- **KLONDIKE WEDDING**
  by **Kate Bridges**
  (Western)
  When Dr. Luke Hunter stands in as the groom in a proxy wedding,
  he doesn't expect to be *really* married to the bride! Luke's not a
  settling-down kind of man, but beautiful Genevieve might be the
  woman to change his mind.

- **A COMPROMISED LADY**
  by **Elizabeth Rolls**
  (Regency)
  Thea Winslow's scandalous past has forbidden her a future. So why
  does her wayward heart refuse to understand that she cannot have
  any more to do with handsome Richard Blakehurst?

- **A PRACTICAL MISTRESS**
  by **Mary Brendan**
  (Regency)
  She was nearly penniless, and becoming a mistress was the only
  practical solution. The decision had *nothing* to do with the look in
  Sir Jason's eyes that promised such heady delights....

- **THE WARRIOR'S TOUCH**
  by **Michelle Willingham**
  (Medieval)
  The MacEgan Brothers
  Pragmatic, plain Aileen never forgot the handsome man who
  became her first lover on the eve of Bealtaine, the man who gave
  her a child without ever seeing her face. Now that he has returned,
  how can she keep her secret?

HHCNM0807